PRAISE FOR ABBY BROOKS

"Abby Brooks is a wizard with Beyond Us—entertaining and pure enjoyment!"

ADRIANA LOCKE—USA TODAY AND WASHINGTON POST BESTSELLING AUTHOR

"A masterful blend of joy and angst.

PRAISE FOR *ABBY BROOKS*

"With just the perfect amount of angst and remarkable character development, Abby Brooks has crafted a masterpiece..."

PRAISE FOR *BEYOND WORDS*

"Once again Abby Brooks creates a world filled with beautifully written characters that you cannot help but fall in love with."

PRAISE FOR *BEYOND LOVE*

"A lovely story of growing beyond your past, taking control of your life, and allowing yourself to be loved for the person you are."

MELANIE MORELAND—NEW YORK TIMES BESTSELLING AUTHOR, IN PRAISE OF *WOUNDED*

"Abby Brooks writes books that draw readers right into the story. When you read about her characters, you want them to be your friends."

PRAISE FOR ABBY BROOKS

FEARLESS

A WILDROSE LANDING ROMANCE

ABBY BROOKS

Cover design by Abby Brooks

WEBSITE:

www.abbybrooksfiction.com

FACEBOOK:

http://www.facebook.com/abbybrooksauthor

FACEBOOK FAN GROUP:

https://www.facebook.com/groups/AbbyBrooksBooks/

INSTAGRAM:

http://www.instagram.com/xo_abbybrooks

Want to be one of the first to know about new releases, get exclusive content, and exciting giveaways? Sign up for my newsletter on my website:

www.abbybrooksfiction.com

And, as always, feel free to send me an email at: abby@abbybrooksfiction.com

Books by
ABBY BROOKS

WILDROSE LANDING

Fearless

Shameless

THE HUTTON FAMILY

Beyond Words

Beyond Love

Beyond Now

Beyond Us

Beyond Dreams

It's Definitely Not You - Joe's story

The Hutton Family Series - Part 1

The Hutton Family Series - Part 2

A BROOKSIDE ROMANCE

Wounded

Inevitably You

This Is Why

Along Comes Trouble

Come Home To Me

A Brookside Romance - the Complete Series

WILDE BOYS WITH WILL WRIGHT

Taking What Is Mine

Claiming What Is Mine

Protecting What Is Mine

Defending What Is Mine

THE MOORE FAMILY

Finding Bliss

Faking Bliss

Instant Bliss

Enemies-to-Bliss

THE LONDON SISTERS

Love Is Crazy (Dakota & Dominic)

Love Is Beautiful (Chelsea & Max)

Love Is Everything (Maya & Hudson)

The London Sisters - the Complete Series

IMMORTAL MEMORIES

Immortal Memories Part 1

Immortal Memories Part 2

AS WREN WILLIAMS

Bad, Bad Prince

Woodsman

Fearless

A WILDROSE LANDING ROMANCE

CHAPTER ONE

Evie

Amelia Brown squished my cheeks so hard my lips poofed out, gave them a pat, and smacked a kiss to my forehead. "Evie. Darling. Smile for me, sweetness. Opportunity hides in every disaster. This is a chance to come back stronger. To learn. To grow."

I mentally added an exclamation or three after each of her sentences and the smile she requested bloomed. With the jingle of jewelry and perpetual optimism, my best friend swept into the kitchen in the apartment we'd been sharing for the last several months, then returned with a bottle of tequila and two shot glasses.

She gave them a wiggle. "We're gonna celebrate."

“Ahh, yes.” I tucked my legs underneath me and hugged one of her many pillows to my chest. “Not only am I living on your couch because my ex is a terrible excuse for a human being, but now I’m unemployed. Definitely a reason to celebrate.” Despite my sarcasm, an odd blip of hope swelled in my heart.

Sometimes you have to burn to the ground to rise from the ashes.

That thought sounded more like it belonged in Amelia’s head than mine. Maybe I’d read it on some of her motivational wall art.

She plonked the bottle of tequila onto her coffee table and folded herself into a sitting position on the floor. “You’re inviting negativity into your life with that attitude.” She glared, which made her as ferocious as a kitten in a field of daisies. “If you listen closely,” she continued, “your higher self and spirit guides are whispering. They’re telling you what you need to know, and I promise you, losing that job is a very good thing.”

I didn’t believe in spirit guides. Or tarot readings. Or any of the woo-woo weirdness Amelia built her life around, but I loved her for it anyway. Besides, whether I believed her or not, I couldn’t ignore the feeling that my change in employment was a Very Good Thing Indeed.

Capitalized. Underlined. Bolded.

"All right, then." I scooped up a shot glass and held it her way. "To new beginnings."

"That's the spirit!" With a massive grin and a twist of the cap, Amelia cracked open the tequila and filled both glasses. She tossed hers back and I followed suit, widening my eyes and huffing a breath as it burned down my throat.

"I can't remember the last time I did shots."

Amelia paused mid-pour. "Hmm. Me neither." With a shrug, she downed her second shot and graced me with a grin that said we were in for some fun.

"Tonight, we're gonna rewrite everything that jackass said when he fired you. We're gonna build you up because, Eveline, you are so fine." She giggled at her silly rhyme and handed me my next shot. "It's time for you to unleash your real self on the world."

I tossed it back as she poured another. "It'd be nice if creepy men would stop unleashing themselves on me."

Five hours ago, my boss sat me down and broke my world by saying I was an acceptable writer, with piles of unrealized potential, but I played things too safe. The man I'd thought of as a mentor stared me in the eyes and said, "Evie, if you were a color, you'd be taupe."

Not powerful, sophisticated black.

Not cool, calm, has-it-together teal.

Not fiery red or sweet-as-candy pink.

Freaking taupe.

"You weren't like this when I hired you," he'd said, then went on to tell me I blended into situations like muzak in a department store. Unobtrusive. There, but not. You could bob your head without realizing. Hum along without caring. Then leave with a song you hated stuck in your head for days.

I was boring. Bland. He said my new personality seeped into my writing. In a world that ran on drama, outrage, and preferred YouTube to newspapers, he couldn't keep waiting for me to remember who I was.

As if that didn't hurt enough, he doubled down.

He told me when he hired me, he'd gotten the feeling I might be useful one day, but if I wanted to make myself useful right then, *on my knees,* he'd consider keeping me around. Pride stinging but dignity intact, I hightailed it out of there and had only looked back long enough to file a complaint with HR.

"Why did he have to go there?" I asked Amelia. "'I might be useful someday?' It's almost exactly what Drew said when he broke up with me..." I clamped my mouth closed.

Drew had said a lot of awful things that day and I'd be better off forgetting them all. My ex-boyfriend didn't deserve one more ounce of my energy. He'd taken enough from me already.

"Whenever a theme repeats through our lives, it's something our guides want us to pay attention to." Amelia threw back a shot, then jotted down the worst things my boss said on a scrap of paper.

Safe. Boring. Bland. Timid. Blow me.

"Okay. Now. Choose one word to overwrite all of that crap. One word that will define Eveline McAllister from this point forward."

She handed me the pencil with a flourish worthy of life-changing events. I studied those oh-so-taupe words written in her decadent script and imagined my life the way I wished it was. Who did I want to be? How did I want to live? When the answer came to me, I couldn't scrawl my answer fast enough.

Fearless.

The scratch of the lead across the paper was a battle cry. The extravagant stroke of that final S was my declaration. I added an exclamation point for emphasis. Then another. Then, drunk on power, tequila, and the desire to put my past behind me, I scratched a harsh line under the word.

With a decisive nod, I dropped the pencil onto the table. It clattered and rolled as Amelia leaned in to see what I'd written. A smile bloomed as her sparkling eyes met mine. "I like it. No. I love it. It's perfect. Who wouldn't want to be fearless?" She stood and spun in a slow circle in the middle of her living room. Her boho skirt fluttered around her ankles. Her bracelets jangled. Her beachy waves danced down her back.

She was so over the top.

So comfortable in her skin.

So not afraid to be her.

She inspired me to fall in love with myself the way she had—or at least make peace with my flaws. Amelia Brown was the most fearless person I knew, and I would do myself justice by learning to be more like her.

Caught up in her optimism and the swirling burn of courage in my stomach, I bobbed my head in agreement. Fearless! Perfect! Heck friggen yes!! I was even thinking in exclamation points! That had to mean I was on to something! Right? Right!

She pulled me off the ground and poured another shot for both of us. How many was that? Two? Three? Tequila flowed so fast and furious, I'd lost count. With the abandon only found on the line between tipsy and drunk, we clinked our glasses and tossed them back.

"Real change needs energy, Evie." Amelia scooped the list off the table, dropped it in a bowl, and lit it on fire. She waved a hand through the smoke like she was gathering it into her palm, then released it toward the ceiling. "Watch it burn and know."

"Know what?" I quirked my head.

She pressed a finger to my lips. "Just know."

When the paper was smoke and ash—which did

feel cathartic—she grabbed the tequila and led me to the window, both of us managing to trip on her skirt.

When did it get so long?

"Let's not focus on the past right now. Let's focus on looking forward." She pointed outside, like my future was on the sidewalk, staring up at us. I didn't think it was, but peered down, just in case. "Now that you don't have to sell your soul to Smallington City Paper you can focus on writing an actual book."

It was everything I could do not to snort. There would be no book. Not from me. Not after what happened with Drew.

"I might be better off to figure out where I'm gonna live first. I know you said I could stay here as long as I wanted, but I'm sure you miss your privacy. And your living room." The streetlights and passing cars outside the window blurred and swayed. I blinked to refocus my eyes as Amelia handed me the bottle and I took a swig. "I guess I could move into the house my Great Aunt Ruth left me."

The letter had arrived the day Drew kicked me out of our apartment. I'd been shocked, especially considering I hadn't seen Ruth since I was two and she dropped a home in my lap right when I needed it most.

"I thought we agreed you'd stay with me." Amelia threw an arm over my shoulder and the scent of vetiver, her favorite essential oil, slapped me in the face. She said it kept her centered, grounded, and happy. To me, it smelled like dirt and mossy stone. Though, after five years, it also smelled like my best friend, which meant it kept me centered, grounded, and happy, too—and given the rollercoaster my life had been on lately, I'd take all the grounded I could get.

"Sweetie, I can't live on your couch forever. Besides, we decided I wouldn't move because the house is far enough away that the commune would be awful." That didn't sound right. "Commune? Commu..."

"Compute?" Amelia smiled helpfully.

"Driving would take too long. The back and forth is too big." We stared at each other for a few ridiculous seconds then burst out laughing.

Amelia hiccupped. Staggered. Then put a hand to her heart as her eyes widened with realization. "Oh my gosh. I understand now. I can't believe I didn't see it before!"

"See what before?" I cupped my hands to the window. My breath fogged up the glass and I swiped it away, but still didn't find what had her so excited.

"We've been looking at this all wrong. That house? It was a hint from the universe and since you didn't take it, your second hint came with more oomph. You know, like losing your job?"

My jaw dropped at the magnitude of the implications. I'd been receiving hints from the universe. First Drew and the awful, terrible things he said and did to me. Then, the house. Now...my job...

It was at that point I realized I was drunk. When Amelia started talking about hints from the universe and I joined in, something wasn't right.

She took the scenic route back to the couch and lowered herself with a sigh. "Maybe you're supposed to move to this place. You have pics, right?"

Nodding, I cracked open my laptop and clicked on the images the lawyer emailed me after I got the letter, grimacing as I awaited Amelia's swift and harsh judgement.

I didn't wait long.

"You own a house that looks like that and you're still sleeping on my couch? I mean, it has a name! Sugar Maple Hill." Sighing dreamily, she swiped the bottle from my hands and took several long swallows.

"Sure it's beautiful, but the communism..." That wasn't the word I wanted. I blinked, listening to the hum of tequila whistling through my brain. Had that bottle been full when we started? It certainly wasn't anymore.

"Community?" Amelia clearly had no idea what I was talking about but was eager to help anyway.

"The long drive. The commute. Commute!" I giggled. "That sounds weird, doesn't it?" I tried out the word several more times just to be sure. "Anyway, it's a gorgeous place but apparently, everyone in Wildrose Landing thinks it's haunted." I flopped onto the couch and leaned my head back, letting it roll to the side to stare at my friend's shocked face.

Amelia shot upright and gripped my shoulders. "You're trying to be fearless, and you inherited a haunted house! No wonder you lost your job! You weren't paying attention to the signs! Evie!"

I didn't believe in either ghosts or signs, but her exclamation points were contagious. I climbed to my knees and grabbed her shoulders in return. "Do you really think so?"

"I know so. And you know what else I know? We're going to spend the weekend in that house. *Your* house. And we'll bring all your things in case you decide to stay." She pointed at the screen and shimmied. "I wonder if we'll see the ghost. Ohh! I wonder if he's like, a handsome ghost! How cool would that be?"

It'd be hard to find any evidence of a ghost, handsome or otherwise, because they didn't exist. I considered saying as much, but the more Amelia shimmied, the more I wanted to join in. Haunted or not, moving to Wildrose Landing and starting from scratch would be a pretty fearless move.

Maybe I'd write a book.

Maybe I'd fall in love.

Maybe I'd find my destiny, waiting for me in a quaint New England town.

Amelia's shimmy slowed. Her face turned a queasy shade of green. She hiccupped, then dashed for the bathroom.

Or...maybe we'd had too much tequila.

CHAPTER TWO

ALEX

It was a dark and stormy night. *Come on, man. You're better than that.*

Moonlight caught in the rain and tumbled to the street. *Now you're trying too hard.*

Rain blurred my vision and wind ripped leaves from trees as I scurried through the cover of darkness, my giant beast at my side. *Right. Moving on...*

"Why can't I even take a walk without running into writer's block?" I glanced at Morgan as his nails clicked across wet pavement.

The better question would have been, "Why was I walking my dog in the rain in the first place?" but I didn't ask that out loud. Talking to myself wasn't a trait I wanted to encourage.

With a wag of his shaggy tail and a quirk of his head, Morgan dismissed my concerns. Neither my clogged brain nor the rain pelting our backs bothered him. Meanwhile, not only did I have blank pages waiting for me at home, but I'd been too distracted to check the forecast before setting out on a walk to clear my head, so the two of us were drenched.

That sucked extra hard because my head remained anything but clear.

Raindrops sliced— *Give it a rest, man!*

Morgan paused to shake the wet out of his coat, hitting me with a deluge of dog-scented water. I returned the favor, leaning over to shake my hair his way. He thanked me with a sloppy, face-sized lick and I straightened just in time to watch a car careen onto the road.

Okay, careen was a strong word for the moderately discombobulated turn I witnessed, but my writer's brain couldn't help but amp up the drama. Which was pointless, because we didn't need more drama than we already had. Morgan took care of that in spades. As the vehicle accelerated, my dog yanked the leash out of my hand and squirreled into the road because—I shit you not—a tiny, drenched kitten sat in the path of the car.

I stopped trying to narrate. There was no need for strong verbs or dynamic language.

The only thing left in my brain was, "NO MORGAN NO WHY ARE YOU SO STUPID DON'T DIE YOU MAGNIFICENT FURRY BASTARD!"

With a barbaric shout, I lurched after my dog and scooped up the kitten, finally understanding why deer went dumb in the face of oncoming headlights. As they bore down on me, Morgan's life flashed before my eyes, with mine hot on its heels. It was a montage of memories complete with a sappy soundtrack coming from the vehicle that would end it all.

The car careened for real, swerving off the road and stopping catawampus on the grass, while I stood blinking, wide-eyed, heart freaking pounding, clutching a shivering ball of black fur in the middle of the road. I shifted the kitten under my coat to warm him as Morgan trotted over and sat at my side.

The passenger door flew open and a woman tumbled out. "Are you flippin' flappin' crazy?" she yelped, waving her arms like she thought she could fly. Her long, ruffled skirt fluttered in the wind, then clung to her ankles, weighted by the rain.

"Me? You think I'm the crazy one here?" I *was* the one who ran into the road, directly into their path, but details like that didn't matter with a crazy person stomping toward you. "Why weren't you watching where you were going?"

"Oh, we were watching! We watched ourselves right off the road, thank you very much. You're the one who needed to be paying more attention, mister." An aggressive finger speared my chest, nearly striking the trembling kitten.

Morgan eyed the animal tucked into my coat and huffed his agreement with the woman.

Traitor.

The driver's door creaked open and a smaller, quieter woman strode my way. Blonde hair. Blonder than her friend's. So pale it almost didn't have a color. Strong eyes. Strong cheeks. Soft lips. Where her friend wore her personality like a badge of honor, this woman could be anything. Anyone. She'd blend into any crowd and no one would question if she belonged.

And yet...

There was more to her. I was sure of it. It hid in her eyes, begging to be acknowledged.

I see you. The thought jumped into my brain and almost straight out my lips. I clamped them shut and glared instead.

Rain plastered her hair to her face, and she swiped it away. "Are you okay?" she asked in a velvet voice. Rich. Soft. Luxurious. It sent chills down my spine and I tried to distill the sound so I could write about it later.

And just like that, the writer's block lifted. In one glorious instant, I could see everything I'd been missing. The invisible plot hole I'd been tripping over. The backstory I hadn't been able to unwind. For the first time in weeks, my muse started whispering, and there I was, clutching a kitten in the rain with no way to record any of it.

"We're good. You?" I needed to get home, pronto, before the inspiration faded. I took a step in that direction as the woman in the namaste shirt kneeled in front of Morgan. Her bracelets jangled while she rubbed his head, cooing sweet nothings his way. His eyes slipped closed and his tongue popped out in what could only be, "Hell, yes I *am* a good boy."

The patter of the rain increased, drawing straight lines through the glow of the headlights. Thunder rolled in the distance. Lightening flashed. And the five of us stood awkwardly in the middle of the road as fragments of music dripped out of their car.

Liam McGuire? Collin West? Something poppy, but deep...

"What sent him into the road?" Madame Namaste asked as she straightened.

The call of my laptop had my feet in motion. Something told me I'd be stuck in the rain forever if Namaste saw the kitten, so I shifted my coat to cover his trembling body even more. "No freaking clue and at this point it really doesn't matter. I'm just glad no one's hurt."

"I guess that means it's destiny, then." She glanced at her friend, an extreme amount of glee dancing through her smile. "It *is* awfully unusual for a dog to run into the road for no reason at all."

It wasn't. At least not when it came to Morgan. The brute was distracted the day they handed out attention spans.

With a roll of her eyes, the driver turned her attention to me. "Can we at least give you a ride? We don't exactly know where we're going but getting you out of the rain is the least we could do after almost killing you."

She was small. Not in stature, but in personality. Her voice was quiet, her gestures contained, but purposefully so. Like she'd plopped herself in a box and said, "You shall not be bigger than this for any reason whatsoever." She reminded me of a houseplant trapped in a pot it'd outgrown, begging for space to stretch and grow.

She was mesmerizing. Sopping wet. And waiting for a response.

"It's all good. Home's close." Not as close as I'd like, given the weather, but I didn't want wet dog all over the interior of her car.

Fucking hell. I was so full of shit, even my thoughts were covered in the stuff.

Turning her down had nothing to do with wet Master Morgan dripping all over her backseat.

This woman intrigued me. With her wide eyes and wet t-shirt, she had my mind traveling down paths I didn't have time or energy to explore. If my muse was finally talking to me again, the last thing I wanted was distraction. This woman? She had "distraction" written all over her. I could feel it with every roll of thunder in the background.

I was on a deadline.

Twenty-thousand words behind schedule *before* I wasted an hour and a half of writing time on my walk.

And that—not anything to do with wet dog—was the reason Morgan and I would be slogging home through the rain. If my muse decided to focus on a stranger I'd never see again instead of the first glimpses of inspiration I'd had in weeks, I was fucking done for. I needed out of her presence sooner rather than later or my agent, my editor, my publisher, and thousands of angry readers would be up my ass so fast I'd forget my name.

The women reluctantly climbed into their car while Morgan and I started home. "Now what are we going to call you?" I asked the kitten purring against my chest. He lifted his brilliant green eyes to mine and mewed. "Larry it is then."

Morgan huffed his disapproval as taillights disappeared down the road, my inspiration evaporating as the car blinked out of view. I choked back a slew of curse words and comforted myself with the fact that I wouldn't see that particular dynamic duo again.

CHAPTER THREE

EVIE

A sopping-wet Amelia pretended to hand me a phone from her place in the passenger seat. "Eveline McAllister. This is fate calling! That whole interaction was proof you're supposed to be here. Welcome to your future, baby girl."

She beamed like we hadn't just run off the road in the rain.

Like we didn't almost kill the most handsome man in existence.

He'd been drenched, so all I knew was he had dark hair. It was long enough to hang into his eyes, which could have been any color as they'd been obscured by darkness and shadow. His smile had been kind and he loved his dog enough to run into the road to save him, but had glared at me like an unwelcome intrusion.

None of that was enough to warrant the fascination that currently had me ignoring my friend and her call from fate as we finished our drive to my Aunt Ruth's house.

I watched the man and his dog shrink in the rearview, diminishing until they disappeared from my life altogether. That shouldn't have made me as sad as it did. "I wonder why he wouldn't let us drive him home? Did I say something wrong?"

Or did he sense my terminal taupe-ness and had to run, run, run before I infected him?

Amelia sagged into her seat. "I don't know. Stranger danger?"

"Like *we* were the dangerous one in that situation." The way he stared at me felt dangerous. As did the fluttering in my belly and the fact that I kept searching for him through the rearview. I gave Amelia an "am I right or am I right?" look.

Instead of a high five of solidarity and head bob of righteousness, she grimaced. "You did almost kill him with your car."

"There is that."

It'd been dark.

And raining.

But that man...he was the stuff dreams were made

of. Broad shoulders. Dark hair. Strong features. And he seemed strangely familiar, though I wouldn't mention any of that to Amelia. She'd be handing me another phone call from fate before the words were out of my mouth.

As it turned out, our near-death experience didn't happen too far from the house. Two more turns and it came into view, stately, regal, and completely out of my league. Where I was a takeout dinner in Styrofoam boxes, this was a five-course meal on gold-encrusted dinner plates. Red maples lined the drive. Autumn had lit the leaves on fire, and they shuddered in the storm, warning us off. The glow from the porchlights welcomed me home, which was weird as I hadn't been paying an electric bill. A crack of lightening lit the sky and Amelia shrieked. I yelped in return, then pulled to a stop in front of the house.

"Talk about an eventful arrival." My friend sounded more peppy than usual. After all these years together, I hadn't known she was an adrenaline junky. Which was fine because apparently, I was too. Every whip of the wind had my heart rate spiraling. Every lightning bolt cranked the energy running through my veins. Electric excitement shivered across my nerve endings.

This was right. This house. This place. (That man.) It was all right.

I blinked away thoughts of sopping wet strangers. He was hot, but his part in this adventure was over. Time to look forward. To follow the whisperings of my higher self and spirit guides.

I grimaced at my inner monologue.

I could only follow Amelia's advice so far without feeling ridiculous.

Leaning forward, I peered through the windshield. "Do you see any shadowy figures in the windows? The internet said people were seeing shadowy figures."

Amelia practically sparkled with enthusiasm as she shook her head. "It's weird the lights are on, isn't it? Why are the lights on in a house that's been vacant for months?"

We gathered our bags and sprinted for the porch. With expectation trembling through my fingers, I slipped the key into the lock and we tumbled inside. We clutched our bags and peered into corners like the Ghost of Great Aunt's Past would jump out and yell BOO at any minute.

"It's weirdly clean in here." Amelia slid a finger over an end table. "You'd think there'd be dust or cobwebs after six months."

"I'll be honest, I don't even know how the lights are on right now. I certainly haven't been paying an electric bill."

My friend shuddered and looked at me with wide eyes. "Do you think the ghost's been paying it?"

"How can I take you seriously when you think ghosts pay bills? Obviously, there's a reasonable explanation for this."

Thunder rolled.

Lightening flashed.

Amelia cringed. "You do realize you sound like every character in every horror movie ever right now?" The quaver in her voice had me wrapping an arm around her shoulder.

"Remind me." I leaned around to meet her eyes. "Which one of us needs to work on the fearless factor?"

"Ha-ha." She slapped my arm to cover the blush in her cheeks. "Very funny."

"I thought so."

Amelia stopped in her tracks and turned to me. "Seriously though, Evie. Lean into that fearless stuff. Life is meant to be lived, not survived. You have to learn to let people in and stop worrying about them turning out to be another Drew. You can't hide yourself from the world and expect to feel good about it."

"Okay, weirdo. I hear you. Less hiding and more..." I shrugged. What was the opposite of hiding?

"Just put yourself out there, doll. That's all I'm saying."

Further exploration revealed the entire house was

weirdly clean, fully furnished, and enormous. I'd have to learn the difference between living rooms, drawing rooms, libraries, and studies in order to live here.

"This place has that weird, someone's been here recently vibe." Amelia peeked up the staircase. "Good thing I brought my sage."

I followed her gaze, running my hand along the banister. "It does feel weirdly lived in."

To my best friend's surprise, even after a thorough sage scrubbing and prayer of protection, that feeling didn't dissipate. Though, the stink factor increased tenfold. I loved Amelia, but our senses of smell would never get along.

We climbed the sweeping staircase and claimed our bedrooms, then said our goodnights. I flopped onto a king-sized, four-poster bed, burying myself in a goose down comforter and piles of pillows before flipping over to stare at the ceiling.

Was this real?

Was this house really mine?

Did Eveline McAllister really belong in a place so lavish?

"Take that Drew Stephens," I muttered, then drove my fists into the mattress as my ex-boss' face swam into view.

You could be useful...

Nope. I would not let those jerkfaces drag me

down. From this point forward, I'd be focusing on the future instead of the past. I swept my hair into a messy bun, brushed my teeth, and changed into PJs—boy shorts and a white tank. As I curled up in my new massive bed, I daydreamed about all the good things that might happen in this house.

I'd write more.

Eat better.

Maybe start yoga or Pilates.

I'd run every day and go vegan.

Or try Paleo.

Or find my perfect match and fall head over heels in love.

As I imagined this healthier, happier, more successful version of Eveline McAllister, the image of a sopping wet stranger popped into my head. With a smile on my face, I snuggled deeper into my haven of pillows and fell asleep.

Little did I know the peace was temporary.

CHAPTER FOUR

Evie

Scritch.

Scratch.

Scritchity-scratch, scratch, SCRRRRATCH!

I bolted upright, covers pressed to my chest, hair and eyes wild.

Thump, thump, thump, scratch!

"Amelia?"

I shuddered at my stupidity as I flung off my down comforter. If I'd sounded like a character in a horror movie last night, I'd just doubled down. Everyone knew the girl calling peoples' names while wearing next to nothing was the first to die.

Morning light warmed the gauzy curtains draped

over my windows and the racket continued downstairs. I pulled on a robe and crept into the hallway, not at all surprised to find Amelia coming out of her room, wide-eyed and grinning like the secret adrenaline junky she was.

"Showtime," she whispered.

Step by step, we crept down the stairs. The second my feet hit the landing, the front door shot open and a demon scrambled through. It was huge and huffing and moved so fast I didn't have time to run. It knocked me down and stood on my chest, wiggling with enthusiasm as I screamed and screamed.

"Morgan!" A male voice followed pounding foot-steps and suddenly, I was free.

Pushing up on my elbows, I found a giggling Amelia, a giant dog, and...

"What are *you* doing here?" The man and I spoke at the same time, our words dressed in identical outfits of shock, outrage, and curiosity.

I'd almost killed him the night before, so he broke into my house to exact his revenge?

Amelia made a show of answering a pretend phone call, handed it to me, then perched on the bottom step to watch the show.

The man shifted the strap of a messenger bag across his chest, then folded his arms and glared.

"Look. I don't know how you got in here, but if you leave now, I won't call the police."

His condescension fanned the fuse lit by a slobber demon named Morgan. "The same could be said in return." I scuttled to my feet, tightening my robe and hoping I hadn't given him the show I knew I had. "Why is your dog breaking into my house?"

"Nice try, lady. I happen to know the owner of this house and she's—"

"My Great Aunt Ruth. And she passed away six months ago." I arched a brow and extended a hand. "Eveline McAllister, last living descendent of Ruth Graywood."

"But you should call her Evie." Amelia grinned from her place on the stairs.

The man eyed me. "Right. Like you didn't just work some internet magic and find that info." He scoffed. "You have no idea how many ghosthunters I've had to chase away from this place since those articles hit the paper."

"Right. You've got me there." I stared at my feet like a dejected puppy, then hit him with a glare that meant business. "Oh, but, would an internet search also provide me with the key? Or the deed?" I grabbed my purse off the table near the door, found the key, and slipped it into the lock. With the man still leaning in the doorway, we were closer than I would have liked.

Especially given my lack of clothing, the fact that he'd just broken into my house, and even knowing that, I couldn't help but stare into his decadent, chocolate-colored eyes.

"Huh. Imagine that." The man stared at my key in the lock and barked a laugh. "It's nice to meet you Eveline—"

"Evie." Amelia stood and took his offered hand. "And I'm Amelia. And that's Morgan and you're...?" She practically purred and I wanted to murder her.

This guy could be a killer, or a kidnapper, or some crazy stalker. Because we'd run into him twice now—once almost literally and once *inside my house*—she was ready to call it fate and bless our marriage with sage, vetiver, and whatever stinky herb signaled eternal happiness.

"Alex Prescott." He shook her hand with a smile. "I live next door. Morgan is very sorry for breaking and entering. We...uhh...saw your car in the driveway and came to investigate."

Dark curls begged for the attention his eyes commanded. A strong nose drew my gaze down to supple lips. The strap of his messenger bag pressed a ragged T-shirt against his pecs and distressed jeans highlighted just the right amount of everything.

And when I said everything, I meant everything.

Sweet googly-moogly, the man was gifted.

I blinked as all of that circled my head then landed with the sloppy kiss of realization. "Alex Prescott? As in, Alex*ander* Prescott?"

As in, the author of world-class thrillers who graced the New York Times Bestsellers List every time he released a book. As in, the writer who'd come to speak while I was a student at Brown University and I, in all my glorious awkwardness, had decided to be brave enough to talk to him afterwards. Said decision led to me basically jogging along beside him, spewing compliments and forcing a discussion about writing as if we were friends as he tried to escape to the parking lot.

At the time, I'd been proud of myself for my bravery. For taking the initiative to talk to someone I admired. But as he lowered himself into his car and drove away, I realized I'd word-vomited a conversation at a guy who outclassed me times a million. He was so much better than me we weren't even playing the same game, and I'd gone on and on about writing as if my opinion mattered in the slightest.

That day, the angel of self-doubt landed on my shoulder and squawked in my ear. *You're the crazy girl who stalked Alexander Prescott to his car, Evie. You will be the story he tells his friends when he talks about weird interactions with fans.*

Everything Drew said after he betrayed me had

welcomed that whispering voice right back. The angel had been perched on my shoulder for months now and the litany of self-doubt was paralyzing.

Alex smiled weakly as Morgan flopped to the floor at his feet. He shifted his bag and eyed the still-open door, desperate to leave now that I'd recognized him—or maybe he'd recognized me. "That's me. *The* Alexander Prescott."

"He's a writer," I explained to Amelia. "A damn good one."

And he was hot as hell. And I stalked him to his car six years ago. And I almost killed him last night. And now, apparently, he was my neighbor. Holy shitcakes. If it wasn't impossible to die of embarrassment, I'd have called the morgue to request a pickup.

"Evie's a writer." Amelia elbowed me. "A damn good one."

Well, look at that. Death by embarrassment looked more and more possible.

I held up my hands, waving off her compliment as I met Alex's eyes. "As my best friend, she's required to say that. I think it's a law or something. I'm...well...I'm not even employed anymore so I guess that means I'm not a writer at all."

Amelia rolled her eyes. "I keep telling her to care less about those details, but she's determined to lock herself in this hierarchical box of success. Being published does not magically validate your skill, you know?" She nodded like he'd agreed, then hurried on, standing as she waved her hands through the air. "I'll leave you two to get to know each other. Coffee calls!" With a pat on Morgan's massive noggin and a less-than-secret wink my way, she disappeared into the kitchen.

"She's right, you know. Many writers more talented than me will never get a book deal."

He was being nice and somehow that made it worse. I smiled, waiting for him to recognize me as the crazy woman who stalked him to his car then sighed when he didn't. Maybe he was being polite by not bringing it up. Or maybe one of the most embarrassing moments of my life didn't even rate as memorable in his.

Alex leaned against the wall near the door. "So, Evie McAllister, inquiring minds. What job did you lose that rescinded your status as a writer?"

"I was a junior editor for a newspaper in a small city. With the economy and everything..." I shrugged and hoped he'd let his imagination fill in the blanks as to why I'd been let go. There was no way I'd tell this man I'd been called safe, bland, and boring.

Alex rapid fired questions my way.

College? Brown.

Accolades? A few.

Years of experience? Five.

"What is this? A job interview?"

Alex laughed. "Just curious." He tapped his temple. "A writer's brain is filled with questions and character details."

"My dad used to threaten to tape my lips together if I asked one more question."

"There you go, then. You know what I'm talking about." Alex pressed off the wall and I did everything I could not to drool. How could a man look that good so early in the morning? "I should let you get your day started," he said. "It was a pleasure to meet you. Sorry we basically broke in. Come on, Morgan." The dog raised his head, then begrudgingly lifted himself from the floor.

"I'll consider it payback for almost killing you last night." I frowned as I rewrapped my robe around me. "How'd you get in anyway? I could have sworn I locked the door."

Alex stared for a long minute. "You do know this house is supposed to be haunted, right? Maybe the ghost has a key."

I laughed, then shrugged. "Or maybe I forgot to use mine. It *was* a bit of an eventful arrival."

We said our goodbyes and I watched him amble down the walk, Morgan prancing at his side as autumn leaves fluttered from the trees. Dappled sunlight traced lines of rippling gold along Alex's head and shoulders. He turned and caught me staring, then lifted a hand.

As I raised my own in return, Amelia appeared beside me. "When your life implodes, it does it in the best way possible. I mean, your Karma must be amazing." She bumped her shoulder to mine. "This house is gorgeous. That man is gorgeous. That dog?"

"Gorgeous?" My gaze returned to Alex as he crossed my yard into his.

Amelia leaned her head against my shoulder. "Pretty much."

For the first time, I didn't need tequila to wonder if she was right.

CHAPTER FIVE

ALEX

The moment I stepped into my neighbor's house, my writer's block dissipated, the thick clouds obscuring my creativity parted, and I could *see*.

It was sublime and had been like that from day one.

Toward the end of her life, Ruth told me that after she passed, Sugar Maple Hill would go to a family member she hadn't seen in decades. The possibility of the house sitting vacant weighed on her, so she asked me to look after the place until the new owner arrived. I'd promised to take care of her home like it was my own, made a copy of the key, then checked in on the woman several days a week.

My days fell into a predictable pattern. Wake. Shower. Visit Mom, who'd spent a lonely life married to my mostly absent father and deserved to know she mattered. Peek in on my sister to make sure everything was moving smoothly on her end and she didn't need anything. Then take Morgan for a walk on the beach, stopping to check on Ruth on our way home. She was a sweet woman, alone in the world save for a great niece she hadn't seen since she was a child. Like my mother, Ruth deserved to know her existence mattered, and I did everything I could to bring that into focus.

The routine eroded my mornings, but something about being in my neighbor's house inspired me. When I'd leave Sugar Maple Hill, my head overflowed with plot and prose, and I'd spend the rest of the day transferring it to the page. But this morning, as I'd stood just inside the front door, my eyes locked on Evie, the effect multiplied. My characters...the plot points, setting, and backstory...they all screamed at me in a way I'd almost declared dead and gone.

As a creature of habit, the run-in with my new neighbor should have derailed my day. Instead, I floated down her walk, mesmerized by the sunlight skittering over my feet. I felt her eyes on my back and sure enough, a glance over my shoulder showed her on the porch, in that ridiculous silk robe that hid nothing and highlighted everything.

And I mean everything.

I waved. She did too. Morgan huffed at a leaf with the audacity to fall to the ground in front of him and I practically clicked my heels together in happiness.

The weight of her eyes on my back faded and I risked a peek. Her door clicked shut as I crossed the invisible line that delineated Ruth's yard from mine—well...this wasn't Ruth's yard anymore, really. It belonged to Eveline McAllister, owner of silk robes and pert nipples. Friend to neo-hippies and trespassing dogs. Blonde hair. Gray eyes. A mesmerizing smile and an aura of—

My phone rang, shattering my thoughts before they could go any further. I huffed a breath when I saw the name of the caller. "Good morning, Brighton," I said to my agent while Morgan did his business and I stared at the world around me.

Fall treated Wildrose Landing like a pampered socialite, dressing the town in designer gowns and jewels. I'd tried for years to capture in words the reds and golds of the leaves, the long slant to the sun, the crisp air, fresh and alive off the ocean. I failed every damn time. It didn't matter how many bestsellers lists I hit, I wouldn't consider myself a successful writer until I finally crystallized the essence of autumn in New England.

"*Is* it a good morning, Alex?" Brighton's snide voice

broke through my thoughts. "Are you anywhere near a finished draft? If you aren't, and let's just say I'm pretty damn sure you aren't, then this is not a good morning." The woman had the aggression and tenacity of a pit fighter, something that worked in my favor, as long as I was on her good side.

"Now see. About that. I have a bit of a dilemma—"

"We have zero fucking time for dilemmas." Brighton's sharp tone made it clear I'd overstayed my welcome on her good side. "Grab your gear, sit your ass down in your dead neighbor's house—"

I rolled my eyes. "At least pretend to be decent and have respect."

Brighton loosed a long sigh. "Sorry. I'm...my nerves are frayed, Alex. I've asked for, and gotten might I add, three extensions on this project. We're officially in danger of losing this contract. You'd have to return the advance. The scandal alone..." She sighed again and I imagined her leaning back in her office chair, pinching her nose and closing her eyes. "I know you're busy doing the eccentric author thing, where you can only write in your deceased neighbor's house, but you've officially found the end of everyone's patience. Get your ass into that kitchen and get the words on the page."

"That's where the dilemma comes in. The house is no longer vacant, Bri. Something I discovered when I used my key this morning and scared the new owner half to death."

And it was all worth it. My mind offered an image of Evie in her silk robe as proof. Yeah. Definitely worth it.

"Okay." Brighton did not sound like she cared one bit about this problem. "Now what?"

"I don't know. The words aren't coming." I shook my head as I turned my face toward the sky. How could I describe the frustration? The fear? How could I make her understand I was doing everything I could, and still got nowhere? "It's like turning on an old TV and all you see is fuzz. I'm staring at fucking static all day long and trying to find the story in it. The one place my brain stopped glitching, even a little bit, was in my neighbor's kitchen, and now someone lives there. What do you want me to do? Knock on a stranger's door and ask if I can come over every day to finish a book?"

"I don't care what you do. Use your key and write while she's asleep if you have to."

"I'm not breaking into my neighbor's house while she's asleep."

"Then make friends with her. Shit. Date her if that helps. Just finish the book. I've done my part, and I'll keep doing it. As soon as we end this call, I'll reach out to your publisher and ask for another extension. But hear me, Alex. It's time for you to stop messing around and do your job."

The call ended, as did every ounce of inspiration I'd found.

A normal person would have been joking when they suggested I break into Evie's house. Brighton most certainly was not. "I'm not that guy," I said to Morgan, who cocked his head as if to question the statement. "I'm not. Who in their right mind would do something like that? I'm not gonna date her either." We jogged up the porch steps to the front door and I let us inside.

As I unclipped Morgan's leash and hung it on the hook near the door, I had to wonder. If I wouldn't break into Evie's house because duh, and I wouldn't start a relationship of any kind with her just so I could get something I needed...what would I do?

CHAPTER SIX

Evie

Amelia strolled into the living room with a Cheshire Cat grin. She was up to something, and I suspected it had to do with a man who broke into my house at the buttcrack of dawn. "There actually isn't any coffee in the kitchen."

"You don't say."

"I do say. I just went in there to give you and sexy neighbor man some privacy. I mean, come on, if you didn't believe in the universe dropping hints, you have to after a grand display like that." Amelia gestured toward the door, then turned her focus to the living room in general. "This house is gorgeous in the daylight, by the way, and I think the sage worked.

That creepy-crawly vibe is totally gone, don't you think?"

I had so many questions that wouldn't organize themselves until caffeine hit my system. I said as much then wrapped my arms around my stomach as I realized I had no clue where to actually go to get coffee. Everything about Wildrose Landing was new and that scared me to death.

"Don't you worry about that, sweet thing." Amelia waved her phone. "While you deepened your connection with Alex, I found a cute little cafe that serves coffee, then made a list of all the places we should explore, ending in a candy shop called Sweet Stuff. This town is utopia. I'd almost consider moving here too."

"I haven't decided if I'm staying, yet." The response was knee-jerk. A defense mechanism. Out before I had time to think about what I was saying.

Amelia rolled her eyes. "I've decided for you. Believe me. You do not want to see how aggressive your spirit guides will get if you don't take their hints. Shit gets real, sweetness. You're moving. End of discussion."

Moving.

What a strange concept. A week ago, I was happily employed, living on my best friend's couch. Just a few days later, I was unemployed, living in a small town, in a house I owned but didn't feel like mine.

And worse, Amelia would be leaving me tomorrow.

"I don't think I can do this."

She frowned. "You can't explore a quaint New England town in the height of autumn? We need to work on this fearless thing more than I thought."

"No. I don't think I can live here. Without you. Without a job. Without a plan."

"First of all, you'll still have me. We'll just video chat more than we used to. Second of all, maybe you could use all this time to actually pursue your dream and write. You have enough money in savings to support you for a little while. When that runs out, maybe you could sell some furniture or something." She gestured around the living room. (Drawing room? Study? What room were we actually standing in?)

I couldn't write and she knew it, but bless her for trying to help me. "I'm suddenly realizing just how much about my life is going to change and it's freaking me out a little. What am I gonna do?"

The question was rhetorical, but Amelia folded her arms as she contemplated an answer. She was extreme and over the top, but she looked out for me like she thought it was her job and I loved her for it.

"You're going to say yes," she said decisively.

Her statement bounced off my head. Between king-sized, four poster beds, demons named Morgan, and hot neighbors who broke into my new house first thing in the morning, I had a lot going on. "Babe, what does that even mean?"

Amelia moved into the middle of the room and held out her hands. "You're going to look every opportunity in the eyes and say yes. You've been led here for a reason and I promise you, if you keep running away, you'll end up learning your lessons the hard way."

"Amelia. Darling. I love you but it's very important you hear me." I put both hands on her shoulders and stared deep into her eyes. "It's too freaking early for lessons from the universe."

Wildrose Landing proved just as quaint and eclectic as Amelia said it'd be. Set just off the coastline, the luscious, briny scent of the ocean filled the air. It combined with the sweetness of changing leaves. The comfort of oversized sweaters and the energy of the tides. Strangers waved as we passed. Shop owners stopped to introduce themselves. Apparently, our "not from around here status" was pretty much airbrushed on our foreheads.

Over and over, again and again, I'd explain that my Great Aunt Ruth had left me the house on Sugar Maple Hill and eyes would go wide. "I heard that place is haunted," they'd say, laughing nervously, ashamed to admit they might actually believe in ghosts.

While I'd try to assuage their fears, Amelia had a blast stoking the fire. "When we got there, the porch-lights were on. And she hasn't paid an electric bill! Not one! How is that even possible?"

She scattered exclamation points like confetti and the people of Wildrose gobbled them up.

As we strolled down Main Street, I grabbed her hand. "You do realize I'll forever be the woman who lives in the haunted house, right?"

"The *fearless* woman who lives in the haunted house. I'm building your brand, babycakes!" She threaded her arm through mine. "You'll thank me for this, you know."

"I'm sure you're right." I wasn't, but didn't need an argument.

I pushed through the doors of Sweet Stuff, the jingle of bells announcing our arrival. Peppy music and rows upon rows of brightly colored candy greeted us. With vibrant pastels and emoji themed décor, the place was an adult's interpretation of childhood dreams. I loved it instantly.

A brunette glanced up from behind the counter. "Hey there! Take a look around. Let me know if I can get you anything."

Amelia peered into the display case, then

wandered over to a wall of jellybeans. "I'm thinking we'll probably go with one of everything."

"Solid choice." The brunette laughed. "You guys visiting?"

"I am," chirped my friend. "But Evie here is moving in."

"New blood! I'm sure you've caught the entire town's attention by now."

"You better believe it." Amelia glanced up from a box of chocolates. "Especially after they find out she's moved into the vacant house on Sugar Maple Hill."

The woman frowned. "Sugar Maple Hill? That house..."

And here we go...

"I know, I know," I said. "That house is haunted."

"No. I mean, maybe? How would I know? I was gonna say that house is next door to my brother's." With a smile, the woman behind the counter extended a hand. "Isabelle Prescott, at your service, though everyone calls me Izzy. I'm not serious enough to be Isabelle."

"What do you know?" Amelia huffed her surprise. "Now that you mention it, the resemblance is striking."

I nodded my agreement. The brown curls. The commanding eyes. The strong cheekbones and full lips. There was no denying the Prescotts came from good genes. Though, where Alex exuded intensity, Izzy screamed fun.

She bobbed her head and leaned on the counter. "I take that to mean you already met my brother."

"And his dog." Laughing, I explained the surprise introduction that morning.

"And that was after we almost ran them over last night." Amelia described the near miss, gesturing wildly. "I keep telling Evie the universe is sending sign after sign...*after sign* her way, but she insists on taking the hard road. I feel like these two are destined to be together."

I rolled my eyes as she gestured to me. "Right," I muttered. "Because that's how the world works. The first person you almost kill when visiting a new place is your soulmate."

Izzy chuckled. "While I can't wait to hear how you almost squashed my brother, I feel it's my duty to inform you that he isn't the relationship kind of guy. He officially married his job, and no one has been able to break them up. So if signs are coming your way, it has nothing to do with him."

I was so glad to hear someone speaking sense, I almost leaned over the counter and hugged her. "I keep trying to tell Amelia here that I'm not exactly relationship ready either, no matter what she thinks fate's telling me. I'm pretty sure there's a limit on how many major life events one person should endure at a time. Losing my job and moving to a new town are more than enough at the moment, thank you."

Maybe that was an overshare, and I would have apologized, but Amelia spoke before me.

"And *I* keep telling *her* that if she doesn't learn the lessons the universe sets out for her, she'll keep getting smacked in the face with them."

The bells over the door chimed and in stepped none other than Alexander Prescott. Amelia elbowed me and whispered, "See?" at the same time he bellowed, "Izzy Prescott! I require genius nuggets!"

When his eyes met mine, he stopped short. The door clicked shut behind him as he cocked his head. "I swear you're following me."

"Except you keep showing up where I am, not the other way around."

He started to concede the point, then thought better of it. "Not last night. I'm sure I was on that road first."

"You got me there," I said as Amelia dug her elbow into my side for no apparent reason. At least she stopped handing me imaginary phones.

Izzy came out from around the counter and hugged her brother. "Aren't you supposed to be writing?"

"Hence the need for genius nuggets." He shoved his hands in his pockets and bobbed his head, the pink neon sign behind him dancing in his wayward curls. With his air of masculinity, Alex Prescott did not look like he belonged in Sweet Stuff, though he moved behind the counter like he owned the place. "You good, little sister? You need anything before I disappear into the world inside my head?"

"You don't have to check on me every day, you know. I'm not mom," Izzy said to her brother, then turned to me. "Alex swears copious amounts of jelly-beans are the only reason he's ever finished a book."

"Only because it's true." He leaned on the counter. "Hit me with a variety. The situation is dire."

As Izzy bagged up an obscene amount of jelly-beans, Alex turned his attention to me. "I hear you're making waves around Wildrose. You two are the only thing anyone wants to talk about."

"I'm sure that'll fade. I never hold people's attention very long."

Amelia smacked my arm. "Be nice to you."

Alex's gaze skated across my face. "Yeah. Be nice to you. You have my attention."

The bag of candy in Izzy's hands hit the floor with a *thwack* and she giggled as she bent to pick it up. "Sorry. Ignore me. I'm just not comfortable hearing my brother flirt. Like, at all."

Alex smirked. "Very funny, but I'm not flirting."

"You have *my* attention," Izzy intoned, leaning on

the counter and hitting me with exaggerated bedroom eyes.

Amelia nodded her agreement. "She's not wrong."

His attention bobbed between the two women. "Oh, she's wrong." He took the bag of jellybeans from his sister and popped one into his mouth. "See, I'm considering offering our friend Evie McAllister here a job. I'd be an idiot to flirt with a potential employee."

"A job?" Izzy, Amelia, and I said in unison, then burst out giggling when Alex blinked back in surprise.

"Since when were you even considering hiring someone?" Izzy asked.

"Since the entire town started whispering Evie's name today. I followed the wave of 'there's someone living in that haunted house,' and the more I thought about it, the more I realized she might be exactly what I need. Someone to read through my drafts. Critiques. Edits before I send things to my editor. We could hang out in her kitchen while she offers moral support. That kind of thing." He popped another jellybean into his mouth and chewed around a grin.

I blinked at the man. Once. Twice. A third time. "I'm sorry. I keep waiting for the punchline."

"No punchline. Think it over, but the offer is as genuine as it is spontaneous. I just have a good feeling about you. You did come highly recommended after all." He dropped a wink at Amelia who dug her elbow into my ribs for the eight hundredth time that day, then gathered his genius nuggets and breezed through the door.

"Okay," said Izzy. "I'm officially a convert to signs from the universe. My brother doesn't flirt, and he definitely doesn't offer jobs to strangers."

"See." Amelia folded her arms over her chest and beamed.

We returned home with bags of goodies draped over our arms. Amelia made a beeline for the kitchen to break into one of her many bags of candy and pulled up short. "Evie! Look at this!"

I peered over her shoulder into a perfectly normal kitchen. "Look at what?"

"See that chair? The one at the little table under the window? I definitely sat there this morning and I know for a fact I pushed it back in."

Two chairs cozied up perfectly to a breakfast table nestled under a large window looking into the backyard. The third sat at an angle about three feet away and I scooted it back in place. "Maybe you forgot in your hurry to make your point about hints from the universe."

"I didn't. I am a serial chair pusher-inner." She

studied the rest of the kitchen, then gasped at the counter. With wide eyes, she yanked open a cabinet and pulled out a mug. "Oh my *God!* Evie! I didn't put this away! I had it out, realized there wasn't any coffee, then put it on the counter. I'm too much of a slob to put it all the way back in the cabinet!"

"Which is it? You're a serial neat freak who never forgets to push in a chair? Or you're a slob who never cleans up after herself?"

Amelia sagged. "I'm holding proof of the ghost right here in my hands and you're too busy being a smartass to care." She waggled the mug in the air, then clunked it onto the counter and disappeared in search of more signs.

While she careened through the living room—drawing room? Study? I really needed to learn the difference—I peered out the window toward Alex's house. What did it say about me that we may have found proof of an actual ghost, but all I wanted to think about was my neighbor?

"It says my priorities are straight," I whispered. Anyone who didn't want to think about a man who looked like that had a wire loose somewhere.

CHAPTER SEVEN

ALEX

My office had been the death knell to my creativity for months, but today was worse. For every minute I worked in the document, I spent ten more scrutinizing my new neighbor as she dug in the flowerbeds in front of her house.

Her hair fought the sun over who could give off more light. Her back was to me, but I could feel her smile and it fed my own. She was my metronome. The hypnotic tick of her actions swirled through my consciousness. Her schedule dictated mine.

I typed the lines into the document. They didn't make sense in the context of the story, but I was desperate to see words on the page. Maybe, if I could get them out of my head, I could make progress on my book. A quick copy and paste sent them into my slush pile—a waiting room for scenes and sentences I liked but couldn't use. Maybe they'd go into a book of their own someday. I'd never written a stalker before. Never been one, either, though anyone peeking in on me as I peeked out at her would beg to differ.

My fingers stilled as my gaze found Evie again. Morgan sighed and shifted at my feet, then lifted his head to hit me with a reproachful glare. "I know, I know," I leaned down to play with his ear and Larry stood from where he'd been curled into Morgan's stomach to head-bump my hand. "Get my eyes off the girl and my head in the game. I hear you, you furry dictator, you."

His tail thumped his agreement, then he stood, resting his head in my lap as he wiggled with excitement.

I read his mind as Larry climbed my jeans. "You're probably right. We both could use a good walk." Wincing, I detached the tiny cat and put him on the floor. "And you could use some restraint with those claws, man."

Nails scrabbled across the floor as Morgan bounded downstairs to whine and wag in front of his leash. The dog had a point. Maybe the crisp air would clear my head. And maybe, just maybe, standing near

Evie would jumpstart my creativity like it had the last few times I'd been with her.

Even more aware of where we were going than I was—after all, we made this trek more often than I would admit—Morgan bounded off the porch and beelined across the yard, pulling me toward our neighbor who crouched in front of her flowerbeds, digging in the dirt. The leash pulled taut, but I refused to trot after him. Desperation was not a look I wanted to wear. Tell that to a dog, though. They lived in desperation and glee—and Morgan was the doggiest dog that ever dogged.

I have to get to that squirrel, or I will die!

I have to eat now, or I will never have another bite!

This is the best walk of all the walks we've ever been on, but I sure wish I had more food! Hey! What's that? A squirrel! Can I eat it? I will try!

Evie glanced up as Morgan arrived, happy and wiggling beside her. "Well, good morning to you, sir!" She rubbed his head, laughing as he bowled her over in his enthusiasm for more love.

I crouched, intervening to the best of my ability. "I'd apologize, but it's pointless. He's not ashamed of his behavior, so I won't be either."

Evie's laughter had the same indescribable quality as Wildrose Landing in autumn. I'd spend the rest of my career trying to nail it down. "This is the kind of greeting a person could get used to. Morgan sure knows how to make a girl feel special."

She glanced at me and her smile faded. "I'm sorry," she murmured. "Did I upset you?"

I quirked my head. "How would you upset me?"

"You're glaring. Hard."

I'd been trying to catalogue her. To sum her up the way I would a character in one of my books. To find the perfect combination of words to bring out the effervescence bubbling under her surface. The life surging through her gaze, contained by what? Fear? Doubt?

Evie fidgeted and I realized I was still staring. Intensely.

I shifted my focus to the dog. "If I'm glaring, it's because of work. Or my utter inability to work. Nothing to do with you. Promise. Not being able to write is like not being able to breathe." Or pay the bills.

I summoned a smile and offered Evie a hand.

Her eyes made promises she wasn't bold enough to keep. This woman with her hair battling the sun...

She wiped dirt from her hands and allowed me to help her off the ground while I mentally repeated the line, hoping to burn it into my brain so as not to forget it before I got home. How was it that this woman held the key to my inspiration?

"The great Alexander Prescott can't focus?" Evie blushed and glanced at her feet. "I assumed words and plots and characters flowed out of your fingers straight onto the page."

"Sometimes they do. Sometimes, an entire day passes with my butt in that chair and my mind in the story and I don't realize until Morgan drops his food bowl at my feet." I grimaced as she sat on the bottom step and rubbed his ears.

"Poor Morgan. Mean ole' Alex making you wait for dinner." Morgan panted his agreement and leaned into her.

"I thought having him around would stop me from disappearing like that." I perched on the step beside them. "He helps. Maybe too much right now. And I make up for the days I ignore him by taking him for walks in the pouring rain just because he asked nicely."

Evie giggled. Her gaze bounced off mine, then settled on the dirt caking her shoes. She brushed it off. "Isn't getting lost in the flow part of the magic of being a writer? Why would you intentionally keep yourself from it?"

My face darkened. The smile faded. Friendliness leeched out of my eyes. I rubbed Morgan's ears and willed myself not to scare my new neighbor more than I already had. Thankfully, her gaze stayed glued to her shoes and she missed the monster who dashed across my face, looking up in time to see the hero. After Candace stormed out of my life, claiming I was just like my father and too selfish for my own good, I'd adopted Morgan and sworn off serious relationships. Caring for a dog would remind me there's more to the world than work, while staying away from commitment would mean one less Prescott man letting people down.

"I have my reasons." I winked. Yep. That happened. A wink. What was I doing?

"Ahh, yes. Reasons," Evie said with a quirk of her head and a glint in her eyes. "Something a failed writer like myself couldn't possibly understand."

"I'm with your friend on this one. Your unemployed status doesn't make you a failed writer."

"But the lack of having any completed books does."

"I wasn't going to say it, seeing as how we barely know each other, but yeah. The thing about a writer is..."

"...she writes." Evie shrugged as she finished my sentence. "I'm afraid of writing. Well, not afraid. Okay, maybe kind of afraid. My confidence took a hit. A couple hits. And now I question everything I try to put on the page."

Morgan plopped his head into Evie's lap. She ruffled his ears and leaned in to kiss his snout. His quick glance my way said, "You better make your move or she's mine, asshole."

Silly dog. No moves would be made. I would not repeat the mistakes of the past.

I stood, offering her a hand to help her do the same. "I feel like this needs to be said, just in case. I know offering you a job out of the blue is a little weird, especially because I don't really know what the job will be and we don't know each other. If I put you on the spot, please don't feel like you have to accept the offer. I have this habit of really going after what I want."

And what I wanted were more chances to be around her because somehow, someway, she opened up the floodgates that had been closed for weeks now. Bonus points because I would talk her into working in her kitchen, which would circumvent Brighton's suggestion of breaking in, something I'd be forever ashamed to admit I tried. After the women left the house yesterday, I used my key, sat down at the kitchen table, considered making coffee, then left, relieved to know my selfishness actually had a limit. After hearing Evie's name on everyone's lips, the idea to offer her a job landed with a heavy thwack of "Hey! That could work!"

Evie's eyes widened. She blinked. Licked her lips. A hard swallow and an open mouth as she searched for words had me realizing what I said could be taken in more ways than one.

Shit, Prescott. She thinks you're coming onto her. Clarify!

"And what I really want is to drag myself out of this writer's block in any way possible. I have this good feeling you're just the thing I need." Plus, let's not forget, she was smokin' hot. And easy to be around. And my sister seemed to like her.

Evie's mouth closed and a blush pinked her cheeks. Her teeth captured her bottom lip, and I swore she still wasn't happy with what I said until a smile finally thawed her features. "It would be an honor to work for you, Mr. Prescott. I do have questions about pay and hours and you know, job responsibilities and all, but assuming those things actually exist, I'm game if you are."

I fought the urge to fist bump the sky. *Game? Hell yes, I'm game! Finished draft, here I come.*

"All right, then." I smiled. "We can talk some more about salary and all that boring shit tomorrow. See if you still want to take me up on the deal once we actually know what I'm offering you."

Evie shoved her hands in her back pockets as she met my eyes. Her smile was bold, but her eyes were scared. "Well, see," she said with that indescribable laugh, "I'm trying this new thing where I say 'yes' instead of 'no.' No matter the terms, at this point, I'm all yours, Boss. I'm basically not allowed to turn you down."

"You should be careful saying that to strangers, Evie."

"What? That I'm all theirs?"

"That you're not allowed to say no. That could get you into more trouble than you're prepared for."

Her face blanched.

"But don't worry. I promise not to take advantage of you." I shoved my hands in my pockets and grinned. "Too much."

My phone buzzed and I pulled it out of my pocket to the sound of her laughter.

Jude: I'm sensing a disturbance in the force. Apparently your neighbor's house is occupado? Doesn't that put a kink in your plans?

I apologized to Evie for the interruption before replying.

Me: I'm adapting. Beers? Tonight.

A series of gif responses had me laughing and Evie looking curious.

"Apparently I have plans tonight." I waved the

phone. The next thing out of my mouth was going to be an invitation to join us.

Was that wise?

I clamped my jaw shut and the silence dripped with awkwardness.

"Lucky you," she replied with a light laugh. Hands still in pockets. Rocking back on heels. Her body language said she wouldn't mind the invitation. Maybe it wouldn't be a bad idea, after all...

The front door squeaked open and I rejoiced in the interruption.

"Oh, Evie!" sang Madame Namaste. "I hate to interrupt your sexual fantasies about sexy neighbor man..." She pulled up short as her eyes met mine. "Oh. You're here. Hi." She lifted a hand as Evie choked and yanked her hands out of her pockets to cover her face.

"Amelia!" she hissed, peeking out from behind her fingers. Color rose in her cheeks and I swore she was praying for the ground to open up and swallow her whole. "I cannot believe you just did that!"

Her friend's skirt swished over the steps as she descended. "I...uh...was just coming to tell you my brother will be here to pick me up in an hour."

Evie looked like she was contemplating murder, then glanced at me like she wanted to explain, then dissolved in giggles. "I am so sorry."

I held out my hands. "And on that note, it's time for

this sexy neighbor man to head on out." Morgan bounded to his feet and trotted after me while Evie whisper-yelled at her friend.

I couldn't make out everything they said, but I did hear Amelia say, "It's not like he can't tell you think he's gorgeous!" It wasn't hard to believe she raised her voice just to be sure I heard. As I crossed into my yard, I started wondering why I hadn't asked Evie out for drinks with Jude.

She was alone in a new house, in a new town, with her moral support leaving in an hour. That wouldn't do. Not at all. Telling myself I was taking care of my newest (and only) employee, I shot my sister a text, suggesting she invite my new neighbor out sometime.

That had nothing to do with me liking Evie. It certainly had nothing to do with me worrying about her, all alone in a new place. It most definitely had nothing to do with enjoying being called "sexy neighbor man."

Obviously, I was doing what any boss would do for a new employee.

Morgan glanced up as I laughed.

"I'm not even fooling you, am I Morginator?"

I was nowhere near fluent in dog, but I was pretty sure the beast agreed I was full of shit.

CHAPTER EIGHT

EVIE

I didn't know whether to laugh or cry, but Amelia had no problem choosing between the two. She laughed so hard she had to sit on one of the steps.

I scowled down at her from my place on the porch. "You are so lucky one of us isn't dead right now."

"Why would either of us be dead?" she wheezed, doubling down on the giggles. I hadn't realized I was that funny, but as usual, her good mood was contagious.

"Me? Embarrassment. You? Because I could kill you for mentioning my sexual daydreams about my neighbor...*while I was talking to him.*" I joined her on the step. "I'm gonna work with that man. If I wasn't trying out this new fearless thing, I'd have quit on the spot and reclaimed my place on your couch."

Amelia rolled her eyes. "It's not like you're the first person to have a crush on her boss."

"But I might be the first person to crush on a boss she mildly stalked six years ago and probably doesn't have the skill she needs for the job he's hiring her to do."

Well, hell. I hadn't meant to bring that up. It would have been better for all of us if that story stayed buried in my memory where it belonged.

Fearless, Evie. Remember what fearless feels like. All that self-doubt? Not working for you. I mentally squared my shoulders and lifted my chin.

"You mildly stalked Alexander Prescott?"

I nodded. "I don't think he remembers, though. Either that or he's being very polite about the whole thing." Keeping an eye on those dark curls as he sauntered across the yards, I explained what happened, whispering in case sound traveled in unexpected ways. One accidental embarrassment was enough for the day.

Amelia leaned her head against mine. "Oh, Evie. I'm sure it's not as bad as you remember it."

"You're right. It's probably worse."

"More likely, it's something that happens to him all the time. I mean, you can't look as good as he does and be as talented as he is and not have random women throwing themselves at you on a daily basis." She laughed and I did too.

"I'm gonna miss you and your perpetual optimism."

Amelia could be a lot to handle, but her irreverent positivity hid a woman who felt deeply and took care of her people. Without her, Wildrose Landing would feel bigger and less friendly, that much I knew for sure.

"I'm gonna miss you too. But the commune isn't as bad as you made it out to be." She winked and bumped her shoulder against mine as she waited for me to get the joke. "We'll see each other more than you think."

"That better be a promise."

I was scared to be alone and she knew it, but neither one of us said anything. Fearless Eveline McAllister didn't acknowledge anxiety, and happy-go-lucky Amelia Brown never gave it the time of day in the first place.

"You didn't have to ask Darian to come get you. I would have been happy to drive you home."

Amelia hit me with a look that cut through the bullshit. "Just because you don't like my brother doesn't mean you should lose a chunk of your day chauffeuring me around."

"That's not what I meant." I picked at the dirt under my nails.

It wasn't that I didn't like Darian. He just inevitably rubbed me the wrong way. The man was somehow both identical to and completely different from his sister. They knew who they were and had no qualms being true to themselves, but where Amelia was into signs from the universe and plant medicine, Darian fell squarely into logic, science, and mild assholery.

Amelia tossed an arm over my shoulder. "I get it. He's exhausting with his need for proof and his inability to have a little faith in things he can't see. But, he is my brother, Evie."

"I know, love. I'll try and be cordial when he gets here."

"But not too cordial, in case sexy neighbor man is watching." She giggled and the breeze flooded my nostrils with her essential oils. Maybe I'd buy some after she left.

"You shouldn't have brought that back up. I'd almost forgotten you embarrassed me like that."

"Yeah, right." Amelia arched an eyebrow. "Like you've ever forgotten anything. Might as well call you Dumbo."

I scrunched up my nose and shook my head. "I'd rather you didn't."

An hour passed with us on the stoop, wrapped in friendship and conversation as red leaves see-sawed to the grass. Darian's Tesla rolled to a stop in front of the house. He unfurled his long frame from the driver's seat and let out a low whistle. "Okay then, Evie. What's the catch?"

I stood and rested a hand on the handrail. "What do you mean, what's the catch?"

"I mean, houses like this don't just drop into people's laps. Is it falling apart? Does it need new wiring? Plumbing? Are the neighbors running a meth lab out of their basement?"

My gaze bounced to Alex's house. No meth labs. Just crushing good looks and a total lack of interest in me. "There's no catch. Well, other than the loss of my Great Aunt Ruth."

"The fact that it's haunted is a pretty big catch." Amelia shimmied in excitement as Darian rolled his eyes.

"There's no ghost," I said before he could eviscerate his sister.

Her jaw dropped. "Then how do you explain the lights? The lack of dust? Or what about the fact that the kitchen was rearranged when we got home yesterday? Or the shadowy figure everyone seems to see through the windows?"

"The kitchen wasn't rearranged," I explained to Darian. "We just couldn't remember if we were slobs or neat freaks." The rest I had no explanation for, other than the fact that small towns loved to gossip.

Amelia slapped my arm. "You have a clean ghost, and you know it, but you're trying to look cool and impress my brother."

"Evie doesn't have to work to impress me. You know that." Darian slipped an arm around my shoulder.

I shifted out of his reach to wrap Amelia in a hug. "Thank you for coming out here with me."

She squeezed until I saw stars. "Thank you for letting me spend a night in a haunted house. And for not killing me when I let it slip that you have a massive crush on your super-hot neighbor."

She dropped her bags in her brother's car, hugged me one last time, then drove away, officially leaving me alone in the brand-new life I hadn't wanted.

I watched them go, then returned to planting the daffodil, crocus, and hyacinth bulbs I'd been working on when Alex arrived. With the house fully furnished and my job situation sketchy at best, my desire to nest seemed destined to happen outside. The fruits of my labor wouldn't appear until the spring, but the best things in this world took time. It was the wait that made it worth it.

At least, that was what I kept telling myself.

When I finally break out of my shell, it'll be worth it!

When I finally publish a book, it'll be worth it!

Maybe I'd been making excuses for myself all along and time was the slow erosion of good intentions.

The crunch of leaves under feet interrupted my thoughts, announcing someone walking up the driveway. Was it Alex? The ghost? Either option would make my afternoon. I spun, surprised to find an older woman headed my way, her salt and pepper hair pulled into a bun at the nape of her neck. A friendly smile lifted her lips while shrewd eyes raked over my face. A gingham cloth covered a casserole dish clutched in her hands. "Hello there, neighbor!"

I stood, brushing dirt from my palms. "Hi! How are—"

"I live right across the street, there. When I heard someone had moved into Ruth Graywood's place, I just about danced through town. I baked you a lasagna because everyone knows a full stomach makes you feel like home." She held out the dish. "I'm Greta Macmillan and I'd officially like to welcome you to Wildrose Landing."

"Thank you so—"

"I came by earlier, but saw you with your girlfriend." She leaned in. "I experimented a little when I was younger too. You'll get no judgement from me. Love knows no boundaries."

"Amelia's just my friend, Mrs.—"

"Please. Call me Greta. And call your friend whatever you want. Your secret's safe with me." Something in her smile told me nothing was safe with her.

"Thank you." I held out the lasagna. "I'm sure I'll enjoy—"

"Well, dear." Greta dug in her purse and pulled out her phone. "I've taken up enough of your time. I'll just be on my way. I'll be back later to pick up my casserole dish."

She turned and ambled down the drive, typing wildly on her device, leaving me to stare in confusion. As Greta reached the street, my phone buzzed from its place on the porch and I scurried up the stairs. Instead of the zany text from Amelia I expected, I found something from an unknown number.

Hey, Evie! It's Izzy, seller of genius nuggets and sister to neighbors. Would you, by any chance, want to meet for drinks tonight? Thought you might like to have a friend. Also, I'm not a crazy stalker, but my brother might be. I got your number from him.

My first response was to say no. In fact, I had the reply tapped out, complete with a perfect excuse of exhaustion and overwhelm, when I remembered I was supposed to say yes to everything.

Well, shit.

My thumb hovered over the send button, but I finally deleted the text and typed in a new response, complete with enough exclamation points to make Amelia proud.

"Remember to be fearless, Evie. Say yes. Stop hiding," I muttered to my phone as I hit send.

Me: Sign me up! Where? When? And thanks for asking me!

Izzy shot me the name of a bar Amelia pointed out in our explorations yesterday. We made plans to meet at six and I practically skipped inside to get ready, carefully looking for signs of the ghost along the way.

CHAPTER NINE

ALEX

Energy dripped from the walls at Cheers 'n Beers—the bar owned and managed by one of my closest friends, Jude Malone—while judgement clouded my friends' smirking faces. "Watching my neighbor through my office window doesn't make me a stalker." I glared down the bar, daring them to say anything different.

"I think watching people when they don't know you're looking is one of the key elements of stalking." Jude quirked a brow then turned to our friend Austin, who shrugged and tossed back the rest of his beer.

"I don't know. Alex is always staring out windows. Just 'cause his neighbor is outside when he does it doesn't make him a stalker."

"Yes." I flared my hands and bobbed my head. "Exactly. Thanks, Austin."

"Yeah. Thanks, Austin. For ruining all the fun." Jude leaned his elbows on the bar. "Now what will I tease him about?"

"Don't worry." Austin grinned. "He'll give you plenty of ammo before the night's over. Of that you can be sure."

"Remind me why I'm out with you two tonight?" I quirked my head as I shifted my drink between my hands.

"Because Cheers 'n Beers is the place to be, especially when you're out with me." Only Jude could pull off a statement that ridiculous.

"The good news is, if you're here, you can't be stalking your neighbor." Austin's gruff voice quirked with laughter.

Jude guffawed and offered him a high five.

"You guys are assholes." I threw back the rest of my beer and signaled for another.

"That's good," Jude said. "You fit right in."

"Have either of you heard from Jack? Any chance he'll be here tonight?"

Austin shook his head. "His sitter fell through. Man, that guy sure could use a break. Life just keeps smacking him in the head."

Jude and I bobbed our heads in agreement. Somehow, Jack Cooper had been enrolled in the school of hard knocks. Of all of us, he was the one who least deserved it.

Seeing as most of Wildrose Landing had decided to celebrate the end of the weekend with drinks, the front door had been swinging open all night long. The crowd got bigger. The sound got louder. People came and went, and I didn't care. Until—it was like a tap on my shoulder and a whisper in my ear, "Hey! Asshole! Look who's here!" I glanced at the entrance just in time to see Evie come through with Izzy.

Our eyes met. Her cheeks flushed. My drink paused on the way to my mouth.

Austin followed my gaze. "No wonder you're stalking her."

"I'm not stalking her," I muttered.

Jude shot him a questioning look. "Her as in...?"

Austin indicated the door with the neck of his beer. "The only face I don't recognize in the place. The powers of deduction insist that is none other than Eveline McAllister, hanging out with Izzy Prescott. Seems like a hell of a coincidence, if you ask me."

"We weren't asking you," I gruffed.

"The powers of deduction?" Jude drew his eyebrows together. "Fancy words for a mechanic."

"A mechanic who owns the best auto repair shop in three counties and hangs out with a writer. Funny.

Seems to me you're the one with the shit vocabulary." Austin cocked a dark eyebrow and went back to his drink.

To my horror, Izzy caught Evie staring, saw me, and dragged her over. "Hello there, big brother!" She slipped onto the stool beside me while Evie hung back. "What brings you out tonight?" She waved at Austin and Jude, sweet as pie.

"Drinks with friends." I brandished my beer. "You?"

I inwardly cursed my little sister and her not-so-subtle game. She knew I'd be here tonight because I freaking told her where I was going when I suggested she ask Evie to hang out sometime. I also informed her that I purposefully hadn't invited my neighbor because, reasons.

"Same!" she chirped, then introduced Evie to the guys. "This is Jude Malone," she said, her cheeks blushing, eyes batting, heart fluttering. Izzy had never been able to say his name without imitating melted caramel. "And this handsome lug is Austin O'Connor. Guys, meet Eveline McAllister, better known as Evie the magnificent, Alex's new neighbor."

Handshakes happened all round and Jude suggested we move to a table. "They're better for conversation when you're in a group this big."

If I'd wanted to be in a group this big, I would have

invited Evie out myself and I gave Izzy a glare that said as much. She fluttered her eyelids, grinned like a maniac, and claimed a seat as far from Jude as possible.

"What's it like, living in a haunted house?" Austin asked as Evie took the chair across from me.

"Honestly? Exhausting." She puffed out her cheeks and widened her eyes. "I've only been here for two days and everyone already knows me as that woman who lives with a ghost. I don't know if I'll ever live it down."

A waitress sauntered over, her gaze tracing Austin's tattoos. Between his blue-collar masculinity and Jude's energy, our table always caught the attention of the fairer sex. "Hey ladies," she squawked. "What can I get ya?" Her eyes fell on Evie, then widened. "Ohmygoodness," she breathed. "You're the new girl. I have to know, and I promised my friend Alice I'd ask if you ever came here, but is your house really haunted? One time, my cousin Ethan told my sister who told me that she saw a man standing in the window. It was, like, super creepy."

"I think it might be," Evie said in a conspiratorial whisper. When the waitress' eyes widened, she continued, "For one, the lights were all on when I first showed up and I've never even paid one bill. The house is really clean. Like super clean. It's like living with a slightly OCD roommate I never see."

The waitress frowned as Jude choked on his beer and guilt washed over me. Letting the town talk about the ghost—aka: *me*—had seemed like a harmless diversion...until now. While I wrestled with my conscious, Evie and Izzy placed their orders and the woman sashayed away.

"It's like that," Evie said when she was gone. "I spent my first day trying to assure everyone it's not haunted, but that wasn't helping at all. I figured I might as well have some fun with it."

"Speaking of fun..." Jude's eyes gleamed in that way that always ended with one of us in trouble. "I just had an idea."

Austin and I groaned. "No, thanks." I rolled my eyes to the ceiling while Austin nodded his agreement.

"You don't even know what my idea is, yet." Jude pouted.

"Don't need to." Austin crossed his ankle over his knee and leaned back in his chair. "We all pass anyway."

Jude leaned in. "We're gonna play a game. Every time someone asks if the house is haunted, we take a shot. Come on!" He slapped the table. "Can you think of a better way to break the ice and get to know each other?"

"I can think of many better ways." I shook my head as I shot him down. Jude had the constitution of an ox, but Evie? She was small and delicate and looked like three drinks would break her, not the ice.

She gave me a look that said "what can you do?" and I gave her a look that said "say no." The quirk of her head reminded me I knew she couldn't say no to things and I wondered if I'd lost my mind. Did we really just have a silent conversation or was the writer's block and impending deadline truly driving me crazy?

"This is a bad idea," I said, in case my imagination had gotten the better of me.

"It is a very bad idea," Evie replied before turning to my friend. "But sure! Why not? The game is officially on."

Jude cheered. Izzy pretended not to ogle him. Austin rolled his eyes. And I tried to bat down a protective surge I wasn't supposed to feel. "You guys go ahead," I said. "One of us has to keep a level head."

"Whatever makes you happy, grandpa." Jude arched a brow, before turning to Evie. "I'd ask you what brought you to Wildrose Landing, but that would be stupid, since we all know your Great Aunt Ruth passed away and left you the house on Sugar Maple Hill." He shrugged. "Small towns. What're ya gonna do?"

She returned the gesture, her smile fading when her eyes found mine. Was I glaring again? Probably. I glanced at my beer.

"What line of work ya in?" Austin asked.

"I'm a writer." She glanced at me. "Not as good as him though. What about you?"

"Yeah," Austin sighed. "Me neither."

She frowned. "You're a writer too?"

"No, I own an auto repair shop, which means I'm nowhere near as good a writer as him." He gave her a devilish smile. "But I'm a *much* better mechanic than he is."

Evie laughed and I closed my eyes to collect as much of it as I could.

"And Jude owns this bar," Izzy supplied.

"Which is why you're receiving impeccable service tonight," he said. "Everyone wants to impress the boss."

Evie's eyes found mine. Did she want to impress her boss? Did I even count as her boss?

"I'm sorry to interrupt." A twenty-something girl with jet black hair and a distasteful facial piercing tapped on Evie's shoulder. "But you're the one who lives in the haunted house, right?"

And just like that, the game was on.

"I am. The first night I stayed there, this weird scratching sound woke me up in the morning." Evie widened her eyes and clutched her heart as the girl wobbled away, satisfied.

"I like her," Jude said, then threw back his first shot. The rest of the table followed suit.

Unfortunately, bravery was contagious. All it took was one slightly tipsy girl to set a cascade of events in motion. A grandfatherly gentleman stopped by on his way to the bathroom. "Is your house haunted?"

They took a shot.

Ted Mason, the guy who ran the farmer's market, leaned on the table. "I heard you have a ghost..."

They took a shot.

A table of soccer moms tittered their way over. "Is Sugar Maple Hill really..." The spokesperson asked in hushed tones, unable to finish the sentence.

They took a shot.

On and on it went until Evie's eyes met mine and she silently begged for help.

Okay. There was no begging, silent or otherwise. My writer's brain was a little drunk on excitement, but Evie? Evie was a lot drunk. And if something didn't happen soon, she would be on her way to bad news drunk. Jude and Austin had taken to loudly discussing the ghost, laughing like assholes whenever someone new took the bait and seeing as how I was to blame for all of this, I couldn't let it go on any longer.

"All right, guys," I said after their fifth shot. "Something tells me Evie isn't having as much fun as you."

She laughed, blinking furiously to focus her eyes. "I'm having fun. You guys are the besht! Who knew I loved tequila so much?"

I glanced at Izzy who didn't look much better, then at Jude and Austin in turn. They zeroed in on the women, then grimaced.

Jude ran a hand through his blonde hair. "Maybe I didn't think this one through."

"You think?"

Evie stumbled to her feet, staggering a little as she detached from her chair. "I'ma gonna commune to the bathroom." She giggled. "Commune. Communism. Compute. What is it with that word when I drink?" she muttered as she wandered away.

"Thank God I opted out of the game." I practically growled. "Now I have two drunk women to take home."

Jude leaned back and threaded his hands behind his head. "Sounds like a problem we all wish we could have."

"One of them's my sister, you dip-shit."

Izzy lifted her hand and twiddled her fingers. "Alex's sister. At your service."

"Why don't I take Izzy home so you can take Evie home?" Jude asked.

My sister panicked. Her hormones screamed yes while common sense said no. Me? I wondered how no one else at the table picked up the fact that she'd been in love with him for years.

"No, no, no." She waved him away like the bad

decision he was. “That’s okay. You’re just as drunk as me. I can get myself home.” Her sentence came out as one long word.

“I am nowhere near as drunk as you.” Jude guffawed. “I have the constitution of a moose. You are a delicate flower who looks like she might blow chunks all over everything.”

“Neither one of those things are true,” I said. “Izzy is not delicate. Nor will she throw up in my car when I take both women home. Will she?” I gave my sister a pointed look and she practically vomited her agreement.

CHAPTER TEN

ALEX

With much stumbling and staggering, I got Evie and Izzy out of the bar. My sister slid into the backseat of my car like a baseball player stealing home and Evie briefly met my eyes before stumbling into the fender. "Whoops. Sorry."

I couldn't tell if she was apologizing to me or the vehicle, but I wrapped an arm around her shoulder to steady her anyway. She breathed deeply, her eyes sliding closed as she leaned a cheek to my chest.

"Did you just smell me?" I asked the top of her head.

She bolted upright. Eyes wild. Nostrils flared. "Yes. I mean no. No. I did not just smell you. I mean. I did. I was close enough to get a whiff of your cologne..." Panic tangoed across her face.

I laughed and patted her arm. "Easy, now. Don't hurt yourself."

Seeing as she had just smelled me, I felt it only fair to return the favor. As I guided her into the passenger seat, I took a whiff of her hair. Underneath the heavy dose of tequila, I caught something spicy. For someone so delicate, I expected lavender, or apple. Something popular and easy to name.

Guess I didn't have her quite as pegged as I thought I did.

Izzy chattered away on the short drive to her house, a cute two-story complete with a white picket fence. All she needed was the husband, dog, and two-point-five kids to complete the American dream. After she extricated herself from the backseat, she leaned in through the window and planted a sloppy kiss on my cheek before sashaying up to the front door and disappearing inside.

Evie leaned out her window, smiling and waving. "Bye!" she called to Izzy's porch, then pulled herself back into the car and to me. Her mouth worked as if she had something to say, but then she stared at her fingers, worrying the hem of her shirt. I threw an arm on the back of her seat and reversed out of the driveway.

"You hungry?" I asked.

"Perpetually," Evie murmured. "Hungry for validation. For connection. For..." Her eyes went wide. "You meant food. Am I hungry for food."

"That is the most expected reason to ask that question, yes."

Evie laughed. "That's the thing about me. I'm never what you expect." She threw her hands in the air like she was tossing confetti and mumbled something about exclamation points.

I was finding that to be more true with each passing moment. The woman beside me was nothing like I expected. As I waited at the end of Izzy's drive, Evie leaned back in her seat and let her head roll my way. I smiled, waiting for her to tell me if she wanted something to eat before I took her home. She stared into my eyes for an extraordinarily long time before a sweet grin teased her lips.

"Yeah," she breathed. "Connection like that." Her grin widened and her gaze softened to the point I felt downright caressed by the thing, then she swallowed hard and sat up. "You still wanna know if I want food."

"I do. It's a matter of turning left or right." I indicated the street behind us. "Left to home or right to midnight snacks."

"Is it midnight?" She looked at her wrist, only to discover she did not wear a watch.

If there had ever been a more adorable sight, I hadn't seen it.

"Figure of speech," I said as I let my gaze do a little caressing of its own. "Tell you what. I'll pick us up something to eat, then take you home. Best of both worlds."

"That's how I always imagined you'd be. Take charge of the situation." She grinned as I pulled out and took a right.

"You always imagined I'd take charge of situations, huh? Sounds like we've known each other longer than a few days."

"We've met before. But we're not supposed to talk about that."

I frowned at the woman in my front seat. I didn't recognize her, and someone who looked like that would stick in my brain. Was she a fan? Maybe she'd been at a signing? Or one of the colleges I'd spoken at? A foggy memory stood up and waved its hands. "Brown. You're the girl who escorted me to my car after my seminar!"

Evie sank lower into her seat. "I have no idea what you're talking about."

"Yes, you do."

"I plead the fifth."

"I can't believe I didn't see it sooner." She'd been as adorable then as she was now. For months afterwards, I'd thought of her and smiled.

"Oh, God." Evie sagged. "I hoped you didn't mention it because you didn't remember."

"Oh, I remember. You were on a mission. I could tell you were terrified, but you were going to talk to me, no matter what. I thought to myself, 'There's a girl who's gonna go places.'"

"Now you're just being nice. Which is also how I imagined you. But we're not supposed to talk about that, either." She patted my thigh as if I was the one who needed comforting.

"I am not just being nice. That's exactly what I thought."

Evie grew quiet as I pulled into the drive thru at Mike's—the best burger joint in town—and placed our order. By the sound of it, she hadn't gone as many places as I thought she would. She'd been so cute that day, with her square shoulders, lifted chin, and trembling voice. She had things to say and no amount of fear would keep them from being heard. I'd pegged her for success.

Fast forward a few years and she'd been fired from an uninspiring job and found herself huddled in my front seat, too afraid to speak her mind. Something had derailed her. Hard.

My curiosity went into overdrive. What could that something have been?

The woman working the drive-thru was so enthusiastic and polite, I considered giving her a tip. Evie accepted the bag and plunged her hand in search of a fry. Typically, food was a no-go in my car, but I let it slide just like I let the topic of our meeting at Brown drop.

"Oh my goodness," she said around a mouthful of food. "This is so good. Like homerun, man. I don't know how I'll ever thank you."

"You act like getting a cheap burger and a ride home is something special."

"It is. I mean, you're Alexander Prescott and I'm... me. This is a huge deal." She waved her hand around the interior of the Range Rover, then grinned around a mouthful of food.

"You work for Alexander Prescott. That makes you a huge deal by association. Besides. Maybe it would be easier on you if you just thought of me as sexy neighbor man."

Evie groaned, her gray eyes rolling wide and mortified. "Nope. Not easier at all. We promised never to bring that up again." She fished around in the bag and grinned.

"I made no such promise."

"You have pretty eyes. They're warm like sunshine, but cool too. They make me think of fall. Whiskey on the rocks. Pumpkin spice. Thick sweaters and falling leaves and the light is just gold, gold, gold." She crammed a handful of fries into her mouth while I hid a smile.

I made the turn into her drive, the red maples waving us home.

"Why'd you stop?" she asked, then stretched her neck to peer through the windshield. "Oh. We're here."

I killed the engine and watched as she hugged the fast food bag to her chest and fumbled with her seatbelt. She fumbled so long, I climbed out of the car and crossed in front. I hadn't intended to help her into her house, but with the seatbelt being an unsolvable puzzle, I'd hate to see how she approached her deadbolt. When I opened the passenger door, she was still struggling, so I leaned over her and freed her with one click.

"Now you're the one sniffing me," she said with a chuckle. She turned to look at me, our faces inches apart. Her gaze fell to my mouth and she licked her lips.

As much as I wanted to kiss her, I pulled back a fraction. Evie was wasted and I would not take advantage of that. "All I smell is burgers and fries."

"Sure, buddy. That's what they all say." Evie cackled like she'd made an epic joke and before long, I was laughing right along. I walked her up the front steps and leaned on the wall as she fished in her purse for her keys.

Moonlight caught in her hair and danced through her eyes. Her hands, delicate as new snow...

I blinked away the narration as Evie staggered. "Whoa, now," I said, gripping her shoulders to keep her from falling, as the inspiration flowed and flowed. Words piled up in my head. For the first time in a long time, I'd be up all night with a story that wouldn't leave me alone—as long as I could get home before I lost the plot.

Evie's gaze singed mine. "I had a wonderful night."

She leaned in closer. Lips parting. Eyes hooded. Head tilted. This woman, my future employee, was coming in for a kiss and I didn't hate the idea. In fact, I was a massive fan of the idea. I wanted to taste her, to touch her, to skate my fingers under her shirt and acquaint myself with the breasts I'd seen under her silk robe.

But, as the sober one in the situation, I needed to do the critical thinking for both of us.

"You, my friend, are very drunk." I helped Evie back on balance and let her go.

She blinked her eyes open and frowned, surprised to find me so far away. "I am drunk." She cradled our burgers and fries, smashing them to her chest as one finger absently ran along her bottom lip. As much as I wanted my midnight snack—Mike's was next level grub—I mentally surrendered them to her, then reminded myself to kill Austin and Jude the next time I saw them. If they hadn't gotten her drunk, I wouldn't be standing on her porch dodging drunken advances from my hot new employee.

The last thing I needed was chemistry.

And holy shit, was there chemistry.

"I should probably get to bed." She leaned against her door, one arm tossed carelessly above her head. "Unless you'd like to join me for a nightcap."

"Careful now," I said with a laugh. "One could almost call this sexual harassment."

"That's okay." She played with the ends of her hair. "I don't feel harassed at all."

"I wasn't talking about you..."

"You're so funny, Alex." She pushed off the door and started playing with the ends of mine. "I can call you Alex, right?"

My body rioted, but I deliberately put more space between us. "It's better than sexy neighbor man."

Her pretty lips formed a pout. "Hey...I thought we had a deal. No mentioning that."

"Now, now. You had a deal." I took another step back, my gaze running along her mussed hair. The makeup smeared under her eyes. The cheesy grin, complete with french fry dust in the corner of her mouth. I closed the distance between us to swipe it away. As my thumb grazed her bottom lip, Evie's eyes met mine. She grabbed my coat and pulled me closer, kissing me deeply. Sensuously. A groan worked its way up her throat and I threaded my hands into her hair, my body working on instinct, ready to set the chemistry between us ablaze.

And then my brain caught up to what was happening. Not only was I too selfish for a relationship—and something told me whatever happened between Evie and me couldn't stay casual—but I'd hired the woman so I could have access to her house. The last thing I needed was to complicate things with sex.

I dropped my hands and stepped away. "You should get in your house, eat your snack, and go to bed. I hear your boss is big into punctuality."

Evie nodded, her smile brightening her face. "Goodnight, Alex."

I raised a hand. "Goodnight."

As I climbed into my car to make the short trip into my own driveway, I realized it had been a very good night indeed.

CHAPTER ELEVEN

Evie

Still clutching the greasy bag of food to my chest, I closed my front door. My entire being glowed with happiness as I leaned against the thing, imagining Alex lingering on the porch, his hand pressed to the red paint, as if he couldn't bear to break the connection between us. One inch of wood, fiberglass, and whatever else went into a door separated his fingers from my back. I could still feel his lips on mine. His hands in my hair. The roughness of his touch that had my nipples pebbled and my lower muscles throbbing.

What a night.

What a glorious, wonderful, perfectly fearless night.

Alex Prescott drove me home. He bought me hamburgers and fries. Took care of me when I was too drunk to do it myself, then sexually harassed me on my front porch, before kissing me like I'd never been kissed before.

"I freaking love tequila." I sighed dreamily, then pushed off the door and climbed upstairs to eat french fries in bed.

"I freaking hate tequila."

I threw an arm over my head and rolled away from the sun shrieking through my window. Something crushed against my cheek. A fry.

A fry?

What in the world happened that ended up with a french fry stuck to my cheek?

I blinked, groaned, then blinked again. Maybe Izzy drove me home and we stopped for snacks...

That didn't quite seem right. Someone had driven me home, but it wasn't Izzy.

As I stared at my feet in the middle of a bed designed for royalty, I tried to stitch the night back together. We'd shared a table with Alex and his friends, who suggested we play a drinking game...and then things got blurry. Really blurry. I'd either vastly underestimated the curiosity of the residents of Wildrose Landing or overestimated my ability to handle tequila.

My clothes traced a drunken trail from the bathroom to the bed. Jeans near the door. Shirt a few steps later. Bra dangling half off the bed—leaving me in underwear and a crooked tank top. A greasy bag sat on the floor....

Wait...

Did Alex drive me home last night?

A memory surfaced. Me with my back pressed against the front door. My arm flung over my head like I thought I was a pinup model seducing the world with my sex-kitten gaze.

Oh, no, no, no, no, no...

Alex *did* drive me home last night.

And how did my drunk brain think to repay him? By flirting mercilessly, then stealing his burger and fries to devour in a fourposter bed like a deranged chipmunk beefing up for winter.

The words sexual harassment danced through the memory...words he'd spoken.

He'd been joking. I was sure of it. He had to be.

Please, please, please tell me he was joking.

Oh, shit. I kissed him, didn't I? He'd been a perfect gentleman and I kissed him.

What kind of idiot threw herself at her boss before she officially started the job? This kind of idiot apparently. With a sigh, I stood, scrubbed my face, and worked on piecing together the rest of the night.

"Oh, God. Kill me now." In the history of embarrassment, last night stole the show. I'd need to figure out a way to apologize, but my pounding head demanded caffeine in exchange for the safe return of my ability to process thoughts. But more important than my need for coffee was the bladder full of tequila. I waddle-walked into the bathroom, peed, then turned on the faucet to wash my hands.

A loud thump came from downstairs.

The hairs on the back of my neck stood on end.

I paused while splashing water on my face and turned off the faucet, drips falling from my nose and chin. Another thump. A bang.

Something was happening down there. A big something.

Was that the scrape of a chair? Holy shit! Was Amelia right the whole time? Was the ghost downstairs moving things around in the kitchen?

I scurried back into my room and swiped my phone off the bedside table as the thumps and bangs continued.

Me: OMG I THINK I HEAR THE GHOST DOWNSTAIRS BUT I MIGHT BE SO HUNGOVER I'M HALLUCINATING!!!!!

Amelia: Why, in the name of all things holy, are you texting me instead of heading down there to investigate???

Amelia: Also, hungover on a Monday?? Lots to talk about chica!

I started to type a response when my phone lit up with a video call. "Get your ass downstairs and take me with you," Amelia said when I answered. "I need to see your face when you realize I was right all along." Holding the phone out in front of me as I went, I thumped down the stairs and headed for the kitchen. Halfway through the living room, I caught the scent of coffee.

Two steps later, I realized I didn't make any.

"I smell coffee," I hissed. "But Amelia! I haven't even been downstairs yet!"

My heart pounded as the kitchen came into view.

"I don't hear anything," Amelia said. "Do you?"

The room was empty, though it hadn't been that way long. The chair Amelia freaked out over yesterday had tipped over and the table was slightly askew. Despite the strong smell of coffee, the pot sat empty and unused.

"Look at the chair, Amelia. Look at it!" I held the phone at arm's length, shaking it in the direction of the upended piece of furniture.

"Turn me around so I can look at you. I need to see

your face right now because you're totally realizing I was right, and you were wrong, and you're living in a haunted house."

I wanted to contradict her but, how could I? I heard what I heard and saw what I saw. "Chairs don't just fall over by themselves." The words slipped past my lips in a whisper as I turned in a slow circle, skin crawling.

"That's right, my friend. And coffee doesn't make itself, either."

"What's really weird is there isn't any. Just the smell." The hair on the back of my neck stood on end and I had the distinct feeling that someone was watching me. "It's like the walls have eyes right now. I've never felt so exposed."

Amelia smirked. "That could be because your tank top is crooked and your boob is popping out."

CHAPTER TWELVE

ALEX

That was way too fucking close. With a mess of papers and electronic devices clutched to my chest, I crouched in Evie's backyard and peered through the massive kitchen window just in time to see her shuffle into the room. Tousled hair. White cotton panties. Phone held out in front of her like a weapon. Crooked tank top with one entire boob spilling out the side. She was adorable. Sexy—in a hot mess kind of way.

And about to see me creeping outside her window like a crazy person.

Talk about hot messes.

I ducked out of sight, then sat right there in the dirt to organize the jumble of papers and the laptop I'd crammed into my hands before dashing out the back-door. "You knew better," I muttered as I opened my messenger bag. "You knew Brighton's advice was shit. Who breaks into their neighbor's house to hang out in their kitchen without permission?"

Desperate writers on a deadline, that's who.

Like that excuse made anything better. I mentally fast forwarded to my inevitable arrest.

I'm sorry, officer. The only place I can write is in Evie's house and I thought I'd help myself to her kitchen because we made out a little last night, but it's okay because my agent told me to do it.

"You stupid asshole," I whispered as I smoothed out a few pages of notes and slipped them into my bag. Evie's voice sounded from inside the house. I pushed onto my hands and knees to peek through the window just in time to see her wrench her tank top back in place. Her eyes were wide and alive and it was the sexiest thing I'd ever seen.

Come on, man. This is the kind of psycho shit you write about.

I'd spent last night replaying the evening with Evie, scrutinizing every word, every touch, turning it all round in my head as I tried to make sense of it. Sleep never came, though *I* eventually did, jerking off while I fantasized about our kiss and that inconsequential silk robe. If only I'd had the visual ammo of this morning's outfit to add to the pile...

That's enough, Prescott! Stop it with the crazy, already.

After hours of being awake, I'd tried to write. After a couple more hours of staring at a blank screen, Brighton's suggestion of using my key sounded perfectly reasonable. Evie was an understanding person, after all, and I *did* let her eat in my car. I'd convinced myself I'd get a few pages written while she slept, then come clean about why the whole town thought her house was haunted when she woke up.

I'd rationalized the whole thing away by imagining Evie finding me in the morning and the two of us having a laugh about everything. I'd head out to check on Mom and Izzy while Evie nursed her hangover and everything would be hunky-dory. But the second I heard the water turn on upstairs, reality set in. What seemed like a cute idea in the early hours of the morning sounded massively ridiculous by the time Evie dragged herself out of bed, and I made a mad dash for the exit. There were better ways to come clean than by actually being in her house when she woke up.

Breaking and entering wasn't cute. It didn't make me endearing and eccentric. It made me an asshole. Funny how it took crawling through the leaves and dirt in my neighbor's flowerbeds to have that epiphany.

Maybe Austin and Jude were right when they called me a stalker.

Once I was sure I'd made it out of view of her window, I stood and brushed the dirt from my jeans. The smart play would have been to scurry my sorry ass back home and forget this ever happened. But something...

...maybe a desire to see Evie in her underwear again...

...okay, definitely a desire to see Evie in her underwear again...

...but also the realization that I had to explain what just happened...

...had me crunching through her yard and up to the front door.

Three quick raps against the red paint plastered a smile the size of Texas on my face. The neighborly part of me wanted to make sure she was okay after a rough night and surprising morning. The red-blooded male part of me hoped her boob would be out again.

The door swung open. Evie's jaw dropped and it slammed closed. "Oh God!" Her voice was muffled, and her boob was safely tucked away—under a mostly sheer white tank.

"Good morning," I sang through the wood.

The door cracked open. "I am so sorry...I don't...I

mean...Did we have a meeting planned? Last night's a little foggy."

"Nope. I'm heading to get coffee and thought I'd check in and see if you wanted any." I stifled a laugh as her shocked expression replayed through my mind. "But I can just come back later if you want."

The door cracked open another fraction of an inch. Only Evie's eyes, nose, and lips were visible. "I would love some coffee, if that's not too much to ask. It's been a morning. One that started with a fry glued to my cheek and ended with Alexander Prescott seeing me in my underwear." She groaned and banged her head against the frame.

"I think we're past the part where you address me with my full name. That's what fans do and as far as I'm concerned, we're friends. I think you can call me Lord and Master, Sir Alexander the Glorious, like everyone else."

She snorted laughter. "How about just Alex?"

"Alex it is." I stared into the one eye I could see through the crack in the door. "For the record, I didn't see you naked. As far as I'm concerned, you're fully clothed—in basically sheer fabric, but that's semantics, right?"

Evie groaned again.

"I'll be back with caffeine and genius nuggets."

"And I'll get dressed in as many layers as I can find and try to forget how embarrassed I am."

"Seems fair." I reached out a hand and the door cracked open a fraction more. Instead of shaking on it as I intended, Evie saluted me, surprising us both. With a long sigh, she closed the door and I headed first to Mom's, then to Sweet Stuff to harass my sister, and finally to fulfill my promise of coffee. While I'd intended to come clean about being in Evie's kitchen—I really did—the time hadn't been right. She was too groggy, and that conversation deserved to happen face-to-face, not through a crack in the door. With her barely being able to look me in the eyes, I opted to wait.

A better time would present itself.

I'd tell her then.

CHAPTER THIRTEEN

ALEX

Two hours later, Evie and I sat at the table in her kitchen. While I coaxed words out of my brain and onto the page, she inhaled coffee and nursed her hangover. She'd ditched the sheer tank and undies in favor of leggings and a long sweater that hung off one shoulder, with her hair pulled into a pile on top of her head. While the outfit wouldn't unseat the one-boobed wonder as an all-time favorite, this one had its highpoints.

After an hour or two of quiet companionship she stood, stretching her arms overhead as she stared out the window. Her sweater lifted, giving me a view of a deliciously round ass that begged to have my hands all over it.

"For a world-famous writer," she said through her yawn, "you spend more time staring than typing. I'm surprised."

I yanked my gaze to her face as she turned around. "Genius takes time."

"Whatever you say, Captain." She saluted me for the second time that day, then gave me a sweet smile.

"Was that snark, dear Evie? Am I detecting sarcasm?" I closed my laptop and sat back. "That's a bold move for a woman who answered the door in her underwear. Not the best way to start your first day on the job, though I'm fine to overlook it if you are."

I said overlook. Not forget. The image of her standing in the kitchen with her boob out would fuel many a late-night fantasy.

Evie bobbed her head and hit me with a crooked smile. "I'm fine to never talk about it again."

"And here I thought I'd bring it up every few days or so to keep it fresh in your mind."

She covered her face with her hands, then peeked through her fingers. "I'd really rather you didn't."

This would have been the perfect time to bring up what happened that morning, or hell! Maybe even what happened last night...but I'd wasted enough time without making progress on my manuscript. It was a selfish decision not to tell her, but selfishness came with the Prescott Y chromosome. Making a mental promise to both of us that I'd never break into her house again, I dropped the topic and moved on.

"You ready to think about work stuff?"

"I was born ready." A blush colored her cheeks and she sat back down, laughing into her lap. "That sounded cooler in my head."

I shuffled through the mess of papers in my bag and found the contract my lawyer drafted over the weekend. The corners were creased, and I had to brush dirt off the back before I put them on her table, but other than that, they were no worse for wear after my unplanned exit. "This outlines salary and job expectations. Editing. Revising. Basically, I want you to be the first eyes on my new manuscript and talk through the storyline with me." I outlined the non-disclosure clause my lawyer made me add, then slid the contract her way. "Just needs your scribble on the dotted line and we can get started."

Evie flipped through the pages, her eyes widening when she saw the salary. "This feels too good to be true."

"You know what they say about that statement."

"If it sounds too good to be true, it is? What are you

hiding in here?" She frowned, shuffling through the papers, looking for a clause she missed.

"I'm demanding. A perfectionist. I fight one sentence for weeks before I scrap the entire paragraph." And I broke into her house this morning simply because I knew I'd write better here than at home. "You're gonna earn that money."

She stumbled into my life like she stumbled into the kitchen. Bare. Open. Eager for me to see all she had to offer…

The sentence went into my slush pile doc while Evie signed her name. "There you go. Consider me yours."

I flipped to the manuscript open on my laptop, then spun the device around and slid it in front of her. "Read."

"Read?" Surprise lifted her lovely face. "Now?"

I nodded. "Read."

Her fingers splayed as she adjusted the laptop, gripping it with her thumb and forefingers, as if she'd dirty the thing by touching it. Shaking her head and blowing a long breath passed pursed lips, she leaned in and started the story. I watched her face, searching for the surprise, the fear, the enjoyment. As she wandered the twisty paths of the first seven chapters, I sought out any sign I'd elicited an emotional response. Her expression stayed neutral. Not the reaction I hoped for.

Maybe she had a poker face.

Maybe she was intentionally hiding her feelings.

Maybe...

"How honest do you want me to be?" She closed the laptop, her face completely, maddeningly unreadable.

"Brutally."

"Do you mean that?" She sat up straight and folded her hands in her lap. "Think before you answer. Do you really want me to be brutally honest? Or do you want me to pretend I'm being brutally honest while I tell you everything you want to hear? Because—"

"Damn it, woman," I said with a nervous laugh. "Put me out of my misery already."

No one gave feedback with a preamble like that unless they had bad news. I prepared for the worst even as I hoped for the best.

"The writing is great. But..." She licked her lips, and I died a thousand deaths.

"But?"

"The sentences are evocative. Beautiful, even. Each of them is technically perfect and pristine. But..." She took a deep breath and I considered removing the word 'but' from all of my stories. It was a vile thing that made me sick. "The plot isn't going anywhere. It's sterile. Nothing's happened in seven chapters but technically perfect sentences."

I dropped my gaze to the table. Swallowed hard as I rubbed my hands along my jeans. Even though it was the feedback I was expecting, I hated to hear it. That meant weeks of work would need to be revised. Maybe scrapped altogether. My eyes closed as I rubbed a temple.

I'd never missed a deadline before this. My publishers had already extended this one three times and Brighton made it clear patience was running thin. What the fuck was I going to do? My career was at stake and now I'd have to start from scratch because the pages I *had* been able to write were freaking "sterile."

"Oh, God." Evie cringed. "You didn't want real honesty! Can this day get any worse? I'm so sorry..."

I placed a hand on hers, intending to calm her down but the action had the opposite effect on me, so I dropped it to my lap. This was not the time to yank her out of her chair and kiss her until I remembered how to write good stories. "You gave me exactly what I asked for. There's a problem with the plot. I've known it, but just didn't want to face it. That's probably why I have writer's block in the first place. I know something's broken."

"I wouldn't go all the way to broken. Most writers would feel blessed to write something like that." She gestured to my laptop.

"Right. Because everyone wants to write something sterile." I sat back and met her eyes. "Don't soften your words to protect my ego, Evie. Speak truth. Even when you don't think I'll like it."

Her gaze held mine as thoughts ticked away behind her eyes. If only I could read her better...

"Okay." She nodded like she'd come to a conclusion. "If you want truth, then so do I."

And here it comes, I thought. *She's gonna ask me about being in her kitchen this morning. Or about the kiss last night. Holy shit. I've known this woman for three days and have already complicated the fuck out of everything.*

Evie took a deep breath and I steeled myself for whatever came next as her eyes met mine. "Why are you, a man who surely has agents and editors and people way more qualified than I will ever be, paying someone like me to tell you these things? Why hire a stranger who got fired from a small newspaper to say something you already know? You *are* Lord and Master, Sir Alexander the Glorious, after all."

Relief hit me hard. We weren't going to talk about me breaking in and we weren't going to talk about the kiss. She wanted answers about work. From this point forward, I'd keep things professional because the stress couldn't be good for my creativity.

I sat back and crossed my ankle over my knee. "I

hired you to tell me what my editors won't. They think my brand's big enough to keep me safe. That my name will sell books, even if they aren't up to my standard. And because I'm so late with this story, they're only going to tell me it's wonderful, so I'll finish the draft. I want someone who isn't in that world to tell me what I needed to hear."

That was only partly true. The reality was that I'd decided to hire her because I wanted access to her kitchen. The rest was just icing. My father would be so proud of me, sacrificing everyone else's needs for my own.

"You wanna know what I think?" Evie folded her hands in her lap and lifted her chin.

"I'd love to know what you think. Let me into that marvelous mind."

A grin lit her face and she stood. "I think you're in a rut, Mr. Prescott. I think you've written the same kind of books with the same kind of characters while living in the same house with the same people in the same town for too long."

I blinked. "Is that so?"

"I think you hired me because you need something different."

Well, shit. Maybe she was better at this than I thought she'd be. Every time I was around her, the story unlocked. Did that happen simply because she was a breath of fresh air in my stale life? Is that why it had been easier to write in this kitchen than my office at home? "And what do you suggest I do about that?"

She laughed. "You do realize I have no idea what I'm talking about and am still fighting a hangover, right?"

"You're also making some good points." I waved a hand. "Do continue."

Evie's gaze raked over me, her curiously brilliant eyes scrutinizing every aspect of my face and body. "I guess we need to break you out of your habits. Get you doing new things. Meeting new people. How can you write compelling characters in interesting predicaments if you're living the same humdrum existence, day in and day out? When was the last time you had something new happen?"

I stared at the something new in question until her cheeks blazed.

"See?" she whispered. "You need things shaken up."

Her words rattled around in my head, making more sense by the minute. She had a point and I needed to listen. "Your job description just expanded to include knocking me out of this rut so I can write again. And...go."

"Now?" Her eyebrows hit her hairline. "You want me to start now?"

"You just read my manuscript and told me it was shit. What else are you gonna do? Drop the mic and walk out of the room?"

"It's not shit...."

"If you don't stop placating me, I'll remind you how many times you sexually harassed me last night." *So much for keeping it professional.*

Evie's jaw dropped and her cheeks pinked. "About that..."

"You said my eyes are warm like whiskey. And that we had a connection. And then you kiss—"

"Fine!" She put a finger to my lips. "I won't placate you ever again. And as far as your rut goes..." She glanced around the room as if the answers were written on the walls. "I guess I'll need to know what it looks like first. Show me your daily routine. Let me experience the rut with you so I know what to avoid."

I liked the way her finger felt on my mouth way too much. It made me want to kiss her again, which I'd already decided was not gonna happen, so I opted to give her a hard time instead. "Wow, Evie." I folded my arms across my chest. "I gave you a pass on the sexual harassment last night because you were drunk. I'm not sure what to do about it today."

She rocked back, head tilted as if listening to the playback of her statement.

Her confusion was adorable, which was why I couldn't stop myself from doubling down. "Maybe we should just call the whole thing off, if this is how you're gonna be."

"I don't...I mean...I thought..." She put her hands on her hips. "What are you talking about?"

"You basically just asked me to date you. Dinner. Drinks. Long walks on the beach. Sounds like the most cliched version of dating out there."

Realization landed. "And that's how you generally spend your time."

"Ten points for the lady with the pretty face."

"I promise you; I'm not interested in cliches of any kind. Particularly the one where the girl loses her fancy job in the city, moves to a small town, and makes out with her boss on her front porch." The blush in her cheeks and darting gaze said otherwise.

That shouldn't have excited me as much as it did.

"If I can't write, I'm screwed and you're out of a job, which means you're also screwed. In my opinion, the faster we get a move on, the better for both of us." I stood and gathered my things. "I'm gonna pop back to my house and take a shower while you get ready. Feel free to come on over when you're done. I'll leave the door unlocked. Just let yourself in."

With that, I bounded outside and crossed our yards, humming to myself the whole way. Morgan greeted me, tail wagging while Larry climbed my pant-leg. "Tell you what boys," I said as I carefully unhooked murder mittens from my jeans, "today is shaping up to be one hell of a day."

CHAPTER FOURTEEN

Evie

Alex closed my front door behind him, and I dropped to my couch with a sigh.

What kind of weird rollercoaster was I on? Lose Drew, gain Sugar Maple Hill. Lose a job, gain Alex and his friends here in Wildrose Landing. Up! Down! Turn! Turn again! And then the loop-de-loop to beat all loop-de-loops...my job description now basically included dating my sexy neighbor/boss...

...who just happened to be a New York Time best-selling author...

How was this even my life?

As Alex strolled back to his house, I grabbed my

phone and buckled in. Amelia would be all for this ride.

Me: Hangover's basically gone. Spent the day watching Alex not really work. Now he tells me part of my job is dating him.

Amelia: IDK, that kinda seems creepy?
Amelia: BTW, I totally knew he had the hots for you.
Amelia: Also. Trying to work through how I feel about this turn of events... Seems very sexual harassment-y

Me: We're not really dating, and he doesn't have the hots for me. I'm supposed to figure out how to get him out of the rut he's in, which will include dinner, drinks, and long walks on the beach. I did kiss him while I was drunk last night. So, you know, the harassment goes both ways.

Amelia: I leave you alone for one day and look what happens!

Me: Wanna know the worst part? I opened the door to him while wearing my stupid tank top and underwear this morning.

Amelia: Was your boob out?

Me: OMG I DIDN'T EVEN CHECK

Amelia's string of laughing emojis had me giggling—and swearing to pay more attention to what I wore to bed. With my mind awash in modest PJ options, I headed upstairs to get ready.

It wouldn't take long.

After all, Alex and I weren't going on an actual date.

Just a change of clothes. A touch of makeup. A swipe of the brush and a dash of perfume and I was good to go. Nice enough for an evening out with my boss, but still totally casual. Easy peasy summer breezy.

Except I checked my hair in every mirror I passed.

Then opted to change my outfit.

Twice.

When I got to Alex's house, there was a note on the door reminding me to come on in. I pushed inside and Morgan skittered and clicked across the hardwood floors to greet me, while a black kitten bounced along behind him. Alex didn't strike me as a kitten kind of guy. Guess I still had a lot to learn about the man.

Gee? You think? That's a real shocker, considering you've only known him for a weekend...

I crouched to scratch Morgan's ears. "Hey, buddy. Long time no see."

He huffed and sniffed my face. The kitten bumped his head against my thigh, purr box rumbling, so I gave him a little attention, too. When both animals were sufficiently greeted, I straightened and peered around the foyer. The house was similar in style to mine, though the furniture was heavy and masculine instead of Aunt Ruth's distinctly feminine choices. A quick perusal of the first floor showed I was alone, outside of the animals. The hiss and patter of running water upstairs said Alex was still in the shower.

Singing to himself.

Loudly.

And offkey.

I perched on the couch as I listened, scratching Morgan's head while his tail wagged and the kitten curled in my lap. The more Alex sang, the more aware I was that he was upstairs, totally naked. Water slicing through his hair. Running down his body. His broad shoulders and proud posture suggested his jeans and T-shirts hid a model-worthy figure. For as much as I'd tried to forget our kiss last night, I couldn't. The memory had been swimming through my mind all day and now it mingled with the image of a naked Alex. The longer I waited, the more my curiosity grew. The more my curiosity grew, the more a devious idea bloomed.

Alex had seen me in my underwear...

It was only fair to sneak a peek of my own.

"I'm just gonna even the score," I said to the kitten as I shifted him off my lap. "So Alex can't hold what happened over my head without getting a little something in return." He'd basically threatened to blackmail me with my drunken shenanigans. Who wouldn't want a little ammunition of her own?

The idea sounded better with each passing moment.

The kitten stretched and mewed his agreement while Morgan huffed an encouraging sneeze.

I crept through Alex's house. Up a curved set of stairs. Down a hallway with plush carpet and rows of his book covers, framed and hanging on the wall. The sounds of the shower grew louder while Morgan paced beside me, his tongue lolling in anticipation. The water stopped, but Alex's singing did not, and my grin widened as he mangled "Tainted Love." The second I got close enough to hear the lyrics, Morgan tilted his head back and joined in, adding his howling voice to the mix.

I buried my face in his fur. "Oh, no, no, no, no, no," I whisper-hissed, but he only upped his game, howling louder as laughter came from inside the bathroom. When the door cracked open, I realized I had no idea what I planned on doing. Was I going to jump out and scare him like some kind of stalker ninja? Peek around the corner and see what I could see? Or maybe I just needed to hightail it back downstairs before anything ridiculous happened.

You know, like a dog breaking into song with his owner while I snuck around like a common criminal.

What I should have done was get my ass back into the living room. What I did was dart around a corner moments before footsteps sounded in the hall. But what I got for it made the whole ordeal worthwhile—a glimpse of one fantastic rear end as Alex strutted down the hallway without a towel.

WITHOUT A TOWEL.

I stared.

Hard.

I wasn't one to appreciate butts. Most of the time, they looked ridiculous as they wibbled, wobbled, and sagged into thighs. But Alex...he took tushies to an entirely new level.

"Why didn't you tell me he wanders around naked and looks like that?" I whispered to Morgan. He cocked his head and wagged his tail. "I know. You're right. It *is* better I know what he's hiding under those jeans."

After making sure the coast was clear, I crept

downstairs like the stealthiest ninja that ever ninja'd. Morgan, on the other hand, took them at a full gallop. I resumed my perch on Alex's couch, humming "Tainted Love" as the kitten bumped his head against my hand, visions of perfect butts dancing in my head.

CHAPTER FIFTEEN

ALEX

I heard Evie let herself into the house as I started the shower, so Morgan singing in the hallway surprised me. No way that dog would be upstairs when someone with perfectly good hands willing and able to scratch his ears waited downstairs. When I cracked open the door and she crouch-ran around the corner, I knew exactly what was going on. I saw her half-naked. She wanted to even the score. I didn't blame her.

But I couldn't let her off easy, now could I?

Where would the fun be in that?

I'd seen a boob, so she could ogle my butt cheeks. Seemed a fair enough trade. I strutted down that hallway like I belonged on a billboard, smiling to myself when a tiny, feminine gasp of approval floated along behind me. Under normal circumstances, I'd throw on whatever caught my eye before heading out, but with Evie waiting downstairs, I took a little extra time.

Favorite jeans? Check.

Black T-shirt that hugged my chest and arms? Check.

Fleece jacket that complimented my hair? Check.

Aware I sounded like the type of self-absorbed jackass I detest with the heat of a thousand suns? Check.

Grateful as hell no one could hear my inner monologue as I proceeded anyway? Double check, bolded and underlined, though the grin on Evie's lips and the blush to her cheeks when I came downstairs made it all worth it.

"Don't you look nice." She lifted Larry off her lap and set him on the couch before standing. "Are you sure we're not on a date? I mean, I think I see hair gel, Prescott."

I gave her the onceover, then sniffed. "Is that perfume I'm getting?" I wafted the air towards my nose. "I'm pretty sure I'm getting a hint of perfume for this definitely-not-a-date."

"I mean, maybe I just wanted to avoid smelling like a tequila factory after last night."

"Sure." I put a hand on the small of her back and started towards the door. "And maybe I used hair gel because I'm fussy about my appearance."

If the name of the game was showing Evie my rut, the first stop would be Izzy's candy shop. When we arrived, the sign in the window read "Closed," but I pushed through the unlocked doors like I belonged—kind of like I'd done with Evie's house earlier. I didn't like the parallel but consoled myself knowing it would be the last time I used the key Ruth gave me.

The bells jangled with our entrance and I added my voice to the mix. "Izzy Prescott! Your brother has arrived, and he requires feeding!"

My darling sister swept out of the back, the annoyance on her face fading when she saw who I had in tow. "I'm all out of genius nuggets," she said with a smirk for me and a smile for Evie, "but aren't you two the cutest couple ever? I'm honored you chose to share your first date with me." Izzy batted her eyelashes and grinned.

After what happened with Candace, dating was off my radar, especially with me being so far behind with work. I folded my elbows on the counter and leaned forward, trying to telepathically remind my sister Prescott men were terrible with relationships. "My new *employee* has taken on the monumental task of breaking through my writer's block."

"My *boss* informed me this was part of my job description approximately one hour ago." Evie's emphasis on the word "boss" was almost as heavy as mine on "employee."

Izzy eyed us, her gaze calculating the perfect six feet of "not interested" between the two of us. "I see."

Evie folded her hands behind her and shifted her weight, nodding emphatically. "The first step in my highly scientific approach is getting Alex to show me his butt...I mean rut!" Her eyes nearly exploded, and she covered her mouth with her hand. "His rut. I need him to show me his *rut*, so we know what to avoid. You know, switch up the energy and see what it unlocks."

Score one for Prescott.

At least I'd made the right impression by strutting naked back to my bedroom.

Maybe, while I got myself off thinking about her crooked tank top and perfect ass, she'd be pleasuring herself to the memory of my naked backside.

Izzy snorted. "Genius nuggets. Drinks with Austin, Jude, and Jack...if he can find a sitter. Dinner at Overton's. Walks with Morgan." She held up a finger with each item, then gave them a wiggle. "There. I just saved you hours of boredom." Her focus darted over my shoulder and she waved at the window. I turned in time to see Greta Macmillan cupping her fingers to the glass and groaned.

"You two are so busted," Izzy said with a laugh. "The whole town'll know you're dating in the time it takes Greta to post to Facebook."

"We're not dating." Evie and I spoke together, stepping away from each other as if more space between us would cement the fact that we were, indeed, just friends.

Izzy whipped out her phone, grinning as her fingers danced over the screen. "Not according to Greta Macmillan's Facebook page." She held out the device to show us a picture of me, leaning on the counter of Sweet Stuff, laughing at my sister's joke while staring at Evie with something hotter than friendship.

I took the phone and enlarged the photo. "How did she post that so fast?"

Izzy shook her head. "The woman is a social savant. If only she could channel her powers for good."

Once we were sure Greta had moved on, Evie and I stepped out of the shop into a crisp evening. She shivered as a breeze lifted her hair off her neck and I offered her my fleece, slipping it around her shoulders as Mr. and Mrs. Tarrington stared, whispering behind their hands.

"I'm afraid I've made you the talk of the town." I lifted a chin toward the grinning couple. Isaac tipped his hat in our direction while Gwen raised a hand, then leaned into her husband and patted his arm. “Between Greta telling everyone you’re a lesbian, then catching you out with me...”

“Add that to the fact that I’m living in a haunted house...” Evie grinned and I swallowed down a touch of guilt. Maybe it would be better if I came clean on that topic...

Later. I’d do it later. “You really know how to make an entrance,” I said instead. “But I wouldn’t worry about it.” I wrapped an arm around her shoulders. “The gossip will die down in, oh, four to six years, or so.”

“Is that all?”

Opening the door to Overton’s, I stood back to let Evie enter first. The hostess—a bookish young woman with bright eyes—escorted us to my table, a quiet space big enough for my laptop on the nights I chose to bring it along. “I’ll return with your whiskey in just a sec, Mr. Prescott.” Bridget gave me a familiar smile as Evie and I took our seats. “And what can I get for you, Miss...”

“Please, call me Evie.” She snapped open the drink menu, then cast me a devilish look. “And do us a favor and scratch that whiskey. He’ll have a” —her eyes scanned the page— “Drunken Sailor, instead.”

I frowned. “I always have whiskey.” The finality in my voice should have ended the discussion, but Evie simply grinned and patted my arm.

"Sounds like a rut if I've ever heard one." The quirk of her head. The glimmer in her eyes. If she wasn't in the middle of bossing me around, she would have been adorable.

"Whiskey isn't the problem."

She arched a brow. "As the woman in charge of this situation, that's my call. And I'm definitely sensing a rut...which is why you'll have a Drunken Sailor tonight."

Poor Bridget didn't know what to do. She stared, feet rooted in place, until I had mercy on the poor girl. "Two Drunken Sailors, it is," I said to her before turning to Evie. "If I'm taking this journey, you're coming with me."

"Can I just say you two are so cute," Bridget said. "It's nice to see you smiling, Mr. Prescott. Mrs. Macmillan's right. You guys are gonna be Wildrose Landing's power couple in no time. I can feel it."

"Whatever we do," Evie said as Bridget headed to the bar, "we will not play a drinking game involving people talking about Greta's Facebook page."

I laughed. She grinned. And I realized I hadn't felt so comfortable with a woman in a long time.

I leaned in close. "I have to know..."

Evie mirrored the movement, folding her arms on the table and arching a brow. "Know what?"

"What you thought of my butt. I've always

assumed it was pretty spectacular, but since I don't exactly have a clear view, I thought I'd ask someone who did."

Her jaw dropped and her eyes went wide. "You *did* know I was watching."

"Of course I knew." I laughed as she shook her head. "Morgan only sings when he's close to me, and he wouldn't leave your side to come upstairs. Not with you being so generous with the ear scratching and all."

"Is that what all the howling was? Singing?" Her smile sparkled with sarcasm.

"I happen to have a very good shower voice, thank you very much."

"I was talking about the dog, but way to make things about you."

"Speaking of me, don't keep a man waiting. What's the verdict on my butt?"

Evie sat back in her chair, grinning ear to ear. "I already have a history of sexually harassing my boss. If I told you what I thought when I saw you strutting down that hallway, you'd file a complaint in an instant."

I couldn't nail down her personality at all. That statement, while it was a massive stroke to my ego, seemed more in line with the confident version of Evie McAllister that escorted me to my car all those years ago. And yet, she often seemed so unsure of herself, I couldn't imagine she'd ever have the guts to say something that direct to my face. I didn't know which version of her was the real her. Was she bold and brave? Or timid and shy?

Our drinks arrived, a tasty combination of gin, rum, ginger ale, and lime. As we placed our orders, a couple at another table caught my attention. The man was tucked into a suit, his tie so tight he had to be suffocating. His phone was out, and he tap, tap, tapped ferociously across the screen. His wife leaned her chin on her hands, staring into the belly of the restaurant, so sad, so alone, even though she sat across from someone who'd pledged his life to her. When her gaze met mine, she conjured a smile that reminded me of my mom.

I didn't want that.

I couldn't *be* that.

Not again.

My father nearly broke my mother. I nearly broke Candace. And I'd made a promise never to be that man again.

Evie sipped her drink and her face fell. "Oh, no..."

"What?" I sat back and crossed my ankle over my knee. "Did randomly choosing a drink off the menu backfire? Go figure."

"Oh, it backfired, all right, but not the way you're thinking. I like it. I like it too much."

Just like I was starting to like her. Too much.

Eager to remind us both we weren't actually dating, I fished in my bag for my outline, a piece of paper I kept with my laptop so I could make notes while I wrote.

It wasn't there.

As Evie stared, I dug through the mess I'd yet to organize only to come up empty handed. A memory of several papers see-sawing to the ground as I dashed out of her kitchen danced through my head.

Fuck me.

If that outline wasn't in my bag, there was only one place it could be...inside Evie's house. My heart dropped to my stomach. I either needed to find it before she did or come clean on the whole ghost story once and for all.

CHAPTER SIXTEEN

EVIE

I made it home without attempting to seduce Alex on my front porch and I counted that as a win. In fact, despite the strange start, I counted the entire day as a win. Spending time with him was so easy, it was hard to remember we'd just met. Conversation flowed naturally, twangs of chemistry kept things interesting, and the night was over before I was ready, especially because it ended on a slightly confusing note.

During our trip to Sweet Stuff and the first half of dinner, it definitely felt like we were flirting, and I'd been sure we'd end the night with another make out session. At some point, the focus switched back to work and the chemistry faded, leaving me to wonder if I'd been seeing things that weren't there.

Which was a relief. (Kind of.)

I had too much going on in my life to start a relationship. (At least that was what self-help blogs had to say on the subject.)

After what happened with Drew, I swore I'd never date another writer again. (Though the two men were nothing alike.)

I paced from the living room to the kitchen and back again as I contemplated texting Alex. I didn't really have anything to say, but couldn't get him out of my mind and wasn't ready for our night to be over. With my phone in my hand, I made my way up to my darkened bedroom and flipped on a light, stopping in the middle of the room to tap out a text.

Me: Not to be weird or anything but I just wanted to say I had a really nice time with you. I was so nervous to move to Wildrose, but I'm not anymore. I can see why you like your rut so much. It's pretty enjoyable.

I hit send and immediately wished I hadn't as anxiety reminded me I should have left him alone. When the bouncing bubbles indicating he was typing a reply started, I heaved a sigh of relief. They danced for a long time, stopped, then started again. For as long as they teased me, I expected paragraphs, not the one-liner that finally appeared.

Alex: Listen…I have something to tell you and you might not like it.

That statement shot a different kind of adrenaline through my system. Me: Ummm…okay…

Alex: I just feel like it's important that I'm honest about this.

Me: I'm all ears. Or eyes, I guess, since I'll be reading whatever it is you have to say that's more important than acknowledging we had a good time together and I'm glad I met you.

Alex: Evie… This is so much more important than that…

My heart pounded as I watched the bouncing dots of his incoming message.

Alex: You left your curtains open and I can see you right now.

I laughed as I looked up. Sure enough, the

windows were bare, the inky blackness of night making me feel exposed. In case Alex was still watching, I waved, then pulled the curtains closed.

Me: Creeper. What are you doing staring into my bedroom?

Alex: Oh, now I'm a creeper because you're an exhibitionist and I just happened to look out my window as I came into the room. Seems fair.

I laughed, said goodnight, then flopped onto the bed and stared dreamily at the ceiling. Lord and Master, Sir Alexander the Glorious just creeped on me in my very own bedroom...and I liked it. Combine that with the memory of our kiss, his fantastic ass, and the blistering chemistry I'd somehow ignored all day, and I wasn't surprised at all when my hand slipped into my pants and I found myself wet and ready.

What did surprise me was the fantasy that followed. As I teased pleasure into my body, I imagined throwing open my windows and finding Alex staring out his. His chest was bare, and his dick was hard, and imaginary me slowly pulled off my shirt and dropped it to the floor. Swaying my hips and tweaking my nipples, I teased him until he unzipped his pants and stroked his cock while I danced.

The scene brought on an orgasm so intense I squeaked, then laughed as I softened into my pillows. “Maybe I’m more of an exhibitionist than I thought,” I murmured, then climbed to my feet and got ready for bed.

CHAPTER SEVENTEEN

EVIE

A week passed and Alex and I settled into a comfortable routine. If he had pages for me to read, he'd show up with hope on his face as he handed them over. When he didn't have pages for me, he'd arrive with Morgan in tow. We'd start the morning with a walk on the beach and go from there.

He'd been right. Sharing his rut did feel an awful lot like dating. Drinks. Dinners. Long conversations about, well, everything. His curiosity was boundless and I was a new toy to turn over and over in his hands as he understood how it worked. I had to actively remind myself he wasn't as interested in me as he seemed.

Not that I was complaining. Alex was easy to be around and his attention felt good, professional or not. I could think of worse ways to earn a living than hanging around a man as talented and driven as him. Part of me kept hoping his work ethic and general writerness would rub off on me and I'd find my way to writing again. The other part—the one I only let come out when I was alone in my bedroom—kept wondering what it would be like to give in to my fantasies about him.

But we won't talk about that part.

Bad Evie for thinking that way about your boss. (Though anyone in my position would.)

And this particular morning, my position included sitting on the couch, nursing my coffee as I waited for Alex to arrive. A knock at the door sent my heart into a frenzy. My stomach shimmied with butterflies and I launched to my feet. My socks failed to gain traction on the hardwood floor, and I went down.

Hard.

"What the hell was that?" Alex's voice sounded through the closed door. "Evie? Are you okay?"

Laughing, I pulled myself to my feet and opened the door, rubbing my sore hip. "I'm okay. Just slipped."

He arched a questioning brow as Morgan wagged his tail in greeting. "I'm very sorry that happened to you."

"It's what I get for running in socks, though. No pages today?" I crouched to greet the Morganator and peeked up at Alex. His dark curls were untamed, standing proud in barely controlled chaos. The stubble on his chin said he'd been up late, probably trying to write, and had been too tired to shave this morning. I'd never been one for scruff, but go figure, he pulled it off to a delightful degree. How was it fair that he could be so unbelievably good looking at all hours of the day?

"No pages." He sighed deeply as he stared at his shoes. "Feel like taking a walk this morning?" Morgan's tail went into overdrive at the mention of the W-word.

Alex's eyes screamed desperation, which was typical on the days he wasn't able to write. The deeper he fell into writer's block, the more certain he was the affliction was permanent. His inability to work tormented him. At first, I thought it stemmed from his fear over finances. If he didn't write, he didn't eat. But lately, I'd started to wonder if it was more existential than that. Like, maybe, his intensity stemmed from something deeper. Something broken. Something he kept hidden from the world.

Or, maybe I was thinking too hard about the whole thing.

"A walk sounds great," I said with a smile. "Just let me grab my shoes."

He took my hand, his grip forceful but gentle, and

my hormones reveled in the contact. "Careful now. Go slow, please." He indicated my socks as humor danced in his eyes. "We don't need you falling over twice in one day."

I slipped on a pair of shoes, grabbed my jacket, and we stepped into the kind of day I used to think only existed because of Photoshop. Who knew colors this strong and sunshine this bright existed without digital augmentation? The crunch of leaves under our feet died away as we made our way onto the beach, grass fading first into rocks and then into sand.

We let Morgan off the leash and Alex tossed a piece of driftwood down the beach, then turned to me as the dog sprinted off, dodging waves. "How come you don't write? This is the perfect time to start a book, especially because I'm having such a hard time working on mine."

The memory of Drew's smirking face chased away my voice. How could I answer a question on a topic I hadn't fully processed yet? I stared at the horizon as I gathered my thoughts.

"You sound like Amelia. She says my spirit guides are trying to send me a message. That by yanking me out of my old life and into this one, they're leading me to my best self."

"And you don't believe that?"

"I mean, in the scheme of life implosions, mine

recovered pretty quickly. Lost a job, gained a job. Lost an apartment, gained a house." *Lost a Drew, gained an Alex,* though I couldn't bring myself to say the last aloud. "When you stack everything up like that, it's easier to believe her than it's ever been."

Alex accepted the stick from Morgan and heaved it down the beach. "Do you like it here?"

"So far, I'm a fan. The view's amazing." I risked a glance his way. "The company's pretty good."

A secret smile lifted the corners of his lips. "Then maybe Amelia's not completely wrong."

"Don't let her hear you say that. I'll never, ever live it down."

"If she's been right about everything else, why haven't you started writing?"

I met Alex's eyes, certain he could see every ounce of my helplessness. Part of me wanted to explain. After all, he understood the impossibility of coaxing a book into existence when your brain didn't want to let it out. But how did I talk about the worst thing to ever happen to me with a man I'd only just met, respected so much, and fantasized about at night? I wasn't prepared to be that vulnerable with him.

"Come on, Evie. Let me into that magnificent mind."

I searched for the best way to encapsulate it all. "I guess I'm scared."

"That's a valid reason." He nodded thoughtfully. "It's also bullshit."

My jaw dropped. "It's not bullshit."

"It really is, though. Would you let fear keep you from going on this walk with me?"

"Obviously not. I'm here."

His head quirked as he registered my response. "Then why would you let it keep you from writing?"

There was no way to answer him without getting too personal, so I shrugged and hoped he'd drop the topic. When Morgan trotted back with the stick in his mouth, I took it from him and tossed it down the beach.

Alex shoved his hands into his pockets. "Writing is terrifying. It's opening yourself up and bleeding your soul onto the page. You have to tap into the best and worst parts of yourself. Explore all the reasons you are you and other people are who they are, then imbue characters and themes with all of it, twisting and shaping, caring and loving. Sometimes hating. Just breathe life into this thing that is at once part of you and nothing like you. And then, if you're successful, you'll publish this book and hundreds of thousands of people will ingest it. Months of work will be devoured in days, sometimes hours, and you'll either be publicly revered or eviscerated. You'll hear exactly what people thought, without punches being pulled because while they think they're reviewing a product, they don't realize they're reviewing *you*. You have to be a little crazy and a whole lot fearless to do this. It's not easy."

I slowed my pace as Alex spoke. He turned to me, his eyes swimming with so much passion and intensity I felt like I could drown. Standing beside him, with the waves whispering across the sand, the sun twisting through the fiery leaves behind him, everything grew so clear, so perfect, so precise. The meaning of life lived in his smile, I could feel it—I just couldn't understand it.

I slipped my hands into my pockets. "I mean, when you put it like that, I can't believe I'm standing out here with you. With all that waiting for me, I should probably get home so I can start on my book." I jerked my head back toward the house.

Alex dropped his gaze to his feet, smiling sheepishly. "But sometimes, everything comes together and it's the most perfect thing, Evie." His eyes found mine and there was that feeling of drowning again. Of coming to life again. "There's nothing like it in the world. When you know magic is spilling from your fingers..."

The wind blew my hair across my face and Alex tucked it back behind my ear. A simple gesture. And a familiar one. His hand stalled at my cheek and all I wanted was to lean into his touch. To recognize that my life wasn't as chaotic as I thought. To stop worrying about doing the right thing and explore whatever this was between us.

About that...

The thing between us? People called it a job.

My life wasn't as chaotic as it could have been because this man swooped in and gave me an income. What kind of idiot would risk that?

Not this idiot, that was for sure.

As Morgan came bounding back, stick in mouth, tail and ears flopping joyfully, I stepped away from Alex. Chemistry be damned.

CHAPTER EIGHTEEN

Alex

One of the things that made me a good writer was my ability to read people. I could see a lie as easily as I could see a person's hair color. When we were kids, Izzy hated that she could never pull one over on me. I didn't let on that while I could see a lie was happening, I often had no clue what it was about. She eventually settled on being brutally honest with me and I appreciated the simplicity. But, while Izzy and I found a rhythm that suited us, the rest of the world refused to get on board.

People lied all the time.

About their age.

Their weight.

Their general sense of well-being. I'd meet someone new, shake hands, and while they said, "it's a pleasure to meet you," I saw the lie tiptoe through their eyes.

What I didn't see was *why* they lied.

Was it my hair? My face? Something I said? Or was I looking at the remnants of a bad morning? A fight with a friend? An asshole coworker? The worries would stomp around in my head, driving me crazy.

As a kid, I lived in this unsettled state, knowing people weren't saying what they were thinking and wishing they would. After I aged into confidence, I realized I wasn't the source of the entire world's frustration. I was, in fact, not that important. I started using everything I saw in people to add depth to my characters. Years passed and my special ability affected me less and less...

Until today.

Evie was holding something back and it killed me not to know what it was and why she wouldn't tell me. There was a reason she didn't write, and it was bigger than, "It's scary."

I tried to tell myself that was fine. We all had things we didn't want people to know. I had secrets locked up so tight, no one would get to them. I'd be a hypocrite to dig into Evie's when I wouldn't loosen the grip on mine. Instead of obsessing over her interior, I distracted myself by focusing on her exterior.

She had a freckle beside her lips. For as much as I loved the character it brought to her face, she covered it with a finger whenever she was nervous. I assumed she spent her childhood being teased about it and guessed she would call that freckle a blemish. I called it hers, and in that, it was everything it needed to be. Her blonde hair shimmered in the sun, like it had a light of its own. She played with the ends when she spoke, twirling them between her fingers, pausing to press it to her nose.

Every time I got close, she stepped away. At first, I assumed it was accidental, a reflexive response to having me in her personal space, but it happened every single time. We were like opposing magnets, and my energy repelled hers. After the night at Cheers 'n Beers, I assumed we were both attracted to each other but maybe I was wrong...

Nope.

No way.

That was some of the bullshitiest bullshit that ever was.

We were both equally attracted. No doubt about it. Maybe she'd been hurt by someone. Badly. Maybe that was why she held herself so tight. So closed. So private.

Maybe that was why she pushed all that she was into a tiny box and refused to reach outside of it.

Or, maybe she recognized what a shit-for-brains move it would be to date her boss.

So maybe it had been a shit-for-brains move to offer her a job, because I'm tired of wanting her every damn day and doing nothing about it. I gave that selfish thought a mental one-finger salute. Helping someone in need was never a shit-for-brains move but making choices in one's self-interest often was.

As Evie played with Morgan, an idea for a scene popped into my head. I pulled out my phone and recorded as many notes as I could, as quickly as possible.

"Do we need to head back?" Evie asked. "Get those ideas onto the page instead of a note on your phone?"

I nodded without looking up. "Probably a good idea."

"Do you want to talk about it as we walk? I'm all ears if you want." Her smile faded as I frowned.

The thought of discussing a baby plot bunny made me uncomfortable. The idea was too new and just one micro-grimace on Evie's part could kill it before it fully bloomed. "Sometimes talking about a plot before it's solid makes it disappear."

Evie nodded like I hadn't just spoken nonsense.

"Totally understand. Just know the offer's out there if you change your mind."

I whistled for Morgan. The beast turned, cocked his head, then barreled straight for us at approximately one thousand miles an hour, skidding to a stop long enough for me to click on his leash, then taking off again. The leash caught in Evie's feet and she shrieked as she stumbled, which caused Morgan to barrel back to check on her, crashing into her with his considerable weight—all in the name of keeping her safe, of course.

She staggered. I caught her. Her soft body pressed to mine...and mine grew very, very hard. "Dang, Morgan," I said as I helped Evie to her feet.

If I didn't know better, I'd say you were trying to make that happen, you magnificent beast. Morgan gave me a look like I was an idiot for not going in for the kiss as the possibility might not present itself so easily the next time.

"Yeah. Dang, Morgan." Evie tugged on her shirt and I relived the feeling of her boobs pressed against my arm.

To distract myself, I opted to share the glimmer of an idea for the scene. In fits and starts, the details came out, in all its infant glory. Evie asked the right questions, got excited at the right parts, and generally said everything I needed to hear to bring the idea into crystal clear clarity. By the time we got into her kitchen, I was practically bleeding the story. My earbuds went in, and the words seeped from my pores and onto the page.

An hour later, when I turned my laptop around for her to read, she grinned the entire time. "It's perfect, Alex. It's everything it needs to be...and then some." The celebration in her eyes felt like victory, but when she got out of her chair and wrapped me in a hug, that felt like a whole lot more.

Another week passed and somehow, everything that felt familiar and tedious just a handful of days ago, felt new and inspiring and fucking perfect when Evie was with me. She took my predictable life and, with her bright smile and insightful questions, turned it into magic. While I wouldn't call my writer's block cured, things were definitely moving, and that was a massive win.

In the nights before I fell asleep, and the mornings before I fully woke, I wondered if maybe, just maybe, it would be okay to chase a relationship with her. After all, she understood what it meant to be lost in a project. She sat across from me as I wrote. She was with me, day in and day out, even if that meant sitting at her kitchen table with Morgan at my feet. How could I ignore her if she was part of the process? I wouldn't do to her what Dad did to Mom, or what I did to Candace because Evie knew what it meant to lose yourself to work.

On the days I couldn't write, I bombarded her with questions. At the start, I called it character study. I dissected her mannerisms and her motivations to weave them into characters later. But as time went on, I realized it had nothing to do with fiction and everything to do with liking her. I wanted to know what made her smile. What made her sad. What made her laugh. I wanted to know everything about her so I could know all the ways her personality blended with mine.

But watching could only go so far, which led to questions. Lots and lots of questions. She answered them with grace and patience, and I liked her all the more for it.

"What's the real reason you won't write?" I asked one afternoon as we sat at her table.

The question came out of the blue. She had a pen in her hand and her eye on the pages I wrote the night before. Her hair was in a bun and she looked like a dream come true, sitting across from me, grinning as she redlined my work.

All the joy slipped from her eyes as my question registered. Evie's mouth worked without any sound.

She put the pen down and exhaled slowly. "I had something happen and I haven't processed it yet. The words dried up and..."

"Do you want to talk about it?"

I needed her to say yes. To open up to me. To stop being so private and finally let me in.

Evie shook her head. "I haven't talked about it with anyone. Not even Amelia. She knows what happened, just..." She closed her eyes. "It hurt and it's over, and that's all I'm ready to say about it."

And that was that.

She returned her attention to my manuscript, her finger covering the freckle next to her lips. Her eyes glazed over. Even though she stared at the page, I knew she wasn't seeing any of the words I wrote.

I stood, took her hands, and pulled her out of her chair so we were standing in a pool of sunlight in her kitchen.

She looked away, but I sought out her attention. "Alex..."

My hands were on her shoulders and my gaze held hers. Pain raged in her stormy eyes and I catalogued it all as I ran a thumb along her cheek. "Whatever happened, whatever it was, I'm sorry. And I know it seems like a good idea to keep it crammed into the back of your head where it feels like it can't hurt you, but I promise you, bad things grow in the dark. You'll feel better once you get whatever this is out of your head." I tapped her temple and she leaned into my touch. "I'd be honored to be the one who helps you shine light on it all. When you're ready."

Her eyes swam with emotion. Conflict. Desire. Pain. Gratitude. "Thank you." Her voice cracked.

And that was when I knew what would happen next. I saw it all, stretched out before me like some too-perfect plot point. I was going to kiss Evie, and it wouldn't be because she was drunk or Morgan tripped her.

It would happen because we finally chose to let it happen.

She would lean in, and I'd close the distance, our lips would clash, and nothing would be the same ever again. Her walls would crumble. So would mine. We'd let each other in. My opinion on love would shift. Together, we'd claim the promise of happiness that had been made when she careened into my life.

I cupped her cheek. Her hooded gaze caressed my mouth.

The way she licked her lips said she saw the moment as clearly as I did—

The doorbell bing-bonged.

Evie and I sprang apart, blinking in the afterimage of what we almost let happen.

"I'm sorry," she murmured, pulling away, finger

moving from her freckle to her bottom lip. "I should... uh...I should get that."

"Evie—"

She disengaged and raced out of the kitchen. A loud bang had me jumping out of my skin. She cursed, then laughed. "I'm okay! Stupid socks."

I heard the creak of the door swinging open. "Alexander Prescott!" Izzy's voice rang out. "I brought genius nuggets!"

Of course she did.

Obviously, this exact moment was the time my sister would choose to do something sweet. I couldn't decide if I wanted to curse her name or bless her for interrupting.

I came around the corner to find Evie rubbing her hip. I gave her a rueful smile before turning to my sister, who held out a bag of jellybeans that rattled and clacked as she handed it to me. "Between these filling my belly and Evie turning every mediocre idea I have into something brilliant, this next book is gonna be a freaking unicorn."

"All your books are unicorns." Izzy's gaze bounced from me to Evie and back again. She'd never been as good at reading people as I was, but you don't grow up in a household like mine and not learn how to read the room.

Which she did. Quickly.

A grin tugged at the corner of my little sister's lips.

I'd been busted. She saw how much I wanted the woman beside me, and if I knew Isabelle Prescott, I'd never live it down.

"How'd you even know I was here?" I asked, while mentally begging her to have mercy on me.

"Greta's Facebook page. She checked you in with your laptop and messenger bag at nine o'clock sharp. She was disappointed to see you walking across the yard this morning because that meant you hadn't stayed the night." Izzy flipped through her phone to show me the post. "If you read the comments, sounds like most of Wildrose agrees."

CHAPTER NINETEEN

EVIE

The day finished like it started, with me in the kind of mood Amelia would be proud of. She'd tell me I'd finally come into alignment with my spiritual mission, then pat me on the head and tell me to chase the feeling. I felt so joyful and filled with reasons to smile, I could see how she'd think that. It was the best kind of mood, and one hundred percent because Alex almost kissed me today.

If Izzy hadn't arrived with a random jellybean delivery, our lips would have touched, and I would have melted, and my friendship with Alex would never be the same...

...and maybe things would have changed for the better...

...or maybe...

...everything would have blown up in my face like it did with Drew.

With a week's worth of chemistry floating through my mind, I dashed to my room, double-checked the curtains were closed, and Facetimed Amelia, flopping onto the bed with a sigh of contentment. Her rapturous smile filled the screen, tendrils of smoke curling behind her head. "I was just thinking about you!"

I frowned. "Are you smoking?"

"What? Eww. No. Darian was here, so I did a sage smudge to clean up all the negativity he left behind. What's up with you, other than the fact that you're apparently one half of Wildrose Landing's newest power couple and didn't bother to tell me?"

Excuse me? How did she even know about that? Maybe Amelia's spirit guides were a real thing—and stronger than I thought. "The reason I haven't told you anything is because there's nothing to say. Alex and I aren't a couple."

"Not according to Greta Macmillan's Facebook page." The camera bounced as she dropped onto her bed. "You should really return her casserole dish by the way."

"How do you know about Greta Macmillan's Facebook page?"

"She sent me a friend request the other day. Accepting was the best decision of my life." Amelia propped a pillow behind her head. "Reading her posts about you are the highlight of my day. Especially the ones where she wonders if you and I are lovers. Poor thing was worried about me until she realized you're much better off with Alex."

"Am I, though?" Amelia was eccentric and extreme. Her over the top personality put people off, but once you got past that layer, her sweetness, her loyalty, and her genuine desire to lift up the people around her made it easy to forgive her woo-woo weirdness. At least for me, especially because she went out of her way to take care of me while gently—or maybe not so gently—pushing me out of my comfort zone.

"Well, spill it." Amelia grinned. "There's something on your mind. I can see it right there in the tension between your eyebrows. To what do I owe the pleasure of seeing your beautiful face?"

"Alex asked me why I'm afraid to write today." I bit my lip, half wishing I'd just bit the bullet and filled him in on the whole story.

"And you told him everything and now you're feeling vulnerable." Amelia shifted, her face zooming large on the screen. "That's totally normal—"

"I didn't tell him anything. It's the second time he brought it up and the second time I dodged."

"Eveline Grace McAllister! Why in the world would you keep something that important from the man Greta Macmillan says looks at you like a goddess?"

"First of all, my middle name isn't Grace. And second of all, you really shouldn't believe everything Greta says. She has this habit of jumping to conclusions—you know, like you and me being in a lesbian relationship."

"Aww. Come on. You can totally see how she jumped to that conclusion. You and me? We're super close and it shows. I wouldn't want to be in a pseudo-lesbian relationship with anyone else." She blew a kiss at the screen. "When are you going to tell Alex about Drew?"

I stared at my closed curtain, wondering if Alex was doing the same. Part of me wondered what I'd find if I tossed the thing open. Would he be there? Waiting for me?

I pushed those thoughts away with a sigh. "I'd rather not think about that whole debacle ever again."

"Sweetheart. You have to think about what happened to process it and you have to process it to move past it. And with all due respect, it's time for you to leave the past in the past."

I sighed again as I moved to the window. The temptation to peek out was almost too much. I missed my connection to Alex. If he was waiting for a glimpse of me...

"You haven't been the same since it happened. Your fire just..." Amelia made a poofing gesture. "It's gone. Like your volume's been turned down."

"That's how it feels." I leaned against the wall. "Like I'm afraid to...I don't know...I'm just afraid."

"And life provided you with the perfect situation to embrace your fearlessness. Step one, tell Alex what happened with Drew. Step two, write a book. Step three, give in to the chemistry everyone in Wildrose Landing sees between you."

"Now it's everyone who sees it?"

"You should see the comments on this woman's post. You guys are spewing chemistry so far and wide, marriages are being saved. It's like a pheromone wildfire, burning through that little town at a crazy pace."

"I miss you," I said through a laugh.

"I miss you too, babycakes. You're gonna tell him tomorrow, aren't you? Just sit his handsome butt down, plop your notebooks in front of him, and rip off the bandage."

"I'll think about it." Though what I actually meant was "not a chance in hell."

Amelia rolled her eyes. "I'm gonna suggest you go with what you said out loud and not what you thought in your head. Your higher self already knows what you need to do. If you sit quietly and meditate on it, the answer will come. And if you don't listen, you'll get a hint. Another little nudge. Then another. And another. Not all of them will be pleasant."

We said our goodbyes and I sat on my bed, phone in hand, staring around the room. Amelia had been right about so many things lately, maybe she was right about my higher self, too. I closed my eyes and cleared my mind, doing my best imitation of her meditating.

When my mind felt appropriately empty, I asked, "Should I tell Alex about Drew?"

My eyes flew open and I practically screamed, "Hell no!"

The reaction was so visceral, I laughed. Loudly.

I asked, and I got my answer. I would never talk about Drew again—especially not with Alex. The second I finished the thought, my phone buzzed.

Alex: Just thought you should know, I'm really glad to know you and don't regret what almost happened today at all.

Alex: Also, your curtains are closed and that makes me sad.

Alex: Also also, I've never shared a baby plot idea with anyone, but I'm really glad I shared one with you. That scene has turned into one of my favorites, because of your feedback. We should definitely share more.

I stared at his last sentence, terrified my higher self had provided the answer.

CHAPTER TWENTY

EVIE

My eyes sprang open and I stared at the ceiling in my darkened room, blinking, confused. Typically, I slept like the dead. If I was awake in the middle of the night, there was a reason...

A series of scrapes and bumps downstairs shot me up straight, blanket clutched to chest...

Chills ran down the back of my neck...

Something was in the house.

A very loud, clumsy something.

"What in the world...?" My voice was a whisper and even that was too loud.

I clamped a hand over my mouth as I channeled my inner Amelia to decide what to do. The answer was simple. Investigate. The down comforter floofed to the ground. My flannel PJ pants (fool me once) swished across the hardwood floors as I crept, crept, crept into the hallway. Quiet as a mouse, I tiptoed down the stairs, my phone in one hand, one of Alex's hardcovers in the other. I'd either take pictures of a ghost or bludgeon it back to death with a critically acclaimed masterpiece.

Like always, the ruckus came from the kitchen. Thumping footsteps. The scrape of a chair. A muttered "Aha!" followed by a series of whispers too low for me to understand.

My heart stammered as I rounded the corner. I opened my camera app. Readied the book. A shadow danced in the corner. It turned and uttered a manly yelp as I entered the room. I shrieked in return, raising the book and clicking the capture button on my phone like a madwoman.

"Wait! Evie!" The ghost flung his hands over his head as I advanced.

Hold on a tick...

I knew those curls...

That voice...

That ass...

I squinted through the low light. "Alex?"

He turned, staggering, as his eyes tried to focus through a smile. His feet were bare and covered in leaves. His chest was also bare, meaning my sexy neighbor had traipsed across our yards in freezing autumn temps, wearing nothing but a pair of sweatpants. He had a gift bag in one hand and a paper in the other, which he shuffled around to wiggle his fingers in greeting.

"Nice PJs." Alex staggered and gripped the back of a chair.

My jaw dropped as he grinned like a kid at Christmas. "What in the world are you doing in my kitchen in the middle of the night?"

He held out the paper in one hand and the gift bag in the other. "I wrote something. And it's the best something I've ever written but I won't be able to use one word of it. I can't fictionalize this. It's too real. Too raw. Too...us." As he straightened, he stumbled, laughing to himself as his eyes locked on mine. "This is how you make me feel, Evie. All of it. Every word."

He shoved the paper into my hand.

What the hell was he talking about? Too raw? Too us?

"And this." Alex rattled the bag, then handed it over. "This is for you, too."

"Are you drunk?"

"On you." His gaze skimmed my face, then he pointed to the crumbled paper in my hand. "And that. Oh, and whiskey. I did drink too much of the stuff, it seems. Total accident." He waved a hand as if to erase that truth from the record. "Open your gift."

I peered into the bag, shifting a metric ton of tissue paper out of the way to find...

...socks.

Many, many socks. White ones. Pink ones. Striped ones. Printed ones.

"So you won't slip and fall anymore." Alex reached in to pull out a pair. "See? They have grippers on the bottom."

Shaking my head, I took the bundle. Sure enough, rows of rubber paw prints on the sole would ensure I never hit the ground racing for the door again. "This is ridiculously sweet—and weird—of you."

Emphasis on ridiculous.

I pulled out a chair and helped him into it, then scrubbed my hands over my face to chase away the cobwebs sleep left behind. "But did you really need to break in at..." I checked my phone. "Three thirty in the morning? Alex! What were you thinking?"

He stood right back up and frowned. "I have a confession to make and I'm afraid you'll be very, very mad at me. I don't want you to be very, very mad at me. I like it when you like me. But if you're gonna be mad, I'll just go." He jerked his thumb toward the backdoor and stumbled that way.

My heart thundered a warning. The last time

someone had a confession for me, my life flipped on its axis. Though, Drew hadn't been nearly as worried about my reaction as Alex seemed to be.

I bit my bottom lip. "I'll do my best not to be angry with—"

"I'm the ghost." Alex turned and wiggled his hands at his side. "Tada!"

"Come again?"

"The ghost. The one that haunts your house. That's me. Tada!" Once again, he wiggled his hands beside his face, though with decidedly less enthusiasm. "This went over better when I practiced it," he finished as he plopped back into the chair next to me.

"Maybe it'd go over better if I understood what you're talking about."

I listened as Alex explained that my Aunt Ruth gave him a key the month before she passed. "She said, 'I don't know my niece all that well, but if she's anything like me, she'll need some nudging to get her ass over here. The house'll probably be vacant for a bit.'" Alex spoke in a trembling falsetto, then smiled, dropping his voice back to his normal register. "Which was true, apparently."

"I definitely needed some nudging."

Alex picked at dog hair on his pants, utterly oblivious to the leaves caught between his toes. "So that's what I did. Took care of the house. Kept it clean. Made sure everything worked. That kinda stuff. But then, I realized how great the light was here at this table." He patted the object in question. "And I could see the story and hear the characters better when I was here, so I started coming over to write."

"And people started seeing you..."

"And thinking I was a ghost..."

"And you just let them?" The idea was so preposterous, I didn't know what to do with it.

"I mean..." He shrugged, grinning wider than I'd ever seen him. "They seemed so excited to have something to talk about. I didn't want to let anyone down." Alex gave me a charming grin, laced with heat and intention. "Do you forgive me?"

Adrenaline spiraled through my system and tangled with the realization he'd been in my house without permission at least twice since I'd moved in. "Why didn't you stop breaking in once I started living here? You have to admit, that's really creepy, Alex."

He dropped his forehead to the table, then rolled it to the side and peered up at me. "The first time I just wanted to make sure I hadn't left anything here. The next time? You'd just kissed me and I couldn't sleep and I couldn't write and I couldn't stop thinking about you and it all made perfect sense right up until you woke up, so I ran away like a coward and promised I'd never come into your house without permission again."

"Then why are you here now, Alex? It's the middle of the night and you're drunk."

He plucked the paper out of my lap and ran his hands down the page. "I wrote this and couldn't wait 'til morning to show you." He lifted his gaze. "Couldn't wait 'til morning to *see* you. I should have kissed you today, Evie. I shouldn't have let you run away."

Our eyes locked.

He licked his lips, his gaze on my mouth. "Evie..."

My name, dressed in his rasping voice, was sin.

It sent chills down my spine and warmth pooled in my belly.

Mustering all the restraint I'd ever been given, I slid my chair back from the table and stood, purposefully avoiding eye contact. This whole thing needed further discussion, but not while he was too drunk to do the conversation justice. "Come on, Boss. Let's get you back home."

I reached for Alex's hand to help him out of the chair. His fingers threaded with mine and he pulled me into his lap, one hand sliding into my hair to angle my face, then his lips whispered against my own. My breath caught as the faintest trace of a kiss set my body ablaze. He tilted his head, delicate, gentle, as if appraising the perfect angle. A master crafter planning a masterpiece.

I melted into him, meeting him kiss for kiss, breath

for breath. My hands traveled the hard planes of his back and shoulders, and I tasted whiskey on his tongue...

...whiskey on his tongue...

"Alex..." I pressed my forehead to his. "You're drunk."

"I am." He licked his lips. "But that doesn't change anything."

"It changes enough. I don't want to be something you regret in the morning."

"I won't regret you."

I closed my eyes. "You might."

"I won't."

With a heavy sigh, I pulled myself out of his lap. "We'll see how you feel about that in the morning."

Alex stared up at me for one long second, then nodded and stood. "Do you see what you do to me?" He took my hand and placed it on the erection straining against his sweats. He groaned at the contact, eyes sliding closed, before releasing my hand. I let it drop and backed away, despite the urge to step into his arms and forget everything but him, us.

"That's very impressive."

"You think so?" His grin was so sexy I didn't think I'd ever recover.

"I know so." I placed both hands on his shoulders

and spun him around. "Now, let's get you and your impressive man-parts home and into bed."

Alex kept turning until he was facing me again. "I'd like to get you into my bed. So would my man-parts."

"I'm sure that's true, but you'll thank me for this in the morning." I spun him back around to face the door. "Are you safe to get home? Or do you need an escort?"

He turned over his shoulder and started to speak. The gleam in his eyes warned me he wasn't going to give up as easily as I'd like.

"Safe to get yourself home it is," I said with a laugh.

His face fell. "Fine." His shoulders slumped. "Are you sure you forgive me?"

"For impersonating a ghost or the sexual harassment I just handled brilliantly?"

"Both."

"We can talk about that in the morning, Alex. Now, get yourself home and into bed. I'll see you in the morning."

I closed the door and leaned my head against the wood, trying to make sense of everything that happened and how I felt about it. As I turned to head back to bed, Alex's poem caught my eyes. I swept the paper off the table and read.

. . .

Dark and dull

A thousand shades of gray

Fading away

And then...

You.

Stumbling into my life

Bare

Open

Bright and vibrant

You.

I am better

I am warm

Because you...

You

Are a thousand shades of

Autumn leaves and rushing waves

You

Are so beautiful the sun blushes

You

Are comfort and joy

You

You

You

I am better

I am warm

I am

Yours.

CHAPTER TWENTY-ONE

ALEX

Evie shifted and the entire bed bounced with the movement. I groaned as my eyes blinked open, then smiled as she nuzzled into my back. Honestly, who hadn't seen this coming? Greta Macmillan saw it. Izzy saw it. The whole town knew Evie and I would end up together sooner or later.

"Good morning, beautiful." I rolled over and threw an arm around...

...Morgan.

He rewarded me with a face-sized lick, and I sat up too fast for my own good. My head pounded as the real events of last night came back to me. I did not woo Evie into my bed with my genius poem like I thought I would. I did, however, get caught breaking into her house. In my sweats. In the middle of the night. To deliver socks.

I also made many moves.

Many, embarrassing, ineffective, sexually aggressive moves. I dropped my head into my hand, then pounded my forehead for good measure. Evie was surely still asleep, but as soon as she woke, I needed to grovel for forgiveness.

"Damn these selfish Prescott genes!" If I didn't take after my dad so much, none of this would have even been an issue. I'd have politely returned the key to Sugar Maple Hill when Evie moved in and done things the normal way instead of following every stupid whim that came to my head because it was easier for me.

Morgan whined his agreement and I shuffled into the bathroom, popping some ibuprofen before making my way downstairs in search of coffee. As the dog clicked across the floor, my bare feet slapped the kitchen tile, following the bits of leaves and debris tracing a path from the front door to the fridge. The doorbell rang as I popped a pod into the Keurig and checked the time. *Too early for anyone to be visiting.* I shuffled to answer, peeking through the window to find Evie on my porch, a coffee steaming in each hand and a bag slung over her shoulder. She had on a coat and a scarf, a beanie pulled down low with her hair braided and slung over one shoulder.

Huh.

She never came to my house and rarely got out of bed before seven.

I opened the door, shivering as the air hit my chest.

"Morning, Casanova." She stepped inside and handed me a cup of coffee. "Close the door before your nipples fall off."

"Bless you, child." I lifted the steaming drink to my mouth, then paused, ready to start groveling. "Look, about last night..."

She held out her hand to ward off my words as Morgan wagged his tail in greeting. She scratched his ears and avoided eye contact with me. "There's so much to unpack about last night that I don't even know where to start."

"I know where to start. With an apology. I had no right to use that key after you moved into Sugar Maple Hill. None. It was wrong, and creepy, and I should have been up front about everything from the get-go."

Evie finally met my gaze. "It *was* wrong and it *was* creepy and you *should* have told me what was going on. I mean, did you not, for one second, feel guilty about letting me get wasted that night at the bar with Jude's little drinking game? The whole time, you knew what was going on and could have stopped it just by being honest. I'm so humiliated. Was it a game to you guys? Is this whole thing between us some twisted..." She shook her head, her eyes closing as she turned away.

I placed a hand on her arm. "This isn't a game for me. I did feel guilty that night at the bar—"

"Then why didn't you say anything?" Evie whirled, her eyes flashing with distrust. "Why did you let me make a fool of myself?"

"You didn't make a fool of yourself."

"I kissed you on my front porch! I went on and on about the color of your eyes, spewing nonsense about connection while stuffing french fries into my mouth, and then freaking kissed you."

"And I loved every second of it."

Evie scowled. "Sure. Right. I should have known that, 'cause you've made your feelings for me impeccably clear over the last couple weeks. I definitely got the feeling you liked kissing me and have always known exactly where I stand with you." She folded her arms over her chest. "In case you can't tell, my sarcasm is fully engaged at the moment."

Oh, I could tell, and despite the fact that I started this conversation intending to grovel, frustration flared. "You aren't exactly easy to read, yourself. First, I think you're flirting, then I think we're just friends, but even then, you won't open up to me. You're shy, but you're not. You're bold, but you're locked down so tight I can't figure you out. You won't tell me why you won't write and if you can't trust me with that, then how am I supposed to know what I mean to you? You're so freaking hot and cold, it drives me crazy!"

Evie glared. "I must be driving you crazy if you thought breaking into my house was a good idea...especially since you don't even know if we're friends or not."

I let a long breath out through my nose, closing my eyes and fighting for composure. "Did you read the poem I wrote?"

Her features softened and she offered a faint smile. "I did and it's beautiful, and if that's how you really feel about me..." She flared her hands and closed her eyes. "That's why I'm here. To find out if I'm the woman in that poem or if I'm the asshole you laugh with your friends about at the end of the day."

"You're the woman in the poem, Evie." My voice was low. Raw.

She squared her shoulders and lifted her chin. "And you're not going to break into my house anymore?"

I fished in the pocket of my sweats for the key and handed it to her. "Never again."

"Then I have something for you." She shifted so she could reach into her bag and pulled out a three-ring binder stuffed with paper. "You asked me why I don't write anymore. I dodged, but it's time I shared this with you." She put the binder into my hands. "You don't have to read it all."

Eager to glean everything I could about Eveline McAllister, I plopped onto the couch and dove in. Inside the pages I found quick wit, razor-sharp pacing, prose that felt like poetry without the pretension...

"How are you not published?" I glanced up, then went right back to the manuscript. "I'll call my agent right fucking now. You're sitting on a bestseller. This story..."

What in the world happened that someone this talented fizzled before she took off? This was the kind of stuff I expected from the girl who escorted me to my car at Brown. It was emotional. Real.

Fearless.

"That's the thing." Evie pulled a book out of her bag and dropped it into my lap. "It *is* published."

I stared at the cover of a title I'd been avoiding like the plague. Despite its success and high praise, the author had been a pompous prick on Twitter, not just bragging about his success, but belittling everyone else in the industry. After I watched that train wreck of a debut, I wrote the guy off. He'd kill his career with that attitude and I'd be smart to steer clear.

I ran a finger along his name—Drew Stephens—

then flipped through the pages, stopping at the dedication page.

To em. Thanks for the springboard. You've been very useful.

I frowned at the lowercase initials. The book was too successful for a typo in the frontmatter. "I don't understand."

"Drew was my boyfriend. We started dating in high school. Went to Brown together. Then, I wrote this. He stole it, published it, and wiped all record of it from my computer so I couldn't file a copywrite claim. The only proof I have is that binder."

"Are you serious right now?"

"I wish I wasn't."

I stared at the book in my lap. That prick. That no good, low life, thieving prick. No wonder she was afraid to write. Afraid to open up. If she'd been with this slithery snake since high school, she'd committed herself to him and he repaid her by stealing her whole fucking future.

"I'm so sorry this happened to you, but you know what? This guy? This asshole Stephens? He'll never be able to pull this off again." I waved the binder in the air then put it on the coffee table. "His career was over before it started, especially if I have anything to say about it. But you? You own the magnificent mind that came up with this story. You have a career ahead of you. I promise."

Evie shook her head, her gaze on her lap. "I can't..."

"But you can! You can write another book. It's as simple as getting your butt in your chair and your hands on the keyboard. And I'll call my agent—"

"It's not that simple and you know it." Evie glanced up, frustration tightening the edges of her voice. "You know how hard it is to write when there's something in the way..."

I opened my mouth to respond, because I had to say something. Anything. Surely, I'd find the one, right thing that would unlock her fear so she could write again. I'd never read anything so fresh, so inspired...

"Drew didn't tell me what he'd done until the book was published. He dropped it in my lap, smirking, then told me to get out of the apartment because he hadn't been in love with me for years. That he'd stayed because he thought I might be useful someday. I moved in with Amelia until I lost my job and now I'm here. So yes, I've been private and hesitant because if I was so wrong about him..."

Her meaning smacked me in the forehead and I sighed. "Then you could be that wrong about me."

"I could be that wrong about *anyone*." Evie licked her lips and met my eyes. "But I don't think I'm wrong about you. I think you're a good man, Alex Prescott, and I think you're good for me, and I think I'd love a chance to find out if I'm right, if it won't make things too complicated."

CHAPTER TWENTY-TWO

EVIE

Alex pulled me off the couch and into his arms. His lips found mine and his tongue swept into my mouth, rendering me speechless. I whimpered, gripping his back, and forgetting all the worries that had spiraled through my head for months.

Complicated? This wasn't complicated.

Kissing Alex was the easiest thing I'd ever done.

"Do you know how hard it's been not to kiss you every day?" His teeth grazed my bottom lip. "You're all I ever think about."

"Maybe that's why you can't write." I smirked, then leaned in for another kiss. Heat built between us. Hands explored. Tongues tasted. His scent surrounded me and my nipples pebbled; my lower belly tightened and throbbed.

Alex stepped back, tearing his succulent lips from mine, took my hands, and led me back to the couch. "I'm gonna get serious for a second. I didn't read enough of your book to know for sure, but what I did read is spectacular. Evie, if you wrote that, then you've got something special."

The topic was a bucket of cold water to the face. The heat from our kiss died, leaving a familiar emptiness in its wake. "I don't have it anymore. Drew took it from me."

"He took that from you." Alex gestured toward the book. "That's it. He'll never publish anything like that ever again. That's not true for you."

My hands twisted in my lap, my thumbs rubbing over knuckles. I watched them move, then finally risked a glance at the man beside me. "It feels true for me. I have never felt so betrayed as I did when he told me what he'd done. That dedication? He looked downright excited to point out the lowercase initials. I have no idea how I didn't see he didn't want to be with me." I hung my head. "Every time I think about writing, I remember his smirking face..."

A face that had always looked at me with love...or so I thought. I'd never felt so foolish as I did when the guy I assumed I would marry told me he'd been planning the theft from the second I told him the idea for the story. *I wasn't sure I'd be able to hang in there long enough for you to finish the damn thing. You are so exhausting.* The words hit me like poisoned arrows, leeching my soul of all the things that brought me joy.

Alex lifted my chin with a finger. "Then we'll rewrite that story. When you think about writing, I want you to think about me. Us. This. You're gonna write the best revenge story and this Drew Stephens guy will rue the day he took advantage of you."

The day flew by in a whirlwind of words, edits, walks, and Alex. I was living a dream—a life dedicated to books, sharing it with someone who loved stories as much as I did. Darkness settled on Wildrose Landing and after dinner at Overton's, we called it a day. I dashed my keys on the end table next to my door and kicked off my shoes, grinning as the grippy paws on my socks stuck to the floor.

Who brought a woman grippy socks?

For that matter, who shoved grippy socks into a pair of shoes, on the off-chance Alex would notice? I laughed my way upstairs and into my bedroom. Seconds after my light flicked on, a text came in.

Alex: I see you.

I glanced to the window and found the curtains closed.

Me: Are you being deep here? Like you 'see' me?

Alex: I mean, I do. I see you. But I'm being literal. Saw your bedroom light come on.

Me: Wow. Do you just sit around, staring at my bedroom, hoping for a glimpse?

Alex: Yes! Guilty. But, don't judge. You'd stare at your window every night too...if you'd seen your boob like me. (And if I'm lucky, maybe I'll finally see them both.)

He'd seen my boob? My hand flew to cover the girls as I mentally replayed the day I'd stumbled downstairs, hungover and certain I was about to see a ghost. I had been so right to sneak a glimpse of his ass in return. With a shake of the head, I tapped out a reply.

Me: I see them every day.

Alex: Sure. Gloat about it. You don't sound like an asshole at all.

Me: Says the man who broke into my house for months. How would you feel if I did this…

Slowly, dramatically, I slipped a hand through the curtains and created a sliver of space between the fabric.

Alex: You tease!

Me: You know you like it.

Alex: More than you know. Show me more.

Feeling exposed, I pulled back the curtains. Directly across from me, I saw Alex standing in the window, sweats on, phone in hand. He glanced up, saw me, and put his hand to the glass.

My body quickly alerted me to the fact that I'd fantasized about this exact situation several times before. Feeling sexy and confident, I ran a finger along my collarbone, grazing the fabric of my collar, then down, down, down.

Alex: Take off your shirt.

Alex: Have mercy.

I considered complying for all of two seconds before I decided to tease him a little longer.

Me: Mercy it is.

And with that, I slowly closed my curtains. Knowing the light was on, hoping my outline would be visible through the sheer window coverings, I slowly lifted my shirt overhead and dropped it on the floor.

Alex: I hate you a little bit right now

Me: Goodnight Alex

Alex: Goodnight you wicked, wicked woman. I can't believe this is how you treat a man who broke into your house to hand deliver safety socks

CHAPTER TWENTY-THREE

ALEX

Evie and I pushed through the doors of Cheers 'n Beers, arm in arm, already laughing. Jude and Austin waited at a table in the back and Izzy would arrive late. She always did when Jude was involved. He loved to tease her about being fashionably late while I wondered how he hadn't figured out she'd been crushing on him for years.

Before we made our way to the table, Evie pulled on my arm. "Maybe we shouldn't get drunk tonight." Her eyebrows drew together and she cocked her head. "You know...just in case."

"In case of what? Hilarity and good times? You're right. We definitely don't want that."

As if she thought my friends could read lips, Evie leaned close to whisper through a clenched jaw, "We have a tendency to sexually harass each other when we're drunk..."

I lifted a brow. "That would definitely be the worst thing ever...?"

"What would be the worst thing ever?" Jude asked from behind us. The jackass had snuck up while we weren't paying attention.

I threw an arm around Evie's shoulder and gave her my most charming smile. "Evie doesn't think we should sexually harass each other tonight."

She dropped her jaw while Jude scoffed. "All you two do is sexually harass each other." He linked arms with her and led us to the table. "Isn't that right, Austinator?"

Austin quirked his head. "Isn't what right?"

"Alex and Evie walk around in a cloud of chemistry and sexual harassment." Jude spun his chair around and straddled it, folding his arms on the back and cocking his head.

"You've noticed that, too?" Austin rolled his eyes. "Yeah. Super stoked for you guys, but the town is preparing a petition. Your happiness makes the rest of us feel like failures."

"That's not what I heard." Izzy leaned in to greet

me with a kiss on the cheek. "The only people who complain about them are serial loners like you."

"Hello pot. Meet kettle." Austin arched one dark brow. "You must be miserable, then."

Jude burst out laughing while Izzy blushed. "Yeah Iz-ster. What's up with you never dating anyone? You're cute. You're smart. You own the best damn candy shop in town. You have some juicy secret that chases men away? Or is it just your inability to keep to a schedule?" He leaned his chin on his hands and opened his eyes wide like a child waiting for a bedtime story.

I all but slapped him upside the head.

One look at the mortification on Izzy's face and I did slap him upside the head.

"What was that for?" He rubbed a hand through his hair like I'd mortally wounded him. Knowing how much time he spent trying to look good, I probably had.

"I'm sure you've done something to deserve it." I fought the urge to glance at my sister just in case tonight happened to be the night Jude was paying attention. Instead, I raised an expectant eyebrow his way. When he didn't respond, I held out my hands and glanced around the bar.

Jude frowned. "What?"

"Last I checked, we've been here for over ten minutes and don't have drinks."

"I don't work here." He sat back, grinning. "I just own the place."

"Do you work anywhere?" Austin snorted. "We all can agree that answer is no."

"Don't hate. Not everyone can be as talented and lucky as me."

Austin bounced a balled-up napkin off Jude's temple. "If feeding a bloated ego is a talent, then I agree, you're the best I've ever seen."

Izzy took off her coat and draped it on the back of her chair. "I thought Jack would be here tonight. When he stopped in at Sweet Stuff with the kids he said he had a sitter."

"The sitter fell through...again." Austin shook his head with a sad smile.

"What's the matter with Jack?" Evie asked. "I'd love to meet him."

I took her hand. "And I'd love for him to meet you. His wife passed away a year and a half ago, leaving him as a suddenly single dad. Their three kids aren't adjusting well, and it's been a real shitshow ever since. If he doesn't get those kids under control, he'll run out of sitters."

Izzy's jaw dropped. "Considering the circumstances, I'm surprised they've done as well as they have. Cut the man some slack."

Conversation moved on and as my friends chatted,

I watched Evie. Her smile. Her laugh. The intelligence sparkling in her eyes. She was sweet and warm. A fire, burning slowly but fiercely.

The more I thought about what her ex-boyfriend stole from her, the more pissed off I got. What kind of garbage, piece of trash, egomaniac did something like that? How could he live with himself, knowing the only reason anyone knew his name was because he manipulated someone who thought he loved her? An innocent whose only sin was placing her trust—and love—in the wrong man.

But more than that, how could anyone do something like that to Evie? I'd never met a person more deserving of all the good things in the world. How could anyone take advantage of someone so kind? So genuine? So—

"What's going on there, big guy?" Jude leaned in, claiming my attention. "You look like you wanna deck someone."

I released the tension in my hands and conjured a smile. "I definitely want to hit someone. I heard this story the other day. A wrong that needs to be righted. And it keeps making me madder by the minute."

"Oh, boy." Jude hooted. "Here we go. Captain White Knight has found another cause." He waggled his eyebrows and sat forward. "Please. Fill us in. We're all ears."

As much as I loved his irreverence most nights, on this one he could very much fuck off. "This cause is a good one."

"Aren't they all?" Austin sat back, beer in hand. "Right until they aren't anymore."

Izzy patted my arm. "Come on, guys. Give his hero complex a break. He can't help it."

I didn't need a break. I needed everyone to understand what happened to Evie so they could get on board and start solving this problem with me. That dickhead Stephens needed taken down, and Evie? She needed...lifted up? Put back together? I didn't know what she needed but I was determined to find out and had no doubt our friends would rise to the occasion.

"Imagine this." I scrubbed a hand over my mouth. "A talented woman works her butt off to create something amazing. Something that would absolutely change her life and launch her career when it got noticed." Evie's eyes widened in a warning, but I barreled forward. "Now imagine someone she trusts steals that thing and claims it's his, then leaves her in the dust of the fame he creates off her blood, sweat, and tears."

Austin made an appraising face. "Sounds like the plot to one of your books. If it's not, it should be, 'cause I'd read that."

"You mean you'd wait for it to become a movie." Jude smirked.

"I mean read it, asshat. Especially if the woman goes all psycho and gets epic revenge on that douchebag. Slowly. And with much deliberation."

"It's not fiction." I ran a hand through my hair. "It's what happened to Evie." With the fire of injustice spurring me on, I spewed the entire story to my friends. They were properly indignant, right up until the moment Evie pushed her chair back from the table and covered her face with her hands.

My words trailed off.

When she looked up, her eyes swam with pain and betrayal. "I..." She closed her mouth and shook her head. "You know what? I think I'm gonna go." She stood and marched for the door.

My friends stared at me, all the indignation they'd aimed at Jerkface Stephens now targeting me. Jude gestured toward the exit. "Go after her, asshole."

The rest of the crew bobbed their heads in agreement.

With a sigh, I pushed back from the table and jogged out of the bar. When I stepped into the crisp evening air, I found Evie striding down the sidewalk, hands shoved in her coat pockets as she stared at her feet, the wind fluttering her hair around her face.

I caught up to her halfway down the block. "Evie..." I put a hand on her shoulder and she shrugged it off.

I reached for her again. "Evie. Listen. I'm sorry..."

She paused but wouldn't look at me. "That was *not* your story to tell." She spoke so quietly, the wind nearly stole her words.

"Maybe your story needs telling—"

Evie turned, slowly letting her gaze find mine. "But that's not your choice, Alex. It's mine. I'm incredibly private. Until tonight, two people knew what Drew did to me. Two." She stared with watery eyes until the weight of the revelation smacked me in the side of the head.

"And I'm one of them."

She glared at the sidewalk, shifting away from me. "I trusted you with that information and you just tossed it out there like it doesn't mean anything."

"But don't you see? It *doesn't* mean anything..."

Evie's jaw dropped. She blinked in surprise before she whirled, her feet clicking a sharp staccato against the ground. I caught up to her and grabbed her wrist. "Hear me out, please. It doesn't mean anything...about *you*. About who you are. It says a shit ton about what a creep that guy is, not you. That's all I'm trying to say."

Her gray eyes swam with unshed tears. "It says I'm

naïve. I'm gullible. I'm an idiot who can't tell real love from fake...."

"That's not what I thought when you told me the story. I guarantee Izzy, Austin, and Jude weren't thinking that, either. You were taken advantage of by a dickhead. An asshole who couldn't cut it on his own. A failure of a human being, Evie. That's what Drew Stephens is. I want to help you heal so we can take that imposter down. Darkness can't survive in the light. You need to bring all of this out in the open to process it."

Evie huffed a laugh. "You sound like Amelia."

"Then Amelia must give good advice." I took her hands. "I didn't mean to share your secret without your permission. I honestly thought talking about it was the right choice, especially with those three. They're ridiculous most of the time, but they're also really smart. I mean, they do hang out with me, after all."

Evie stayed silent, but at least she didn't pull her hands from mine.

"I don't want you to be very, very mad at me." I leaned down, desperate to meet her eyes, hoping she caught the callback to the night I was drunk.

Her smile said she did. "I am very, very mad at you. I also forgive you. But Alex? This is the second time I'm forgiving you for doing something presumptive and selfish. I'm not comfortable sharing that much of myself with people, but if I do, it needs to be on my terms. Not yours. That kind of stuff...I'm better off if I hold onto it myself."

"I'm genuinely sorry. It never occurred to me that you wouldn't want our friends to know." I cupped her face, caressing her cheeks with my thumbs. "But, and I'm just putting this out there, you don't have to hold it all by yourself now. I'd be honored to help carry it."

"Thank you." Her words were soft, like she had to will them past her lips. "Now, will you please kiss me? I need to feel something other than confused right now and when your mouth is on mine, everything in the world comes into focus."

"Funny..." I leaned closer. "I feel the same way."

My lips crashed into hers, my tongue sweeping into her mouth as I wrapped my arms around her and pressed her body to mine. Her curves melted into me, inviting me to take more, to go further, to touch, touch, touch every inch of her right there on the frigid sidewalk outside Cheers 'n Beers.

The hitch in her breath nearly broke me. I needed skin. Contact. I needed more than a boob falling out of a tank top and a hot as hell silhouette behind a closed curtain. My fingers slipped under her shirt, grazing her ribs...

"Geeze, you two. Get a room."

I pressed my forehead to Evie's. "Now is not the time, Jude. Can't you see I'm apologizing?" I shooed him back toward the bar as I wrapped an arm around Evie and tucked her against me. Her need for privacy on the matter didn't make a whole lot of sense to me, but it was important to her. From that point forward, what was important to her, would be important to me—even if I didn't completely understand why.

CHAPTER TWENTY-FOUR

EVIE

The night passed in a blur. After Alex spilled the Drew story to his friends and we practically set the street on fire with his apology, we went back into Cheers 'n Beers to finish the evening with a little drinking and a lot of laughing. Having the tragedy that was the theft of my book out in the open didn't change the way anyone treated me. Or the way they looked at me. In fact, it almost felt like I had three more people in my corner. Like maybe Alex was right...Drew stealing my book didn't say anything about me. It did, however, say loads about him.

At the end of the night, Alex pulled to a stop in front of his house. "You missed my driveway," I said, with a laugh. "Did you have more Drunken Sailors than I thought?"

"I know where I am and I'm not drunk. I thought we'd progress to the sexual harassment portion of the evening." He killed the engine and opened his door, giving me a smile designed to make my blood boil. "You coming?"

I sure hope so, especially considering what I felt hiding under those sweats the other night.

Hoping he couldn't read the thought through my facial expression, I blinked it away and replied with a hearty, "Sure!" then followed Alex into his house.

The clatter of nails announced the cavalry as the door swung open. "Well hello, sirs. I missed you, too." He crouched to greet Morgan and Larry and as he let the dog out to do his business, I started to worry I hadn't read Alex's intentions right at all.

Maybe he didn't invite me in for drinks and sexiness.

Maybe his comment about sexual harassment was a joke.

Maybe this had something to do with work...

But after Morgan galloped back into the house, Alex took my hand. Pulled me close. Wrapped me in his arms and started swaying, crooning a terrible rendition of "Every Breath You Take." He spun us in a slow circle as Morgan titled his head back and joined in the song.

Alex's eyes, when they met mine, were filled with the warmth of friendship and the heat of lust. "Hold on." He tucked a strand of hair behind my ear. "I can do this better." A few seconds with his phone had the song coming over the house speakers. Morgan and Larry took a seat while Alex drew me back into his embrace and danced me around the living room. His body was supple and strong. His confidence was soothing. He spun me and as I came back to face him, I pressed my lips to his. He stilled, his hands skating up my hips and slipping under my shirt. His touch sent goosebumps shivering along my spine.

Eager to return the favor, I ran my fingers along the corded muscles in his back. The kiss deepened as our bodies caught fire. Where before we were tender, sweet, the exploration of firsts, now we were driven by urgency. Dissatisfied with the fabric between us, I yanked his shirt over his head, then stood back to admire the swoops and curves of his torso.

"Where do you find time to work out with your writing schedule?" I trailed my fingers along his pecs, my nails scraping over his nipples.

His eyes slipped closed and it looked like he wished he could purr. "I'll tell you when I remember."

My shirt found its way to the floor next to his. Alex

bent his mouth to my breasts, teasing, sucking, biting and I dropped my head back as the speakers crooned. He gripped my ass, his fingers digging as his curls tickled my neck. Stumbling backwards, he dropped to the couch, his heated gaze blazing into mine.

I straddled him, slowly lowering my weight onto the erection straining against his pants. Rocking my hips, I gasped as his length rubbed against my core. Alex ground into me, groaning, a guttural sound that set my nerve endings on fire. The friction, the contact, *him*...my senses overloaded with it all. My hips rocked and rolled, edging pleasure ever closer, ever deeper, sharp with urgency and reckless, tortured abandon.

A wet nose pushed against my hand and I stilled. Alex laughed as Morgan pressed his snout into our laps. "Way to kill the mood, my friend."

Slipping out from underneath me, he stood, then led me up the stairs and into his bed. Without preamble, he took off my bra and dropped it to the floor. My pants went next. Then his. He rolled on a condom, then laid down on the bed and pulled me on top. His thick length slipped inside me, slowly, decadently, as I lowered myself. I rolled my hips as he worshipped my breasts, biting into the soft flesh with a low growl.

My first orgasm was graceless, a panting, bucking thing that came out of nowhere. I rode him as my body became sunlight, as starbursts exploded along my skin. His hands seared my hips with pleasure, and I called his name to the ceiling. Over and over, again and again, out of control, at the mercy of instinct.

When I opened my eyes, I found Alex staring up at me, his gaze singed with lust. "That was so fucking hot." He rocked his cock deeper, grinning wickedly as I gasped. "And so was that. I like watching you lose yourself." He thrust again, slowly slicking himself into me, gaining speed, faster, greedy, chasing his own want with such abandon I felt myself falling again, spiraling into ecstasy as pleasure bloomed across his face.

I finished with him, my head tossed back, his eyes closed as his lips parted. When his gaze finally met mine, he grinned. "I think you just earned a raise."

I slapped his chest. "Not funny."

"Are you sure? I thought it was and we both know I have a better sense of humor than you."

I lifted my hips, then shifted off him, collapsing by his side. "There you go again, thinking you know all the things, when simple stuff eludes you. You know, like don't break into your neighbor's house or tell her secrets to your friends."

Alex brushed my hair back from my face. "I know that you're the most beautiful woman I've ever seen. I know the more I learn about you, the more I want to know. I know that I'll do everything in my power to show you how amazing you are."

His eyes glistened with truth and mine glistened with sweet tears, which I quickly brushed away as he headed for the bathroom to clean up.

CHAPTER TWENTY-FIVE

Evie

The next morning I opened my eyes to find Alex kneeling beside the bed, watching me through his phone. Sunlight filled the room, catching in his curls and twinkling in his eyes. "Wait," he said. "Don't move."

I jerked my face away from the camera. "What are you doing?"

"I said don't move." Alex shifted and the bed bounced. "That would've been the perfect picture," he said with a sad sigh.

Something in his statement made me smile, and I peeked over my shoulder to find him grinning. "Why are you taking pictures of me in my sleep?"

"I figured I'd post it to Greta's Facebook page so the residents of Wildrose Landing can figure out who won the pot." Alex shifted again, his phone coming into focus as he set up another shot. "My money's on Jude."

I yanked the covers over my head. "Have you learned nothing? What is it about 'I'm a private person' means 'please share pictures of me sleeping on the internet?'" I risked a peek out of the covers to find Alex crouching beside me, grinning as he closed and locked his phone. "Also, people were betting on when we'd sleep together?"

"You're adorable, you know that?"

"You're not too bad yourself." I sat up and returned his grin. "You're not really going to post those on the internet, are you?" As much as I wanted to be cool and nonchalant about the whole thing, the thought of my slobbering face squished against a pillow hitting Greta's feed didn't exactly make my morning.

"I'll definitely be posting these." When my jaw dropped, Alex laughed. "I'm joking, silly. These are private. If I had my way, no one but me would see you like this ever again. Your post-coital sexiness is mine from this point forward."

With his curls crazed from sex and sleeping and a crooked grin sliding across his face, Alex looked downright edible. How was it that someone as normal as me had ended up in this man's bed? What had I done to deserve *the* Alexander Prescott looking at me like I was the most precious thing he'd ever laid eyes on? He was a bestseller. Had friends and family who loved him. An entire town who cared about what he was doing and who he was doing it with.

I was just...me.

I curled into him. "Have you even seen this Facebook post everyone keeps talking about? I can't bring myself to look."

"Oh, I've seen it. And there's more than one post." Alex's fingers flicked across his phone and opened Facebook. He took a quick look, then covered the screen as his brows creased. "You're not gonna like this."

I reached for the phone, but he jerked it away. "Come on, Alex. Let me see."

"There's nothing to see." He hid the device behind his back, and I lunged for it.

"Then there's no reason to hide it from me."

Alex pushed me back onto the bed and straddled me. "If I tell you, you promise not to freak out?"

I shrugged. "I'll try..."

Carefully, Alex pulled the device from behind him. "Greta posted a new pic this morning. It's blurry, probably because she was standing on her front porch and zooming in to see us, but that definitely looks like you coming inside with me last night."

"Please tell me you're kidding." I snatched the phone from him.

Alas, he was not kidding, though the pic was so grainy we could have been anyone, anywhere. I scrolled and found a few familiar names in the discussion. "Did you see this?" I pointed to a comment. "Izzy says 'Can confirm the chemistry was off the charts.' And Jude added 'You all have me to thank for this.'" I dropped the phone and closed my eyes. "How are you so cool about this?"

"It's not that big of a deal, Evie." Frustration crept into Alex's voice.

"It is to me. I'm a—"

"Very private person. I know." He grinned as he gathered me in his arms. "You weren't very private when you were shrieking my name last night."

"That's because no one was around to hear."

Alex huffed a laugh. "Morgan and Larry would beg to differ. They might never look at you the same."

"Morgan and Larry will have to learn to deal, then. Given what you did to me last night, I didn't have the mental faculties to care who heard."

"What I'm hearing is I just need to sex you out of this privacy anxiety." Alex slipped his hand under the covers and caressed my thigh. "I am definitely up for that challenge." He shifted, whipping the blankets away and positioning himself between my legs, then kissed my inner thigh. "This is a very magical place, you know." His finger slipped past my underwear. "All warm and soft and cozy."

I relaxed into the pillow, suddenly caring less about who saw what on Greta's Facebook post than I should. "Please don't tell me you're comparing my vagina to a sock."

Alex's finger deepened its magic. "There *is* a lot of slipping going on..."

I giggled. Then gasped. Then lost all sense of time as my body gave itself to his.

Alex collapsed beside me, grinning like an idiot. "I like waking up to that. We should definitely make that part of our morning routine."

I propped myself up on an elbow and returned the smile. "I concur. One hundred percent. Lots and lots of sex has to be one of our cute couple things."

He frowned. "Cute couple things?"

For half a second, I was afraid I'd jumped ahead in the relationship timeline by naming us a couple, but I squashed that worry flat. Fearless Evie didn't fret over stuff she couldn't control. "Yeah. You know. Couples have things. Some people make up funny words. Others buy each other stupid gifts or have silly nicknames..."

"And you want sex to be our thing?"

I arched an eyebrow. "Don't you?"

"I am so down for being that couple who has lots of sex." Alex stared into the distance, as if appraising the idea. "Feels original, you know?"

I giggled, content. Being with him seemed so natural in a way being with Drew never did. I'd never hung out naked in bed, making jokes after sex. I was more used to a quick cleanup, a peck on the cheek, and then dispersing to different rooms in the apartment.

Alex's eyes met mine. His jaw dropped. "That's it..."

"What's it?" I asked. "Still working that sex angle?"

"No." He sat up. "No...I think I figured out why my story's not working. I actually think..." His eyes slipped over my shoulder as he lost himself to thought. "I think I know how to fix it."

His excitement was contagious, the glee in his expression sending my heart over the edge. Life was rewarding us for the challenges we'd faced and now that we'd found each other, everything was falling into place. His story was coming into focus. I had friends to support me. We had each other...

"What are you still doing in bed with me?" I sat up

and shooed him towards the door. "Go. Write. Be the amazing author you are."

He bent down to kiss me, once, twice, a third time. "Wait till you read this, Evie. I see everything the story's been missing..." His eyes were wide with wonder and excitement. "You're never gonna see this coming."

"I'll definitely never see it if you never write it. Go on, silly. Get to work. Harness the magic while it's happening."

Alex kissed me one last time—long, deep, full of promise—then raced from the room and disappeared into the study.

CHAPTER TWENTY-SIX

ALEX

Why in the world did my eyes feel like sandpaper? Probably because my face was three inches from the computer screen. I sat back, realizing for the first time that I was sitting in the dark, my laptop the only source of light in my office.

I'd written the entire day.

My hands felt like hooks. My back was stiff. My belly rumbled and my eyes burned. Physically, I was miserable but mentally? Emotionally? I was flying high. Between Evie and her magic hooha unleashing the grip writer's block had on my words, I hadn't felt so good in a long time.

I stepped out of the office and bellowed, "Eveline

McAllister! I require sexing!"

My voice echoed through the house, interrupted by the click of Morgan's nails as he clomped up the stairs with Larry bouncing along behind. After giving each a bit of love, I headed downstairs. "Evie?"

With my house obviously empty, I checked my phone and found two texts from a few hours ago, one from Evie and another from my agent.

I read Brighton's first. **You're one month from your deadline and I'm sorry to say there are no more extensions. You've used up all the goodwill on this project. Hope you're writing. Call me. Soon. Or just finish the book already and call me then.**

One month.

One month to finish more than half a book. Yesterday I would have said it was impossible. But after today? I might just be able to pull it off.

I clicked over to Evie's text. **I checked in on you, but you seemed totally lost in the story. So happy for you! I fed the animals. Come see me when you surface?**

Come see her?

I'd rather see her come. I chuckled as I added a mental rimshot. Sex with her killed three birds with one stone. Not only did we both get to have orgasms—

birds one and two—but her body was the cure to my broken brain and looming deadline—bird number three. I stopped in the bathroom to rinse my mouth, then dashed across our yards and knocked on her door. When she didn't answer, I pushed inside and bellowed, "Eveline McAllister!"

A crash sounded from the kitchen, followed by a sharp curse, then Evie's head poking around the corner. "What is it with you Prescotts and screaming your arrival?"

I crossed the room in a few short strides, cupped her face, and kissed her deeply. "Did you know you have a magic hooha? Did you know it this entire time and were holding out on me?"

She giggled. "Magic hooha? Who even says that?"

"You must have known. That's why you tried to talk me into not drinking last night, so I wouldn't seduce you and discover what you've been hiding."

"That's exactly what happened. Oh, wait. No. It's not. Not at all." She ran a hand through my hair, taming the crazy curls. "Did you have a good day?"

"A good day? *A good day?* I had a freaking fantastic day. I haven't written that much in..." I shrugged. "I don't know that I've ever written like that. You're my talisman. The..."

I was about to say, "the best thing that ever

happened to me," but I stopped short of going that far. No need to scare her off so early in the game.

"Have you eaten?" Evie asked. "The plan was to surprise you with a homecooked meal, but, you scared me pretty good and now it's decorating the kitchen floor. I would have gone down too, but someone gave me these nifty socks." She lifted a foot and wiggled her toes.

"Are you serious?" I stared over her shoulder at the disaster on the floor.

"I wish I wasn't. Not only does orange chicken take some time, but it also makes quite a mess when chucked overhead and splatters to the ground."

I apologized and helped her clean the sticky orange sauce covering the tile and cabinets. When we finished, I pulled out a chair for her to sit and massaged her neck and shoulders. While mine ached from being hunched over in my chair all day, I wanted to lavish Evie with attention. Not only did she understand why I'd been locked in the office, but she wanted to celebrate with a homecooked meal. Could she be more perfect?

"You know what?" I pressed a kiss into her hair, inhaling deeply to memorize the scent of her shampoo. "I've been craving a burger from Mike's ever since you commandeered mine. I know it's not a great replacement for homemade orange chicken, but maybe it's close?"

"Are you kidding? I liked those burgers enough to eat two and then sleep with the fries." Evie stood and slapped me on the ass. "Let's go, White Knight."

I cringed at the nickname, then quirked my head. "Do I want to know what you mean by sleeping with the fries?"

"No. No you don't." She grabbed my hand and dragged me out of the house.

After going through the drive thru at Mike's and ordering our meals in separate bags—just in case—I drove us to Lookout Point, otherwise known as Make Out Central for the high school crowd. With stellar views and plenty of privacy, there'd been more than a few steamed out windows in the last twenty years. Thankfully, tonight, we were the only car on the ridge.

"Do you know what a big deal it is that I brought you here?" I asked as I put the Range Rover in park.

"First things first, bucko. Hand over the burgers." Evie made grabby hands for the bag and the paper rustled as she dove in for a handful of fries. "Now that's taken care of, please explain why it's a big deal for me to be sitting in a parked car in the dark."

I unbuckled my seatbelt and threw an arm over the back of my seat as I shifted to face her. The squeak of the leather caught her attention and she quirked her head in a question. "What? Why are you looking at me like that?"

"This is called setting the mood, my muse." I gestured out the darkened windows, the strong beams of the headlights stretching out in front of us, obscuring the true beauty of the view. "You don't bring someone to Lookout Point if you don't have serious intentions of making some moves. Everyone in Wildrose Landing knows this, and as our newest resident, it's time you did, too."

"I was already fairly clear you had serious move-making intentions before we left my house. I think your mention of a magic hooha said it all."

"You're not seeing my point." I sighed dramatically. "I've only brought two people up here. Ever. Samantha English from high school. And now you. I'm making a serious declaration of intent."

"Intent, huh?" Evie grinned, still clearly not seeing the magic of the moment.

"Prepare yourself." I turned on the radio, the swoony, croony goodness of a playlist I built just for the moment filling the cabin, then turned off the head-lights. The night sky came into view, every star imagin-able visible in the velvet dark, with a crescent moon shining its silver light.

Evie gasped, the Mike's bag forgotten in her lap as

she craned her neck to see out the windshield. "Oh, Alex! It's beautiful."

"It pales in comparison to you."

A smile pulled at the corners of her lips and she glanced at me. "That was..."

"Cheesy?"

She shook her head and shrugged as she settled back into her seat and gave me her full attention. "Wonderful."

Her smile stoked my own and I rested my head against the headrest as my eyes wandered the splendor of the heavens. "Do you have a favorite author?" I rolled my head to meet her gaze. "Other than me of course."

"Other than you, one of my favorites is pretty obscure. She only put out one book, but it was so poignantly written, I come back to it whenever I need to feel something, if that makes sense. Harlow West. I'm sure you haven't heard of her."

"Actually, I have. My agent used to work with Harlow's sister-in-law. I've never met Mrs. West, but I am a fan of her work."

Evie nodded, thoughtfully. "I should have known she wouldn't be obscure to you." She chewed on her bottom lip. "What's your favorite movie?"

"That one's easy. *Harry and the Henderson's.*"

"Harry and the who? Definitely never heard of

that one. Let me guess. Some dry documentary on Harry S. Truman."

A laugh exploded past my lips. "You're so far off, it's ridiculous. *Harry and the Henderson's* is a comedy from the eighties about a family who finds Bigfoot. He comes to live with them—" Evie dissolved into giggles and I raised my brows. "What? Why are you laughing at me?"

"This is so not the kind of movie I thought the great Alexander Prescott would list as his favorite. That's all. But please, do go on." She waved a hand for me to continue.

"It was one of my mom's favorites, thank you very much. She made Izzy and I watch it so many times when we were kids, I can still recite the lines. And yes, I even tear up when things get bad and George Henderson has to make Harry—that's what they call Bigfoot..."

"Obviously." Evie shook her head, giggling into her lap.

"Anyway, as I was saying, the Hendersons have to make him leave for his own safety. George is so mean and Harry is so sad, but he finally goes back to the wilderness, thinking the family he's come to love doesn't want him anymore."

"Heartbreaking." Evie did not look the least bit

heartbroken. "I feel so much closer to you now that I know this."

"I feel like I'm being made fun of here and I'm not sure I deserve it. You didn't see Bigfoot's expression when George Henderson tried to force him to leave by punching him in the face. He was so confused. So upset, but it was even harder on George."

"Lord and Master, Sir Alexander the Glorious has a soft spot for quirky eighties movies about Bigfoot. I am so much better for knowing this." Evie's laughter triggered my own.

The conversation moved on as we discussed everything from the best hamburgers—Mike's, obviously—to childhood fears and traumas. The more Evie opened up to me, the more I realized what a gem she was. "Why are you looking at me like that?" she finally asked.

"That's what I do when I find something special. I analyze it from all angles and try to distill it down to its essence so I can understand how it works."

"And just what is my essence?"

"You're a lake in the mountains, so serenely beautiful it takes your breath away, with unexpected depths and life teeming beneath the calm surface."

Evie's face softened as she unclicked her seatbelt and shifted, grabbing my collar and pulling me close.

Her lips brushed mine, delicate and soft. "Ready to do our cute couple thing?"

Unable to resist her lips, I kissed her again, heat building between us. "I was born ready," I finally said, then grimaced.

"Let me guess. That sounded better in your head." She laughed, then slithered her way into the back. "Come on, lover boy. There's a magic hooha that could use some attention."

CHAPTER TWENTY-SEVEN

Evie

Alex joined me in the backseat of the SUV, his long frame devouring the space. I leaned back, my head against the cool window as his lips found mine, hungry and heated. His tongue caressed my mouth, sweeping against my own as my hips lifted to his.

"Fuck, Evie." Alex's voice whispered past my ear as his stubble raked across the skin at my throat. His hand snaked under my shirt, gripping my waist and pulling me closer, as if even a hint of distance between us was too much.

His fingers worked the button on my jeans, the hiss of the zipper mingling with the hitch of my breath as he slid them past my hips. Kissing me long and deep, he spread my legs, then shifted in the tight space, lowering his face to my cleft. One long, slow lick had my eyes rolling closed, my hand pressing to the chilled window. "Alex..."

His name was an invitation, a declaration, the pleasure he brought me with just one touch more than I ever dreamed possible. As I writhed, he sucked my clit into his mouth, his finger slipping inside me, stretching me, warming me. The intensity of the sensation had me trying to crawl away from him.

"Relax for me, Evie." He blew a soft breath against my clit. "Let me show you how good you can feel."

With one shuddering breath, I relaxed into him and the magic started once again. His fingers stroked while his mouth licked and sucked. My inner thighs grew wet and I panted his name. Over and over, again and again, a prayer, a lamentation, desperation and pleasure pulsing through me as my body responded to his.

"That's right, baby. Come for me. Show me how good it feels."

As if all I needed was his permission, sensation spiraled out of control. My body clenched and quivered and I gripped his curls in my fist, at once needing him to stop and never wanting it to end. When the bucking of my hips slowed, Alex lifted his face, wiping his mouth with the back of his hand. His gaze pierced mine as he freed his cock, the hard length straining towards me as I wrapped my hand along the velvet shaft, swirling my thumb around the crown.

"Fuck me, Alex. I need you inside me."

With little preamble, he slipped on a condom and pressed himself against my entrance. I hissed a breath as he entered. With the first orgasm having barely receded, pleasure zoomed back through me, calling another to life as his pelvic bone met mine. A sharp thrust elicited a cry from me and a groan from him and then he was off and moving. My hips lifted to meet him as he braced himself on the window, condensation fogging the glass and dripping away from his heat. It was pleasure and pain, fire and ice, intensity layered upon intensity and I found myself muttering obscenities as my body succumbed to his.

Never before had it felt like this.

So right. So real. So...everything.

CHAPTER TWENTY-EIGHT

EVIE

Snow started falling the first week in December, transforming my front yard into a glistening field of white, with a path of footprints connecting my door to Alex's. His fingers had been glued to his keyboard nonstop since the writer's block lifted. He'd surface for sex and most meals, then dive back into work. I took over caring for Morgan and Larry and occasionally reminding him to eat. Gone were the days of walking the beach. Gone were the dinners at Overton's. I had a few magnificent hours with Alex in the morning while we went over my notes on his new pages, but then he was pretty much gone, too.

Which was okay.

Totally fine.

One hundred percent to be expected.

He was a writer. He needed to immerse himself in his work or he'd never finish the book...especially considering how far behind schedule he was before we met. His deadline crept ever closer. Just two weeks away. With the proper focus, he'd make it, so I did everything I could to take the pressure off our relationship. I'd be there when the book was done.

My phone jingled and jangled from its place on my coffee table. I put down my book and answered a video call from Amelia. "All right. Spill it," she said as soon as her face filled the screen. "What's wrong."

"Nothing's wrong—"

"Don't you bullshit me, Evie. You know I can tell when you're lying."

She did have an uncanny sense when it came to the truth, but this time, her lie detector was broken. "Sorry to burst your bubble, but everything's great here."

"That's not what I've been hearing." Amelia tossed her hair over her shoulder.

"Sounds like your spirit guides finally got something wrong."

"One, they never get things wrong, and two, they aren't my source. It's worse than that. According to Greta Macmillan's Facebook page, you and Alex haven't been seen out together in at least a week."

I snorted. "Ah, yes. Reading what my nosey neighbor has to say about my relationship is the best way to know what's going on..."

"It is when all you tell me is that everything's perfect."

"Everything is perfect." I leaned my head against the back of the couch. I was happy. Alex was happy. He was writing. I was thinking about starting a book for the first time since the Drew incident...

"Then why aren't the residents of Wildrose Landing gushing about you two anymore? Hmm?" Amelia's face said I'd been busted. "They also stopped talking about your ghost. Which seems odd. Given how that was the only thing anyone wanted to talk about last month."

I hadn't told Amelia that Alex was the cause of the ghost rumors yet, though it was probably time. "Maybe people found something better to focus on then boring old me."

"Better than a power couple making it work in a haunted house? I think not. Greta implied there might be trouble in paradise."

"Really?" I'd tried to find Greta's gossipy posts endearing. It hadn't worked. Every time someone brought up that damn Facebook page, I found myself more annoyed. "How did she make such an implication?"

"She said, and I quote, 'Well, dear friends. It seems as if there might be trouble in paradise with WRL's newest couple. Evex—Alex and Evie for those of you who don't understand relationship names—haven't been seen in weeks. Could this be a repeat of the Candace situation?'"

The Candace situation? What the hell was the Candace situation?

"Amelia. Nothing in that was an implication. She straight out said—"

Amelia waved my concern away. "What's this Candace situation?"

I shrugged. "No clue. Look, I'm touched that you're so concerned for me—"

"It's not just me. The whole town is starting to question if this is the beginning of the end for you guys." Amelia sighed dramatically. "And after only a few weeks of bliss..."

"It's not the beginning of the end. Alex's writer's block cleared and his publishers wouldn't extend his deadline. He's had his nose in his laptop almost nonstop, writing like a madman to catch up so the project doesn't get pulled. I see him every morning, he goes to work, and then sometimes we see each other at night. We're just not going out as frequently. That's all."

"I hope you're right. I've been so happy for you since everything came together."

"I've been happy for me, too. Still am. You really shouldn't worry over what Greta says. She's not always right. She's the one who started the rumor that my house was haunted, and she was so wrong about that." Bracing myself for her judgement, I filled Amelia in on how I discovered Alex had been the ghost all along.

She frowned. "Alex was breaking into the house, everyone thought he was a ghost, and he just let them keep thinking that so he could get what he wanted? I'm not sure I like what that says about him."

Even though I'd had a similar thought the night the story came out, I didn't want to mention that to Amelia. "I think you're oversimplifying things and jumping to conclusions. You've decided something's wrong between us, so you're looking for proof to validate your concerns."

"I just want you to be happy."

"I am. I promise."

"Have you started writing again?"

"I've considered it..."

"Well, if you're considering writing, then things must be going better than Greta says they are." Amelia blew a kiss at the screen, made a promise to talk again soon, then ended the call.

I dropped my head back on the couch. It *had* been

an awfully long time since Alex and I went out. After our Range Rover adventure, we'd eaten at Overton's once, and that had pretty much been that. Maybe, it'd be smart for us to go out tonight. Especially if people were starting to think the magic was fading.

I laughed to myself. Since when did I care what other people thought?

CHAPTER TWENTY-NINE

EVIE

Bridget the hostess clapped her hands to her chest when Alex and I walked through the doors of Overton's. "Oh, yay! I'm so glad to see you two out and about! I'll post an Evex sighting and the whole town can relax a little." She pulled out her phone and aimed it our way.

Alex gently lowered the device before she could snap the pic. "Evex?"

"That's your ship name. You know. Evie. Alex. Put 'em together and you get Evex." She raised the phone again. "Do you mind? I get bonus points if I post proof."

Bonus points? Proof? What in the world was going on with Greta Macmillan's Facebook page?

"Evie's the one to ask." Alex turned to me with a mischievous grin. "She's a very private person, you see."

I absolutely did not want my picture posted on that damn Facebook page. I didn't even want to be a topic of conversation in the first place. The vulnerability of an entire town scrutinizing my brand-new relationship planted an uneasy feeling in my stomach. If I had my way, I'd be comfortably slipping under everyone's radars.

But, I was working on growth. Strength. Trust...

So...

"This is way the heck out of my comfort zone, but sure. What's the harm?" While the fearful part of my brain listed all the possible harm in an alphabetized and bullet pointed list, I snuggled into Alex's embrace and Bridget happily clicked away.

The moment we were seated and awaiting our Drunken Sailors, Alex pulled his notes out of his bag and started reading. His pen tapped against the page as he thought. His brow furrowed only for his whiskey eyes to light up as he scribbled a note in the margin. As he worked, he took my hand, absently running his thumb along my knuckle, and I smiled right along with him, happy to see the story still flowing.

What I said to Amelia was one hundred percent true. I was genuinely happy for Alex. That was how writing should be. Consuming. Rewarding. I missed feeling that way but didn't begrudge him for being in it. Not for one second.

At least I didn't before I spoke with Amelia.

As I watched Alex think, I tried to reclaim the general sense of ease I had around the topic of him working at all hours before her call. He needed to devote his time to the book while his brain still allowed him to see the story, or he'd have to pay back his advance and risk getting dropped by his publisher. What a ridiculous thing, that someone as talented and prolific as Alexander Prescott had to worry about that. The world focused too much on money and immediacy. Maybe people and products, relationships and trust, maybe those things wouldn't break so easily if we focused more on quality and less on speed.

Patience would be the name of my game.

Alex would finish the manuscript, send it off to his editor, and everything would go back to normal.

I placed my chin in my hands and gazed into the belly of the restaurant, surprised to find a couple tables staring. Some smiled before they glanced away, but always, I caught the faintest hint of sadness flitting across their faces. The people of Wildrose Landing felt sorry for me, which didn't exactly leave me with the warmest of fuzzies.

Alex glanced up, caught me staring into the distance, and frowned. "You okay?"

"Me? Oh yeah. I'm great." I sat up straight and grinned widely to prove just how great I was.

"Do you want me to put these away?" He gestured to the notes, then went ahead and shoved them into his bag before I could reply. A haunted look crossed his eyes, but it was gone before I could be sure I saw what I thought I saw. "Only a fool would let a beautiful woman eat dinner alone, while he sat across from her."

"I really don't mind if you need to work. I know that deadline's putting pressure on you."

"Spending an evening with the most beautiful woman in Wildrose Landing will refresh me and the story will be even better tomorrow." Alex leaned close. "Especially if I earn access to that magic hooha."

I giggled through a slew of anxious thoughts that had no right to interrupt our dinner. What if he was only with me because of the magic hooha? What if he actually didn't like me? What if he was using me to get what he wanted, and intended to cast me aside when the book was done? What if Amelia knew how much doubt she'd put into my head? Would she tell me I was being silly? Or would she double down and reinforce the narrative?

I couldn't stand so much self-doubt. My head needed to just stop already.

"Who's Candace?" The question was out before I could stop it.

Alex flinched. "Where'd you hear about her?"

"Apparently Greta's been talking about her on her Facebook page."

Alex sat back, a frown tugging at his lips as he raked a hand over his mouth. "Candace is an ex. We were pretty serious for a while, but it didn't work out."

Eager to keep the conversation light, I offered a smile. "Did she steal one of your books and publish it as her own?"

Obviously uncomfortable, he glanced at the ceiling and swallowed hard, then forced a laugh. "Not quite."

"Wow. You mean *you* stole *her* book and published it as your own? I didn't think you had it in you."

This earned me a genuine smile and hearty laugh. "I'm full of surprises. Stick with me, kid. I'll make it all worth your while."

"I bet you say that to all the girls." It was everything I could do to keep joking while my mind waged a war with my personality. My curiosity demanded I press for more information on Candace, but I didn't want to be a hypocrite.

Privacy mattered.

Alex would tell me his story when he was ready.

Or he wouldn't.

And I'd be okay with that.

Probably.

Maybe.

For the most part.

"It's eating you up, isn't it?" He quirked a grin. "After going on and on about being a private person, you can't bring yourself to push for more info even though it's eating you up inside."

"I mean, it wouldn't be the worst thing ever if you wanted to tell me about her." I smiled warmly while I ran a finger along the back of his hand. "I did tell you about Drew after all."

"Oh, Evie." Disappointment dripped from his words while humor sparkled in his eyes. "I didn't think you were the type to keep score."

I took a long drink of my Drunken Sailor, never breaking eye contact. "It's fine," I said after I swallowed. "You can keep this part of yourself private. I'll just know that I trust you more than you trust me. That's okay. I understand."

I had him with that one and we both knew it.

"Look at you with the shrewd negotiating skills." Alex took my hand and pressed a kiss to my palm. "I like it," he said, then raked his fingers through his curls. "My problem with Candace stretches back to my parents. My mom loved my dad with all that she was.

She gave up her career to move to Wildrose so he could focus on his. Everything was fine for a while, but then Dad disappeared into his job. He worked so much we never saw him. When Mom asked him to stay home or take time off, he'd lay on the guilt extra thick. She was miserable and I hated him for it until I grew up to be just like him. Candace and me? We would have imploded eventually, but my job made it happen so much faster, and so much worse. You've seen what happens when I fall into a book. I disappear, just like he does. Candace couldn't handle it and things ended on a pretty sour note. I swore I'd never do that to someone again and haven't been in a relationship since."

I wondered where that left us. Would Alex say we were in a relationship? Or was this more about the convenience of my magic hooha? I let out a shaky breath. "And yet, here you are, with me."

It wasn't a direct question. I didn't come out and say what was on my mind, but I did think the subtext was pretty clear. *Who am I to you?*

"Exactly. Here we are. I'm out of the house. My notes are in my bag. And we're having a lovely dinner. Or we will be, if it ever arrives." Alex kissed each finger on my hand and I relaxed. A little.

Damn Amelia for getting into my head.

"You don't have to worry about me pulling a

Candace on you. I totally understand when you disappear into a book. Back when I could write, I was the same way. Drew never minded, but apparently he never cared, either. So there's that."

Dinner arrived and we chatted while we ate. Everything felt right with the world again, until an idea struck Alex. He shoved his plate away, pulled out his notes and went to work, while I finished my dinner, then sat with my chin in my hands, staring into the restaurant and waiting for him to be done.

CHAPTER THIRTY

ALEX

When I was in the zone, I could write six to seven hundred words in twenty minutes. In the three hours I'd been with Evie at Overton's, I could have written over five thousand words, bringing me that much closer to the finish line I wasn't sure I'd reach. I knew the total because I did the math over and over, adding another six hundred every twenty minutes.

It was worth it. Being with Evie. Finding the time to make her feel important. I didn't want her to feel like Candace, or worse, like Mom. And I hated feeling like my dad, so putting down work for an evening was a good thing.

Funny how many times I had to remind myself of that.

After I fleshed out the idea that struck me when dinner arrived, I pulled my plate back in front of me to finish my meal. "Have you thought about trying to write?" I asked around a mouthful of lukewarm steak. "I know you've got a lot of extra time on your hands now that I'm gone so much, and I'm not trying to push you out of your comfort zone, just..." I flared my hands and sat back.

Evie needed to write. Someone as talented as her couldn't shut the door on that gift. Now that I'd seen how good she was, I made it my mission to heal her heart enough to bring her back to her purpose. Jude would call it another cause to soothe my White Knight Syndrome. I called it taking care of the people that mattered.

I'd do whatever it took to make her feel safe enough to unleash her talent.

Just as soon as I finished this book.

Evie's gray eyes lowered to her hands as she spun her glass on the table. "I've thought about writing. It doesn't scare me quite as much as it used to." Her faint smile told me everything I needed to know. I was on the right track, guiding her back to herself.

"That's obviously because of my awesome factor."

"Obviously." She put her chin in her hands and batted her eyelashes. "The credit is all yours."

"What would you write about?"

She shrugged. "I said I wasn't quite as scared by the idea as I used to be, not that I had any clue where to start."

There was a less noble reason the thought of Evie writing excited me. Yes, she had a talent I wanted to nurture and grow, but also, I wouldn't have to worry about her spending all this time alone if she lost herself to writing, too. As ulterior motives went, it was fairly benign. A win for both of us—one that would bring her joy *and* save our budding relationship.

The look on her face when I glanced up, the one that had me putting my notes away without waiting for her to ask...it wouldn't have even been a thing if she'd been working on her book while I worked on mine. "Could you imagine what Wildrose would think if the two of us sat here all night, lost in notes and laptops?"

Evie grinned. "It's a cute image. Two writers, out on the town, but not really out at all because they're lost in their own worlds." She sipped her drink, swirling the ice in the glass. "I do miss writing."

"Take some time. See if you have an idea." I wanted to offer a chance to talk through it with her, but my mind held up the stop sign that was my deadline.

After.

I'd have all the time in the world to help her after.

In the meantime, if she was working on her own book, then maybe my guilt about ignoring her would fade and I could write even faster. It was a win for both of us.

"Have you ever not met a deadline?" Evie asked.

"Once. During the Candace debacle."

The whole thing had been so ugly. I'd thought she understood that first and foremost, I was a writer. That I had to close my office doors and disappear to the world. When she'd blown up, she'd gone right for the jugular, telling me I was just like my dad. Two weeks later, I adopted Morgan and swore I'd never get involved with someone again.

And yet...

...here I was.

Involved.

Evie grimaced. "I promise not to be a repeat of that. In fact, my magic hooha offers its services as often as you need to make sure you meet this deadline without issue."

I shoved the last several bites of dinner into my mouth, chewing as fast as I could, then held up my hand as our waiter passed. "Check, please!"

Her chest heaved. Her eyes flashed. Her nipples pebbled as I skated my lips along her skin. Soft. Delicate. Slow.

I would savor her. Sipping at pleasure the way I sipped whiskey. My dick strained against my pants as I lowered her to my bed, her hair fanning out across my pillows, her eyes on me, screaming that she was mine, mine, mine.

I traced a finger along her inner thigh, and she trembled, arching her back in anticipation, only to groan as I pressed a kiss to her belly, her ribs, her throat. The room throbbed with want, a pulsing energy pressing us together, but I refused to succumb. I wanted her dripping. Quivering. On the edge. I wanted her body to sing for mine. To watch her tremble and quake, her eyes hooded with want...for me. Tonight wasn't about sex. This was about how she made me feel. How I wanted to make her feel. This was about the two of us, coming together, saying everything words couldn't.

I want you, said the slow slip of my finger.

I need you, said the brush of my lips.

I think I'm falling in love with you, said my hand fisting in her hair.

I know, said the arch of her back, the whimper in her throat.

I know, said the clash of our bodies.

I know, said the quiver in her legs.

If she could hold on two more weeks, everything would go back to normal.

Just two more weeks.

CHAPTER THIRTY-ONE

Evie

I woke before my alarm and rolled over to find myself alone in bed. A note rested on Alex's pillow with his messy script dancing across the page.

My muse,
The hardest thing I've ever done was walk away from you this morning. Your hair begged to be caressed. Your lips begged to be kissed. Your breasts spilled from your shirt and...well, you get the drift. You're freaking sexy, but words must happen. In case you couldn't tell, I'm head over heels for you and falling farther every day.
Yours for as long as you'll have me,
Lord and Master, Sir Alexander Prescott the Glorious

I pressed the note to my chest and flopped back on my pillow with a sigh before climbing out of bed to start my day. Another note waited for me in the bathroom, taped to the mirror, with a heart and smiley face drawn on the glass with dry erase markers. Giddy and grinning, I read the note.

Roses are red, violets are blue, the best thing about me is the day I met you.

He'd drawn a winky face at the bottom of the page and I could just imagine him giggling like a child as he wrote the ridiculous poem. I shoved the paper into the pocket of my PJ pants, brushed my teeth, then headed downstairs in search of coffee, only to pull up short when I found a note on each stair leading to the first floor. Each page contained only one word, and by the time I got to the landing, they formed a single sentence.

In case you couldn't tell, I want you to know how much I care about you.

Another note dangled in the doorway leading from the dining room to the kitchen.

A lot. I care a lot.

And one last note waited for me by the coffee maker, with a single red rose sitting in a vase.

Evie-

I hope you don't mind, but I made an appointment for you today. Normally, I wouldn't presume to dictate your schedule, but this is an extraordinary circumstance and I hope you'll forgive me. In exchange for promising my agent the book would be done on time, I had her reach out to Harlow West and ask if the two of you could sync up sometime. Mrs. West proved to be perfectly lovely and in need of a reason to visit New England, so she flew in from the Keys this morning and will be waiting for you at Brewhaha—the coffee shop on Main Street—at noon. It's been all I could do not to spill the beans ever since she confirmed last week. I have my phone turned off so I can focus, but I'll power it back on around 2 to check in on you. Please enjoy your day and know that you're always on my mind.

XO

Alex

I read the note three times before I dropped it to the counter, screamed, and danced in place. Harlow West was here. In Wildrose Landing. To meet...me. Me! The woman who lost her job due to a case of terminal taupeness was now consulting on an upcoming release from a critically acclaimed bestselling author and had a meeting with Harlow freaking West in a couple hours.

I screamed again, flinging my arms overhead and spinning in a circle to scatter exclamation points before I finally got control of myself and shot Alex a text.

Me: I know you won't see this because your phone is off but OMG THANK YOU. I am so lucky to have met you, Alex. Like, so freaking lucky. And not just because you pulled some strings and got me a coffee date with HARLOW FREAKING WEST!!! But because you're good to me and I really like you and I love the way your brain works... I'd go on, but just know that you've made me so amazingly happy.

I hit send without overanalyzing every word I wrote, then dashed upstairs, surprised when my phone buzzed with a reply.

Alex: So, I may have cheated and turned on my phone just in case you reached out. Enjoy yourself today, my muse. Be bold. Be brave. Be you. Know that your mind is just as magnificent as hers. Most importantly, know that my heart is with you today.

I grinned so hard all I could do was send Alex a

string of emojis, then stood in front of my closet, wondering how one prepared for a meeting with an idol.

Turned out, preparing for a meeting with an idol included a lot of second guessing and the trying on of multiple outfits before finally remembering Alex's advice.

Be bold. Be brave. Be you.

It was like he knew I was learning to be fearless and helping me in my search.

"Bold, brave, fearless. That's me," I whispered, pulling out my favorite oversized sweater with chunky blue, white, and gray stripes. I paired it with jeans and ankle boots, then added a long necklace and earrings that caught the light. I left my hair natural and swiped on some makeup, then stood back to appraise myself in the mirror.

"Stylish yet casual, if I do say so myself." I smiled at my reflection, took a big breath, then headed for Brewhaha. As I entered, my eyes went straight to the woman with the white-blonde hair nursing her coffee at a table in the back. Harlow freaking West. She smiled, waved, and stood as I made my way to her.

"Evie McAllister?" Her blue eyes sparkled in the

light and as I extended my hand, I realized how starstruck I was because no one's eyes actually sparkled. (Except maybe hers.)

"That's me! It's such a pleasure to meet you, Mrs. West."

"Please," she said with a grin. "Call me Harlow."

I shook her hand, ordered my coffee, and sat down to a surprisingly easy conversation. We talked about writing, about life, about everything she experienced as she met her husband and wrote her book. When the topic turned to me, she listened intently and asked gentle, probing questions.

"Alex said you're a damn good writer, but you're dealing with a ton of self-doubt right now. Take it from the queen of self-doubt, sometimes you just have to take a deep breath and power through." Harlow shrugged. "I always surprise myself on the other side. I'm sure you will, too."

When the meeting was over, I left feeling like I'd made a new friend and could conquer the world. The second I sat down in my car, I called Alex. He answered on the first ring.

"So? How'd it go?"

"Thank you, thank you, thank you for that." I paused as I navigated out of the parking lot and onto Main Street. "Do you have a minute? Can I come by and thank you in person? I promise I won't stay long."

"I set aside the afternoon for you. So get your cute butt over here and tell me all about it."

When I pulled into Alex's drive, he was waiting on the porch. I ran to him and he swept me into his arms. "Do you see it yet?" He cupped my face and kissed me slow and deep. "Do you see how special you are?"

I smiled against his lips. "Don't be silly..."

He silenced me with a kiss. "If you don't see it yet, then I'm not doing my job well enough because you are the best thing that ever happened to me. Every day is better because you're in it."

I tried to protest, but Alex lifted me into his arms, then carried me into the house and up to his room, where we celebrated a great day with our cute couple thing.

CHAPTER THIRTY-TWO

EVIE

Three days passed. Alex was in the zone, delivering pages and pages of new work to me every morning. I'd sit down at the table with my red pen, making as many notes as I could manage while counting down the hours until I saw him again. This morning, coffee steamed in a mug at my side and snow filtered to the ground outside the window as I read through his latest additions. Gone were the days of pristine sentences navigating a sterile plot. The story commandeered my attention, even in its rough draft form. This might be his best work yet—

My pen clattered to the table. My jaw dropped. My heart? It stopped, then sped up so fast I saw stars as

I read and reread a clump of bracketed text—a note Alex left for himself he'd forgotten to delete.

Consider using Evie's story here. Change deets, obvs. But Austin was right. The theft of her work is hugely compelling and would make a great pivot point.

The pen hit the floor before I knew it rolled off the table. I was in the living room before I knew I'd left the kitchen. Behind the wheel before I knew what I was doing, and knocking on Amelia's door before I was aware an hour had passed.

"Evie?" She took one look at my face and swung the door open wide. "What happened?"

"Nothing." I paced the living room I used to call home. "Everything."

She closed the door and waited for me to stop moving. "Is this an ice cream and *Dirty Dancing* kind of nothing-slash-everything? Or a tequila and drum circle kind of nothing-slash-everything?"

I stopped and stared at my friend. "I think I've made a terrible mistake."

I trusted Alex. I trusted him with the parts of me I swore I'd never give to anyone and he knew, he *knew* how hard it was for me to share that story....

"Are you pregnant?"

"What?" I recoiled. "No."

"Okay. Good. Then this calls for tequila." Amelia swept into the kitchen and returned with a bottle and two shot glasses.

I stared at the liquor. The last thing I needed was to muddle my thoughts when I couldn't even make sense of how I was feeling. "Thanks, but I'm good."

But I wasn't good. Not at all. And the tears I furiously blinked away ratted me out.

"You look furious."

I explained what I'd found in Alex's manuscript. "I mean, it's just a note. A thought. The scene doesn't actually exist, but I'm so uncomfortable with that story making it into his book...." I plopped onto the couch and rested my elbows on my knees.

Amelia put the bottle and shot glasses on her coffee table then perched beside me. "What did he say when you brought it up?"

I stared at the ground for a long time, chewing on my bottom lip.

"You did bring it up, didn't you?"

"I was so upset, I just drove right here, without even worrying about the communism being too long." I gave her a weak smile as I offered our silly joke and Amelia wrapped me in a hug.

She brushed my hair off my face. "I understand

why you're so upset, but you need to be talking to Alex about this, not me."

"I know I do." I took in a shuddering breath. "But what if I misjudged him? I mean, this is the guy who let the entire town think my house was haunted so he could keep getting what he wanted. What if I tell him how I feel, and he uses the scene anyway?"

"What if he doesn't?"

"But what if he does?"

My anxiety ran away with my logic. All I could remember was the humiliation of being used by Drew and never paying attention to the signs he'd dropped along the way. Because in the end? Looking back? They were there. I chose not to see what a terrible person he was, and therefore, in a way, I chose to allow him to steal my book.

What if I was doing the same damn thing with Alex?

"Evie. Sweetie. Love. You have to talk to him about this. You can't let your fear of the confrontation keep you from speaking your needs. You have to step up, be fearless, and tell him why this won't work for you. How can he know how much it bothers you if you don't use your voice?"

I dropped my head into my hands. "I shouldn't have to tell him. He should just know."

"But...should he?" Amelia used a high, squeaky

voice that told me she really didn't buy the premise of my statement.

I stood and flung out my arms. "Yes! He should! A few days after I told him the story, he blurted it out to all our friends. I was so mad, *so mad.* I told him point blank I wasn't okay with telling people about what happened. I need him to know that putting my story in his book would hurt, because I need to know he understands me."

"I get that. I do. But you still need to talk to him. You're jumping to conclusions and you haven't even read the scene yet."

My jaw dropped. "Whose team are you on, here?"

"Yours. I'm team Evie, all the way. But if you don't talk to him about this, you're not being fair to Alex, and you're not being fair to you." She crossed the room and took my hands. "You're not being very fearless right now."

I didn't need Amelia to tell me I was wrong. I needed her to tell me I was seeing things clearly, maybe for the first time. Her statements only added to my confusion.

"It was a mistake for me to come here." I yanked away and moved for the door. "I just got in my car and drove and didn't even bother to call." My gaze glued itself to the floor. "I'm really sorry to interrupt your night."

Run away, run away, run. It's what you're good at, after all, whispered the angel of self-doubt.

"Evie..."

"No. It's okay. I'm just gonna go..." I wrapped Amelia in a quick hug, then got the hell out of there before she could say anything else.

While the drive to Amelia's was over before I knew it began, the drive back to Wildrose lasted an eternity. My anxiety played tricks with time. Minutes lasted hours and my heart questioned everything that happened in the last few months. Snow crunched under my boots as I made my way up to my porch, stomping my feet on the mat before stepping inside and heading upstairs. A minute after my bedroom light turned on, I got a text from Alex.

I needed to make some changes to the manuscript. The door was unlocked, so I let myself in and grabbed it. Will return tomorrow. I missed you something big today. Life loses its color without you around to brighten things up.

I spread the curtains and found him staring out his window. He lifted a hand and blew me a kiss. I echoed the movement, then texted him goodnight before laying down to wait for sleep.

I'd talk to him in the morning. No matter how badly the prospect scared me, I owed it to both of us to talk to him about how finding his note made me feel. I'd do it as soon as he returned the manuscript. Just flip to the note and mention how I'd rather he not use my story in his book.

That shouldn't be too hard. In fact, it should be easy. He'd hug me and tell me it never occurred to him and promise to take it out. I'd be proud of my fearless self and we could go on the way we had been, like nothing ever happened.

Only, when Alex handed me the manuscript in the morning, the bracketed note was gone. Relief washed through me. He must have thought better of the idea and took it out. For half a second, I considered bringing it up anyway, but why rock the boat? Especially since he'd already solved the problem? Instead, I gave him a kiss, hugged the manuscript to my chest and promised myself never to bring it up again.

CHAPTER THIRTY-THREE

ALEX

Evie had been weird for the last couple days. Her smile was too bright. Her words too cheerful. She didn't always look me in the eyes, and when she did, I caught glimpses of something heavy. She was hiding something from me, but I had no idea what it could be.

Part of me was afraid she'd seen that stupid note I left in the manuscript, but I kept telling myself she'd have said something if that was true. The idea had come to me in the middle of writing a scene and I'd left a bracketed note so my mind wouldn't fixate on it and I could move on. I could never include Evie's story as a plot point. It was too personal, and she'd made it crystal clear how she felt about the topic after I spilled the beans at Cheers 'n Beers. I'd intended to delete the note after I finished writing for the day, but had tumbled into bed exhausted instead.

A much bigger part of me insisted Evie thought I'd abandoned her in favor of my manuscript. That for as much as I hoped she understood, for as much as she *said* she understood, it still hurt too much to wait for my attention. I knew that feeling too well. I resented my dad for never being around when I was little, especially after Mom fell off the edge. When I realized my personality shared that flaw with his, I tried to cut him some slack...I just couldn't.

There was only a week and a half until my deadline came due. A week and a half of hard work before I could finally emerge from the office and give Evie the attention she deserved. She'd hold on that long. I was sure of it.

"Right?" I asked Morgan, who looked up from his place on the floor. "Everything will be fine as soon as I'm done."

The weirder Evie got, the more my daily word counts slipped. Instead of being lost in my world, I'd find myself worrying about whether I should stop and check on her. At the same time, I knew that if I did step away from the keyboard, I'd be distracted the entire time, worrying about the words I should be writing as my deadline tick, tick, ticked closer.

The pressure was getting to me. My mood suffered. Was any of this even worth it?

I sighed as Morgan dropped his head into my lap. "I knew better than to try and have a relationship. I promised myself I wouldn't let this happen again but here it is. Happening." I scratched behind his ears and he huffed in contentment. "At least I never let you down."

Except for every time Evie had to take him on a walk or put food in his bowl. Larry had even been spending most nights at her house because he had a bad habit of laying on my laptop to get my attention.

I just didn't have the time for him.

For any of them.

I ran a hand along the back of my neck, pausing to massage the muscles clenched as tight as bone. "It'll all be over in a week and a half."

Except there'd be another book. And another. And another. More deadlines. More days locked in my office while the world ticked by outside. More days for Evie to feel alone. Neglected. More chances for me to become my father.

And that was that. The words were gone. The story dissipated. The real world was too heavy for me to leave behind. I pushed back from the desk, stretching my arms toward the ceiling as my back and neck creaked and popped. Outside, snow drifted to the ground, covering up the path of footprints connecting Evie's house to mine.

If the words were gone, I might as well ease my fears and spend the evening with her. I picked up my phone and powered it on. Lo and behold, a text from her popped onto the screen.

I'm gonna meet Izzy at Cheers 'n Beers tonight. We'd love your company if you can pull yourself away from the story. Miss you big, White Knight.

I checked the time. Evie was probably already at the bar, having drinks with my sister, wondering if I would show. Imagining the surprise on her face when I walked through the door, I stood and headed for the bathroom to check my hygiene. My phone rang halfway down the hallway, and I frowned when I saw Mom's smiling face pop up on the caller ID.

"Hey, Mom. How're you doing?"

I decided to wear that black V-neck sweater Evie loved so much and the thought of her eyes lighting up had my mood improving with each step.

"I'm great," Mom said with so much enthusiasm I knew it was a lie. "How's the book?"

"Looks like I'm gonna make my deadline after all." I reached into my closet, only to remember the sweater was in the hamper. I'd worn it the last time I felt bad about leaving Evie alone for too long. "Thanks for being so understanding about me having to bail on you. I miss seeing you every day," I said as I searched for Evie's second favorite shirt.

Mom tsked. "Don't worry about it for a second. You always make me feel like I matter, even when you're busy. You're not your father, Alexander. No matter how much you think you are."

What would you say if you could see me right now?

We chatted about the book as I picked at my hair in the mirror, then the topic moved to Evie as I wondered how dirty that black V-neck sweater actually was.

"Things seem to be going so well between you two," Mom cooed. "It warms my heart to see you happy."

I massaged my temples and closed my eyes. "It's a balancing act. Trying to get the book done and not make her feel taken for granted."

"I'm sure you're walking that tightrope just fine and if that woman is worth your time, she'll know it, too."

Fuck it. I will not be that guy wearing clothes out of the hamper. I stomped back into my closet and yanked options off hangars.

"What made you stay?" The question popped out of my mouth without permission. That was what I got for trying to have a conversation while distracted.

"What do you mean, son?"

I closed my eyes and let it rip. "With Dad? I know he didn't walk that rope at all. Why, after everything got bad, did you stick around?" I'd wanted to ask that question for years, but avoided it out of respect for her pain. She'd been through so much, who was I to make her relive it just to satisfy my curiosity?

Mom cleared her throat. "Your dad always managed to say just enough to make me feel like he cared. I'd be on the verge of calling it quits and he'd magically show up for dinner and dote on me like he did when we were young. Or take a day off work and we'd hit the town. It was like he could tell I'd reached my limit and he'd go back to being the man I fell in love with."

"And that was enough?"

"Your father is very charming when he wants to be. I told my friend once I wished he'd just stop showing up so I could walk away and not worry about the years of marriage I was throwing away. By the time he actually did stop, I'd already given up. It's not that bad, living the way we do. I wouldn't call our relationship a marriage, but it has its high points."

I didn't think it did, and the scar on her wrist told me she didn't feel that way either. It was the lie she told herself to keep going without hating her life completely. After we hung up, I stared at my reflection for a long time as Mom's admission circled my head.

I was about to do the very thing my father had done to my mother and it made me physically sick.

I'd been locked away, neglecting Evie for weeks now, and I was about to show up and remind her why we were so good together before I locked myself away again. And sure, this book would finish, and things would go back to how they were when we first met, but there was always another book. Always. This would be the pattern of our lives the way it was the pattern of my parents' lives.

I didn't want that.

I never had.

More importantly, Evie didn't deserve that.

I loved her and had to let her go, but I knew she wouldn't leave if I didn't give her a good reason. She was Harry and I was George Henderson, and it was like my entire life had been leading me to this moment. It would break me to hurt her, but it was better this way...for her.

And so, rather than show up at the bar and make her feel like everything would be okay when it wouldn't, I turned my phone off and sat back down in the office.

CHAPTER THIRTY-FOUR

EVIE

Cheers 'n Beers was rockin'. The energy was high. The music was loud. The conversation was great. Every joke Izzy made was on point, but I still had to remind myself to laugh because my mind was with Alex.

"You seem quiet tonight." Izzy leaned in, quirking her head in a parody of her brother's inquisitive face. "Tell me, Evie. What're you thinking? Let me pick that marvelous mind of yours."

I laughed for real. "You sound just like him."

"After a lifetime of having my marvelous mind picked by Alex Prescott, I hope I'd have it down by now." She bounced her head to the beat of the song coming over the jukebox. "So spill. What's got you down, Charlie Brown?"

"On the surface? Nothing. It looks like Alex is gonna make his deadline with time to spare. The book is...well, it's amazing. I'm really happy here in Wildrose." I offered my most genuine smile to prove my point.

"But..."

"Well, I miss him." I hurried on before Izzy misconstrued my meaning. "But that's not the problem. I understand why he's had to disappear into the office so much. I really do. It's that I know it bothers him, so I'm trying not to say anything about it..."

How much should I share? Should I tell her my real worry? The note I found in the manuscript? What if I sounded petty for bringing it up? After all, Alex did remove the note...

I nibbled on my thumbnail as Izzy bobbed her head. "Alex told you about Candace?"

I nodded. "And about your dad."

"He told you about Dad?" She frowned. "Like, all of it?"

Seeing as I had no idea what 'all of it' entailed, I shrugged, then explained what I knew. "He said he adopted Morgan to force himself to stop working sometimes."

Izzy nodded as she leaned her elbows on the table. "Okay. Yeah. He gave you the high points."

My stomach dropped an inch. If Alex was holding things back from me—

For Pete's sake, Evie! Give it a rest with the worry and doubt already.

"There's more?"

"There's more." Izzy hesitated, her eyes darting back and forth from my face to her hands spinning her beer. "Things got really hard for Mom right after I graduated high school. Alex's first book had just been published, so he was super busy and didn't come around to visit as often. I was sowing my wild oats and wasn't around at all. Dad, for whatever reason chose that time to say eff it and focus entirely on work so Mom was alone, with a capital A. She really struggled." Izzy cleared her throat and met my eyes. "She tried to kill herself."

My jaw dropped as I processed the info. "Oh my goodness! Izzy!" I covered my heart with my hands. "I'm so sorry that happened."

"Yeah. Me, too. I moved back to Wildrose and opened the store. Alex made it a point to visit her every day. After the whole Candace thing went down, he swore he'd do everything in his power to avoid becoming our father."

At the mention of his name, my gaze darted to the door.

"He'll be here." Izzy patted my hand. "If I know anything about Alex Prescott, he's head over heels for you. He'll come."

My cheeks caught fire as a grin stretched my lips. "I'm pretty head over heels for him, too."

And I was. Despite my concerns about me misjudging him. Despite the fact that we'd barely seen each other in weeks, I was falling hard for Alex—in a way I swore I never would again.

The chair across from me scooted out and I half stood, expecting to find Alex with his giant grin and humor-filled eyes. Instead, a man I didn't recognize took a seat. "Hello, ladies."

Izzy bolted out of her chair. "Jack! Oh my goodness! I can't believe you're out of your house!" She wrapped the stranger in a hug, then turned to me. "This is Evie, the woman who tamed Alex's heart. Evie, meet Jack, the man we never get to see anymore because sometimes bad things happen to good people."

A tall man with vibrant blue eyes and a mess of dark curls bobbed his head and shook my hand. "I'm so glad to meet you, though after all I've read on Greta's Facebook page, I feel like I already know you."

Izzy patted his arm. "How are you even out right now?"

"I found a sitter for the night and begged the kids to behave, but I'm sure I'm on borrowed time before something goes spectacularly wrong. Are the guys here?" He glanced around the packed bar. "I just assumed they'd be here."

"Alex is supposed to show up any minute, but I haven't heard anything from Austin or Jude." No one could miss the blush that streaked across Izzy's face at the mention of his name.

"How come you two haven't dated yet?" I blurted out.

Jack chortled. "Hooo! You just get straight to the point, don't you?"

"I mean, considering I've been wondering about that for months now, I wouldn't say *straight* to the point..."

Sadness wilted his smile. "Has it been that long? I really need to get out more."

"Is it that obvious I have feelings for Jude?" Izzy looked like she was trying to disappear through the floor as her voice lowered to a harsh whisper.

"Izzy," I said as I wrapped an arm around her shoulders. "With all due respect, you blush and giggle every time his name comes up."

Jack bobbed his head. "And you're never alone with him, or you weren't before I stopped being able to leave my house."

Izzy rolled her eyes. "Because if I *was* alone with him, I'd jump his bones."

"I knew it!" I slapped a hand to the table.

"But *he* doesn't." She put her hand on mine. "And I'd like to keep it that way. Nothing good will come of Jude and me together. Not one thing."

The thought of Jude and Izzy in a relationship had me shaking my head. His irreverent assholery combined with her good-natured workaholic self? Sparks would fly and I wasn't sure it would be in a good way. Maybe it was for the best that she kept her feelings for him a secret. Well, if you could consider what she'd been doing keeping things secret, since everyone but Jude seemed to know how hard she was crushing on the man.

Speaking of severe crushes...

I glanced toward the door. When that area of the bar proved Alex-less, I expanded my search to the rest of the tables. Maybe he'd been here for hours and we'd missed each other.

Somehow.

Izzy patted my hand. "He'll be here. He will."

Though, her smile was less sure. Her forehead pinched. Her eyes...worried.

I sighed and promised myself I wouldn't look at the door again. After all, my invitation came with the caveat that he might not be able to pull himself away from work. He only needed a week and a half of concerted effort to finish the draft and everything would go back to normal.

CHAPTER THIRTY-FIVE

EVIE

Alex didn't show up at Cheers 'n Beers. He didn't text an apology. Or an explanation. I even threw open my bedroom curtains and flicked on the light the second I got home, hoping I'd catch his attention. The windows in his house were dark, save the office. I stared for five minutes, willing him to notice I was home. To reach out. Anything to let me know he'd noticed me at all.

Nothing.

I collapsed onto the bed next to a sleeping Larry. The jostle and bounce of the mattress had his head lifting and his bright green eyes blinking open. He stretched and yawned, then stood to bump his head against my cheek. "At least someone remembers I exist," I murmured as his purrbox engaged.

That wasn't fair.

Alex's deadline was just a few days away and if his publisher decided to drop him over this book, it could ruin his career.

Though, he was *the* Alexander Prescott. If this publisher dropped him, there would be a line of houses willing to pick him up in a heartbeat. In a world that didn't have time to read anymore, Alex sold books and that meant something.

"But that doesn't mean he should just let that deadline go by. It's not the way he's wired." I scratched behind Larry's ears. "We just have to be patient a few more days. Just a few more days and the book will be off to his editor and things will go back to the way they used to be."

But somehow, Alex's absence at the bar felt significant. Maybe it was the fact he'd never gone a day without talking to me since I'd arrived. Maybe it was my unanswered text. Maybe it was because he'd made such a big deal about knowing everything about me, but had kept the story of his mother's attempted suicide to himself. Whatever it was, something felt wrong.

With those thoughts for company, I petered

around the house, taking my time as I got ready for bed, hoping beyond hope Alex would reach out. An hour passed before I finally texted him.

Missed you tonight. Hope you got all the words.

Half an hour plodded by before I got a reply.

Words are happening. Sleep well.

Nothing was wrong with his text, yet everything was wrong about it. This wasn't the way Alex and I talked. He always had a joke for me. Or a kind word. Or at least an "I missed you, too."

Unless he was really lost in the story...

I growled and punched a pillow. It felt so good I punched it again. And again. Then fell to the bed, laughing at myself as Larry pranced over to investigate. "I'm driving myself crazy," I said to the ceiling, then curled up in bed and waited for sleep.

The next morning, I bounded downstairs, excited to finally see Alex face to face. Everything was easier in the light of day, with him in front of me. When I could see his facial expressions and hear his tone of voice. I was sure my fears would dissipate the second he showed up to drop off his new pages. We'd have our morning conversation over coffee, and all would be right with the world.

When his knock sounded, I all but ran to greet him, thankful once again for the non-slip grippers on my socks. I flung open the door to a brilliant, snow-covered morning, and blinked in the brightness. Alex held a bouquet of flowers in one hand, and I grabbed the strap to his messenger bag and pulled him inside. "Good morning, handsome."

It might have been my imagination, but I had to pull harder than I would have thought, for a man about to get some serious lip action.

He smiled as I closed the door and gave the flowers a wiggle. "I can't stay. I just wanted to drop off last night's pages before I swing by and give these to Mom."

Oh.

The flowers weren't for me.

I stepped back, embarrassed. "Do you have time for coffee?"

"I really don't. Gonna go see her, then get back to work. If I'm diligent, I'll have this thing done tomorrow. Just in time." Alex's eyes were everywhere but on mine. My intuition screamed something was wrong, while my rational mind continued to preach he was extremely busy and everything would be okay in a few days.

"Okay then," I said as he fished in his bag for the

manuscript. "I'll shoot you a text when I've been through these?"

"Sounds like a plan." As he handed them over, his fingers snaked into my hair. His lips pressed to mine and all was right in the world.

There was no faking the heat I felt in his kiss.

No pretending there wasn't emotion coursing between us.

No worrying that what I felt wasn't real, or that he didn't feel it, too.

His kiss said everything I needed to hear, and for half a second relief flooded my senses.

But then Alex pulled away and his eyes were distant and his goodbye was strange and as the door closed between us, I worried that nothing would be the same again.

Alex

The last twenty-four hours had been a steady stream of the hardest things I'd ever done. Last night, choosing not to meet Evie had been the hardest thing I'd ever done.

Until choosing not to text her the second she got home took that title.

Then, her bedroom light went on, and she yanked open her curtains. I'd stood in my darkened room and peered through the slats in my blinds, watching her look so sad. So fucking sad, and all because of me. I thought I'd hit the ceiling on awful.

But going to bed without talking to her was hard.

Working on the manuscript was hard.

Showing up at her house with flowers for my mom —but not for Evie—was hard. I knew it was a dick move and that was *why* I did it. It was a slap to her face, and it hit the mark exactly as I intended.

I hated to see her hurting, but this was for the best. If my life was going to be a whirlwind of work, work, work...of abandoning her to loneliness even though she was with me, I needed to let her go. It would be better for her in the long run.

The pain I caused her would be temporary.

She would heal.

She'd move on.

She'd blossom.

Knowing I was saving Evie from becoming my mother meant I could deal with hurting her a little now instead of a lot later, but knowing the final blow would knock the breath from her lungs? I hadn't come to terms with that, yet.

I knew Evie well enough to see exactly what I needed to do to make her hate me.

As much as I loved her, I needed her to hate me.

Making her leave me was for the best.

It had to be.

CHAPTER THIRTY-SIX

Evie

If last night sucked, and this morning sucked some more, I should have known there was no hope for the rest of the day. After Alex left, I dutifully sat down at my kitchen table and got to work on his manuscript. It was good. Better than good. Hours passed as I read, enthralled by the twists and turns of the climax. This definitely was his best work yet, and I was so happy for him, right up until I got to scene forty-eight.

Scene forty-eight did us in.

It was the nail in the coffin. The flick of a lighter to my fuse. It was the straw, and I was the camel, and my back shattered.

Before I finished reading the scene, betrayal

had me biting my cheeks so hard they bled. I threw my pen across the room. It bounced off the wall and hit the floor, and Larry chased it into a corner. Under normal circumstances, the raise of his hackles and hop, hop, pounce attack would have me giggling, but these weren't normal circumstances.

Alex did it.

The one thing I needed him not to do. The thing I couldn't recover from. The thing I needed him to know would be a dealbreaker for me...

My story became the pivot point for his book.

He'd changed my name. Drew's too...but just barely. Instead of Drew Stephens, he was Stephen Drews, and I knew, I just *knew* he'd read this book. He'd see our story, barely camouflaged as fiction, and he'd come rip-roaring back into my life to blow it to smithereens.

I'd deal with Drew the way I dealt with his first insult. By ignoring it. By being a duck and letting him roll off my back like water. But what Alex did? I couldn't ignore that. I couldn't take this betrayal from him.

I thought he was so much better than this. I thought he understood me. I thought he knew this would kill me and discarded the idea out of respect, or understanding, or even love.

I scoffed. "Looks like I overestimated him the way I do everyone else."

Amelia's voice whispered in the back of my head, *you should have talked to him the day you found the note...*

I pushed it away as I flipped back through the beginning of the manuscript, stopping at all the red ink scratches of my notes. As I re-encountered the story, it became apparent this wasn't the first time I'd made it into the plot. Bits and pieces of the female lead belonged to me. Her tight smile. Her guarded nature. The more I read, the more I realized that this whole damn book was me, and it didn't paint me in a great light.

If this was how Alex saw me...weak...compromised...damaged to the point of uselessness...

With my heart pounding, I marched across our yards and banged on his door, not even stopping to grab a coat. His door swung open and I pushed through.

"This isn't a good time, Evie—"

I held out the handful of papers. "Is this how you see me?" I gave them a shake. "I can't believe I didn't see it before, but is this...am I...who am I to you?"

Alex's face hardened. His lips formed a thin line, and he folded his arms over his chest. I'd never seen him look so cold. So detached. Even on that first day in the rain, he'd looked at me like I might be special. "Evie—"

"I can't believe you told my story. I just can't believe it. You know how private I am..." I dropped the manuscript on his coffee table. "Obviously, you know it all too well, if the female lead has anything to say about how you see me."

I waited for him to say something, *anything*, but he simply stared.

"I saw the note. The bracketed note about using my story. And I was gonna say something about it, but then you snuck into my house and took it out. I thought that meant you'd thought better of the idea, but it looks like you just didn't want me to get upset before you'd had time to write scene forty-eight."

His silence said everything I didn't want to hear, and I arched an eyebrow. "Damn it, Alex. Aren't you going to say anything?"

"I don't know what you want me to say." He turned away, his face so hard, my heart splintered against the sharp angles and immovable features.

"You don't know what to say? How about 'I'm sorry?' Or 'that's not how I see you?' Or 'I'll rewrite that scene because I knew it'd bother you the second I had the idea?'"

"I do see you like that. Your smiles and sweetness

are an armor to hide how afraid you are underneath it all."

My jaw dropped. My heart broke. I blinked in surprise. "I..."

What he said was true, and it was something I'd been working on. Hell, my entire trip to Wildrose Landing happened because I'd decided to work on becoming fearless. But to hear Alex, someone I thought understood me, point out my flaws so coldly? I wrapped my arms around my stomach like I could fold in on myself and disappear.

"Look. Evie. I don't know what to say here. The scene is staying. And if you don't like the way I'm writing that character, just remember, it's fiction."

But it wasn't and he'd just said as much. That character was me, in all my vulnerable glory. "What's gotten into you?"

"This is just business."

"This is not just business. This is us."

Alex scoffed. "This is life with me. I'm not always available. I'm not a private person. Everything is open for story inspiration. If you can't handle it, then maybe you should follow Candace's lead."

I stared for several long minutes, trying to make sense of the man in front of me in context of the man I thought I'd known.

I couldn't. I had no idea how to connect the dots

between how he'd been with me just a few days ago and how he was acting now. "You know what?" I swiped at the tears wobbling in my eyes. "I'm gonna go. If you want to talk to me later, when you've had a chance to think this through, then you know where to find me."

"I don't know what you think we have to talk about."

"You can't publish that!" I jabbed a finger at the manuscript lurking on the table.

"I can. And I will. If you can't get good with that, then I don't think we have much more to say to each other."

I retreated toward the door. "Izzy told me you weren't like your dad. She said you were kind and thoughtful and went out of your way to prove you weren't him. I wonder what she'd say if she knew how you were acting right now?"

Pain flashed through Alex's eyes and for a second, I saw the man I thought I loved.

He blinked and the moment was gone. "She'd say I was just like him. And she'd be right." He ran his hands through his curls and his gaze hardened. "Look, I've wasted twenty minutes with you, and that's seven hundred and fifty words I won't get back. Are we done here? Or do you have more screeching to do?"

"Oh, we're done. We're so done you don't even

know. Say goodbye to my magic hooha. I hope you got everything you needed out of it because we won't be seeing you again until you come to your senses."

"I think I'm good. Thank you. You've been very useful indeed."

The words echoed and distorted, ripping open an old wound that had only barely started to heal. I gasped and staggered and the tears I'd tried to valiantly to hold back spilled down my cheeks. With my blood pounding through my ears, I raced out of Alex's house and slammed the door.

CHAPTER THIRTY-SEVEN

ALEX

"You've been very useful indeed."

Evie recoiled like I'd punched her in the stomach and I hated myself for everything I'd done. If using her story in my book had been a low blow, hitting her with that line was an unscrupulous abuse of a weakness.

I wanted to run to her. To pull her into my arms. To plead with her to forgive my unforgivable sin. She deserved to know I didn't mean a word I'd said. I'd kiss her and hug her and take it all back, smoothing away the pain so she'd smile at me again.

But soothing her would be selfish.

Evie was better off without me, the same way Mom would have been better off without my dad. I couldn't take away Evie's pain, because I'd only be setting her up to ride this merry go round over and over again. A woman like her deserved so much better than what I had to offer.

So I was cruel. Intentionally awful. While using Stephens in my draft was the killing blow, calling her useful cauterized the wound, making it perfectly clear she needed to leave and not look back. It was George Henderson's punch to Harry's face, and it was the hardest thing I'd ever done.

Drew's dedication to Evie had given me the ammunition I needed. I was an asshole for using it, but I could see how much she wanted to stay with me even after she read scene forty-eight. How much she wanted to believe I was just in a bad mood, or caught up in the throes of writing. If I hadn't hurled that final insult her way, she would have stuck around.

I had to drop that bomb.

For her.

"Fuck, I sound like such an asshole right now."

Morgan peered up at me, panting his agreement.

"What's done is done and can't be undone. Evie can move on and I can...finish this manuscript, I guess." I gathered the papers and flipped to scene forty-eight. A single dot of red ink marked where I'd landed the punch to her gut. Stephen Drews. It was so blatant. So visceral. Using that scene would mean betrayal for her.

What she didn't know was that it would never make it into the final book. I would not humiliate her by publishing the worst thing that ever happened to her for millions of people to read. I only included it in the draft to make her leave me.

Right now, she's probably calling you the worst thing that ever happened to her.

"I am such an asshole."

With that, I gathered my papers and trudged back up to the office, where I'd finish my life, alone and unable to wreak havoc on the hearts and minds of others.

"It's better this way," I said to the ceiling. "For all of us."

At least I'd earned the name Prescott.

It wasn't better. Not at all. All the inspiration I found left with Evie. Getting the last few chapters finished in time was a monumental effort. I didn't shower. Barely ate. Definitely skipped sleep.

But I finished.

The last chapters were a mess. My editors would reject them but that was fine. We'd piece it all back together. With their brains propping me up, we'd come to a story that made sense. I expected my mood to shift the moment I submitted the document. I ordered a giant pizza but couldn't eat it. Skipped the shower I desperately needed in favor of staring at the walls. Laid down for sleep, but it wouldn't come.

Evie's curtains were tightly closed, but I could still see her silhouette when she came into her bedroom. I picked up my phone more times than I wanted to admit to tell her I'd finished the book.

That I was sorry.

That I missed her.

That I didn't want to hurt her...

But I had hurt her. And apologizing now would only make me more like my father. I had to let her go. No matter how hard it got on me, I had to let her go.

It'd been a week since I aimed my parting blow at Evie. A week since I'd heard her voice. Since I'd seen her smile. A week since I'd willingly blown my life to pieces.

Snow fell to the ground in hard lines. No soft fluttering. No delicate glistening. Hard diagonal lines blasted my face as I struggled from my porch to hers. I needed to see her. To apologize. To say I didn't mean any of it and that nothing had been right for me since I said what I did.

I was a weak man, taking what was best for me instead of giving her the freedom I knew she needed.

I stood on her front porch. Hand raised, ready to knock, as my mother's words circled my head. I didn't know what to do. I wanted Evie back, but I didn't want to ruin her. I didn't want to make her another miserable woman tied to a Prescott man.

Instead of knocking, I leaned my head against her door, imagining her inside, cooking, cleaning, slipping around in those damn socks. Larry was still with her, and the little guy was better off without me, too.

"I love you," I murmured. "I could have loved you for the rest of my life, but I would have broken you."

With that, I lifted my head from the door and fought my way back to my house. I'd done the right thing. Evie was better off, even if it meant I'd never be happy again.

Evie

I actually got so far as pulling on my coat and my shoes. I had Larry in my arms, and planned on using him as my opening salvo. After all, I hadn't meant to adopt a cat. I'd only taken him for the short time Alex would be busy writing and fully intended on returning him when the manuscript was done.

I stopped in front of my door.

Could I do it?

Could I see him?

After everything he said to me, could I face him? Just hand him the cat and ask all the questions that had been floating in my head for the last week?

I didn't think I could. I leaned my forehead against the door, crying softly as I imagined all the things I thought Alex was.

He'd used me just like Drew had.

"At least I got a sweet cat out of the deal," I murmured, kissing Larry on the head before lowering him to the floor.

I took off my coat and hung it in the closet. Yanked off my shoes and set them by the door. When I peeked out my window to see the snow, I could have sworn I saw fresh footprints from his door to mine, but no. That was surely my imagination.

Alex and I were done.

If we'd ever even started.

CHAPTER THIRTY-EIGHT

Evie

"I'm thinking I might move back to Amelia's for a while. Put the house on the market." I leaned on the counter at Sweet Stuff and barely met Izzy's eyes.

She folded her arms and shook her head, the neon lights playing in her hair. "I'm sorry my brother's such a dick. I really don't want you to leave, but I completely understand. I couldn't stand being his neighbor either. I'm not sure I can stand being his sister, after what he did to you."

Her brown eyes looked so much like his I had to glance away. "I just don't know what to do with myself. He sent over my final paycheck and I haven't seen him since..." I shook my head. I hated thinking about that morning. The cold set to his jaw. The lack of feeling in his eyes. The way he regarded me like a fool when he told me I'd been *useful.*

"I don't understand it, Evie. I was so sure he wasn't like Dad. I guess that was wishful thinking." She straightened and shook her head again.

I wanted to ask her about scene forty-eight. I wanted to know if he'd left it in the book because there was still a part of me that utterly rejected what happened. Still a part of me that couldn't reconcile who I thought Alex was, with who he turned out to be. Surely, Izzy had read the finished manuscript. Surely, she'd know...

I brushed away the wishful thinking. Fearless Evie didn't make the same mistake twice. She lived. She learned. She moved on.

"I started writing," I said. "A little. Maybe that was the reason Alex came into my life. To show me what it really means to be brave. I can't let other people's shittiness keep me from being whole."

"I wanted him to come into your life to make you happy. And him happy. And maybe give me a sister." Izzy offered a sweet smile. "But, helping you move past the Drew ordeal and start writing is a pretty solid consolation prize."

"You thought we'd get married?" The words tightened my throat and I swallowed down a lump.

I would not cry. Not over him. Not anymore.

"I'd never seen my brother so happy. I gave you guys a year before he popped the question." She shrugged and slid her hands in her back pockets. "Shows what I know."

"Between you and me, I'd definitely practiced signing my first name with his last, and I definitely felt like an idiot for doing it, especially after...you know... everything." I'd honestly thought Alex loved me. Turned out he was just using me, too.

"You'll come visit right? Or at least check in through Greta's Facebook page?" Izzy came around the counter and wrapped me in a tight hug. "I'll never forgive my brother for this, you know."

"I'll be around." I'd miss Izzy. And Jude. And Austin. Hell, I'd even miss Greta Macmillan and her blasted Facebook page.

But I wouldn't miss seeing Alex's house every day and wondering how I'd been so wrong about him. I wouldn't miss watching him stroll past my house with Morgan or the sad glances the people of Wildrose had for me. I wouldn't miss Bridget's sniffling smile when I stepped into Overton's, like my tragedy was hers, too.

"I just need a chance to heal. As soon as I sell the house, I'll find a place of my own. I love Amelia, but I need to figure out how to be myself with myself, if that makes any sense."

"It does. But Evie? Who you are is pretty amazing. I hope you don't need to do too much soul searching to realize that."

I gave my friend another hug and pressed her cheeks together. "I'm gonna miss you."

"Nah. We'll stay in touch. Can't miss me if we never really say goodbye."

Amelia paced her living room, navigating the boxes of my things while Larry batted at the skirt swirling around her ankles. I'd never talked myself into giving the cat back, and Alex had never asked. Larry was better off with me anyway. "I am so disappointed in your spirit guides. I genuinely felt like they were pushing you to Wildrose."

"Maybe that was the problem. I should have been the one to interpret what my spirit guides were saying." I arched an eyebrow as I glanced up from my notes on a potential plot that had captured my interest.

"You know? That's actually kind of brilliant."

"Besides, look at me, writing again. Maybe Alex wasn't the point of my trip to Wildrose Maybe this was." I pointed at the notebook in my lap.

"Maybe you had to have your heart broken again to prove you could be fearless."

"Maybe. But..." I glanced around the room as if I could see my higher self/spirit guides/whatever else Amelia thought might be throwing hints my way. "I'd appreciate a chance to learn some lessons that didn't hurt so much. I really liked Alex."

"Oh, sweetie. I'm so sorry. I really liked him, too. Or at least I thought I did."

In the week since I left Wildrose, I'd heard from Alex exactly zero times. "He got what he wanted from me and showed his true self. Feel like I fell for the old switcheroo. Again."

"Have you talked to his sister? Do you know if he took out that scene?"

"Why would he? If the whole point of pretending to like me was to finish his book, why would he change it?"

"I don't know. Something just seems...off...about the way he reacted."

I bobbed my head. Everything about what happened to me in Wildrose seemed off, especially because I'd begun to think I could call that place home. That I'd found friends who understood me and the perfect eccentric town to help me find my way back to myself. "Twice now I've had someone I cared about steal a piece of me and share it with the world."

Amelia made a sad face, but I held up a hand.

"Drew stole my book and it hit the top of the charts. And it sucks that I didn't get to experience that ride, but still. My words. My characters. My book. I did that. Alex was right. Drew will never do that again because he just doesn't have what it takes, but apparently I do." I pointed at my notebook. "And I'm going to do it again. And this time, my name will be on the cover."

"And the checks."

I laughed. "That'll be a nice change of pace, too."

When Alex's book hit the shelves, it was sure to skyrocket into fame. His name alone was enough to create buzz around a new release, but, like it or not, that story was one of his best. He outdid himself with... well...everything.

And even though I hated seeing myself the way he saw me, scared, meek, so freaking taupe I wanted to vomit, I was gonna be part of that success.

Me.

I made that character compelling.

No one would know. No one but me, Alex, and Amelia. Maybe his friends. Probably Izzy. But when his book succeeded, that would be because of me, too.

There was something empowering in that.

Whenever the voice of fear spoke up, whispering to me in the middle of the night that Alex had stolen from me, used me, that the whole world would get to see the weakest parts of me, I reminded myself that I was about to hit the top of the charts again.

Sometimes I cried, but more and more, I found myself smiling.

CHAPTER THIRTY-NINE

ALEX

Watching Evie move out of her house should have made me feel like I'd done the right thing. It should have been a celebration of chivalry to do my White Knight Syndrome proud. Instead, it sank my heart into my stomach, where it stayed for weeks.

I finished the book, carefully weaving the ending together with the threads I'd started in the beginning. Pulling plot points, subtext, and character arcs into a finale that felt like a fucking nuclear bomb. My thrillers were known to keep people on the edge of their seats, but this one...*this* one...

It had depth.

Emotion.

The payout was beautiful as I crafted the female lead to fit the way I truly saw Evie. Yes, she was the framework for my character. Yes, she was right to hit me with all those accusations when she stormed into my house, but she was so wrong when she believed I saw her as meek, mild, and fearful.

Eveline McAllister had a quiet grace. A gentle fearlessness that had gone into hiding after that asshole Stephens gave her a reason to doubt how people would treat her, but it was there when she chased me to my car all those years ago. It was still there when she crept downstairs in her underwear to face a ghost with nothing but her camera and a whole lot of side boob. And she was overflowing with it when she knocked on my door to call me out for using her story against her wishes.

My life was better for having known her.

At least that was what I kept telling myself. Meanwhile, I often forgot to shower. I barely saw my sister. I only left the house to see Mom. I'd been turning the guys down for drinks at the bar for weeks now. I wrote Evie letter after letter, pouring out my heart and soul, explaining everything and begging for her forgiveness. Only I never sent them. I'd promised to protect her, even from myself.

My editor called the new book a triumph.

It damn well better be because it might be the last thing I ever wrote.

"Wouldn't that be the worst twist of fate ever?" I asked Morgan as he plopped to the ground at my feet. "I did the right thing and chased Evie away because I didn't want to abandon her to work, only to never write again."

A knock at my door sent my heart racing, calling Evie's name. Obviously, it wasn't her. She'd left Wildrose and never been back, but my heart hadn't gotten the memo. It still expected to see her every time I stepped outside. Or peered out my bedroom window. Or opened my eyes in the morning.

Whoever was out there would have to deal with disappointment. I wasn't in the mood for company. The knocking turned into banging. "Alexander Prescott!" My sister's voice rattled the windows. "I know you're in there!"

Cursing under my breath, I stood, stormed through the house, and yanked open the door. "Go away."

Izzy pushed past me. "Nope. Also. Wow." She waved a hand under her nose. "When was the last time you showered? You're ripe."

I sniffed an armpit and recoiled as my sister greeted a wiggling Morgan. "Welcome to depression station. We specialize in dark rooms, listless stares, and a general feeling of hopelessness. I'd offer you something to drink, but that's too much work."

Izzy stood and held out a cup of coffee and a bag from Sweet Stuff. "Good thing I brought the drink to you. And some genius nuggets." She regarded me like a venomous snake, just as likely to bite her hand as I was to accept the gifts.

I took the coffee and avoided the jellybeans. They reminded me too much of Evie. Izzy dropped the bag on the coffee table, then yanked open the curtains covering the picture window in the living room. I flinched away from the light, fighting the urge to hiss, while covering my poor, watering eyes. The sun glinted off a brilliant January day, a fresh batch of fallen snow glittering in the yard.

"Oh, Alex." Izzy sighed my name, her voice dripping with pity as she stared at me in the light. "I had no idea it was this bad."

I ran a hand through my hair, suddenly self-conscious as I looked down at the sweats I'd put on... how many days ago? "I'm fine."

"You're not. The guys are worried about you. I'm worried about you. Mom's worried about you."

"I miss Evie more than I thought I would."

Izzy's face hardened. "Yeah, well, you have a funny way of showing someone you care."

I hadn't told Izzy why I pushed Evie away. I hadn't

told her the choice was breaking me. That I'd done what I did to keep from being a repeat of Mom and Dad. Why bother? It wouldn't change things. Evie was still better off without me.

"Have you heard from her?" I asked. The neediness in my voice betrayed me. I cleared my throat and turned away.

"I have. And let me tell you, you did a number on her. It says a lot about how much you mean to me that I'm here at all after how you behaved."

"Is she okay? Where is she?" I shuffled toward my sister, eager for even a sliver of information.

Izzy frowned, her intelligent eyes narrowing as she studied me intently. "She's writing. For what that's worth."

The smile that stretched my face almost hurt. "That's wonderful!"

"She even said she might submit it to an agent when it's done."

I dropped onto the couch, so overwhelmed with emotion I didn't feel like I had the strength to stand. "Tell her to do it. Don't let her back away. I'll call my agent...wait, what genre is she writing? It doesn't even matter. I'll still call my agent because I'm sure she knows someone who will want this book..."

I glanced at Izzy, who regarded me like she'd stumbled across a strange, new lifeform. "I'm not sure getting her published is the kind of atonement you need to make."

I waved the statement away. "It's the least I could do."

"No. The least you could do is treat her with kindness and respect. You know, be the kind of man I thought you were instead of the douchebag you turned out to be."

I recoiled. "You're out of line."

"No. You're out of line. You've been so different lately. First, you act like you're falling head over heels for this woman, and we were all so surprised. Happy, but surprised. Then, out of the blue, you turn on her and basically say you've been using her the whole time —which doesn't sound like you. At all. And now, you're wallowing in a month's worth of Mike's bags and burger wrappers, talking about getting Evie published." Izzy paced toward the door. "I don't know this version of you."

"Or maybe you never really knew me at all."

Her jaw dropped. "I stopped by to tell you it was time to get your life together. You messed up. Big. It's time to own it and move on. But, now I think I'm here to tell you you're being a particular kind of asshole. Maybe you're more like Dad than I wanted to admit." She yanked open the door. "Enjoy the jellybeans," she said, then disappeared into the blinding day.

CHAPTER FORTY

Evie

Amelia's doorbell rang and I looked up from my laptop.

Fifty chapters.

Eighty-seven thousand words.

All in a few months.

I'd never written so fast, but the story was pouring out of me. It felt like healing. Like growing. Like finding myself again and realizing I was kind of a badass all along.

With a sigh, I stood, crossing the small apartment in a few steps. I'd meant to sell the house in Wildrose Landing as quickly as I could and move out of Amelia's living room, but I couldn't bring myself to put it on the market.

At first, I blamed it on the season. No one buys a house in winter.

Then, on the book. I was too busy to focus on selling the place.

But the truth was, I was scared. Scared to think about my time there. To process how quickly I fell in love with someone who didn't feel the same. Or maybe just scared to close the door on that brief time in my life. Whatever the reason, the time had come to move on. As soon as I finished the chapter I was working on, I'd contact a real estate agent and put Sugar Maple Hill on the market.

I opened the door to an annoyed young man. "I need you to sign for this," he said, thrusting a box into my hands and holding out a digital doohickey. I scribbled my name on the device, then closed the door, perching on the couch to open the package.

Inside was a book with a sticky note attached.

You never got to see how it ended.

The words scrawled in a painfully familiar script. I peeled the note off and gasped at the title.

Fearless, by Alexander Prescott.

The words Advance Reader Copy scrolled across

the cover, with a note that this was an unedited, prepublication copy and likely to have errors. With my stomach doing backflips, I flipped through the first few pages. Tears sprang to my eyes at the dedication page.

To EM. You fought the sun over who could give off more light. Your smile fed my own. I 'saw you' the moment you careened into my life, hiding your strength under a well of pain. I'm sorry for everything I said at the end. I hate myself more for it every day. Hope you're still wearing sticky socks and scandalous PJs.

I miss you.

I wiggled my toes that were indeed encased in non-stick socks and ran a finger across the words. In the scheme of books dedicated to me, this one sounded much nicer than the first, but made no sense in the context of what happened between Alex and me.

"He misses me?" I scoffed as I paced the living room. "Then maybe he shouldn't have been such a jerky jerkface."

The book dropped to the coffee table and I couldn't bring myself to touch it again.

A month later, I finished my book, and put the house on the market. Much to everyone's surprise, it sold within a week.

And that was that. I no longer owned a home in Wildrose Landing. I didn't go to the closing, so my realtor handed the keys to the new owner and a healthy deposit hit my account. It was time to go house hunting. Or apartment hunting. Or just bask in the fact that I'd taken the plunge and did what needed doing. I hadn't run away or procrastinated. I'd done the hard thing and felt better for it.

Izzy cried when I told her. "I guess I kept holding out hope you'd be back someday."

"You know you can always come visit me. Whenever I figure out where I want to live, that is."

"Between the sale of the house and YOUR FREAKING BOOK DEAL, you can afford to be choosy."

My heart fluttered at the thought. When I got up the courage to submit to agents, I had several falling over their feet to sign me, which was a shocker and totally unheard of for a newbie. A bidding war erupted, and the book sold for more money than I had imagined. It had to be Karma, swooping back around to do me a solid. After being taken advantage of by two different writers, the writing world was trudging around to lift me up.

Izzy launched another round of congratulations my way and I almost asked her about Alex.

Almost.

The words were right there. Right on the tip of my tongue. *How's he doing?*

But it felt like a disservice to myself to ask. So I didn't.

I did, however, pick up his book after I finished the call. I turned it over in my hands, studying the cover. I ran my finger over his name. "Freaking *Fearless*," I murmured. "Of course the title's *Fearless*."

Somehow, I found myself reading the thing. I skimmed the first couple chapters. After all, I was fairly well acquainted with them. But then...

...then...

Some changes caught my eye and I started reading with more attention. Before I knew it, the apartment was dark, my eyes were blurry, my heart was thundering, and my entire world had been turned upside down.

Yes, I was in those pages. Yes, I was meek and mild in the beginning.

But the end...

Oh my goodness...*the end.*

Alex turned that character into a phoenix rising from the ashes of the tragedy. She was smart and quick and through so many passages I felt like he was speaking directly to me through the dialogue.

This is how I see you, Evie. This. You're a phoenix, strong and beautiful and I love you.

On top of all that, scene forty-eight was nowhere to be seen. No mention of Stephen Drews stealing work from the woman who loved him. Alex had taken it out. Instead of humiliating me, he'd...elevated me.

"I have to see him."

Amelia paused on her way into the living room. "See who?"

I stood and brandished the book. "I have to see Alex."

She frowned. "We just got you over him..."

"I'll never get over him. Especially not after this." I shoved the book into her hands like simply holding it would explain what was inside. "I don't know why, but after reading that, I think he loved me, and if that's true, then I have to see him. I have to talk to him."

Amelia flipped through the first couple pages. "Oh my goodness, he capitalized your initials in the dedication." The goofy grin tugging at her lips said it all.

I pulled out my phone and called Izzy. "Two calls in one day?" she said when she answered. "I feel like a superstar."

I hopped over small talk in favor of the point. "I

didn't ask about Alex the last time because...well, because. But I just read his new book. How is he?"

"He's...well, he's not great, Evie. I thought I understood him, but I just don't. He's been wallowing like his heart is broken since you left, even though as the asshole in the situation, he has no right. He turned into a full-on hermit after the 'for sale' sign hit your yard and I haven't seen him since it sold. He's leaving for a book tour tomorrow, and I'm really hoping it'll do him some good. Not that you should worry about him. Not at all. Not after what he did to you—"

"I don't know, Izzy." A grin blossomed as I spoke. "I think, after reading the book, I think he chased me away on purpose, like George from *Harry and the Henderson's*. I don't know. This sounds crazy. I just...I need to see him."

"He's leaving tomorrow, first thing. He'll be gone for weeks."

"I better get a move on, then."

Amelia looked up from the book, eyes wide. "You're going to Wildrose tonight?" Izzy echoed the question.

"I have to." I shrugged. "I have to see him and at least thank him and I have to do it before I think better of it so yeah. I'm going to Wildrose tonight."

CHAPTER FORTY-ONE

ALEX

My phone rang with a call from Izzy. We hadn't talked as much as we used to since Evie left. I assumed she was mad at me for chasing away her new friend. She had every right to feel that way. I was mad at me for chasing Evie away. I accepted the call.

"Alexander Prescott."

I flinched from the gravitas in her voice. This was not the traditional family greeting of bellowing each other's names from the entry. Her greeting dripped with accusation. Disappointment. I wasn't in the mood.

I sighed. "Speaking."

"Did you *Harry and the Henderson's* Evie?"

"I'm sorry." I pinched my brow. "Did I what?"

"*Harry and the Henderson's.* That stupid movie mom used to make us watch when we were kids. Remember the part when John Lithgow thought Harry would be better off without him so he said terrible things and hit Harry to make him leave?"

I did remember the movie and that was exactly what I did, but discussing it would do more harm than good. "I'm sorry, Izzy. I'm drawing a complete and utter blank here."

"No. You're being obstinate to keep me from reaching my point, but never fear, we share the same genes, which means I can be every bit as stubborn as you. You made Evie think you were an asshole to make her leave."

I huffed a breath, crossed my arms over my chest, and shuffled into the kitchen.

Izzy loosed a dramatic sigh. "You did! You giant, self-absorbed idiot!"

"Self-absorbed?" I stopped and leaned my head against the wall. "I literally chased away the woman I loved so she wouldn't suffer the way Mom did."

"The way Mom did?" Genuine confusion tightened Izzy's words.

In the biggest infodump of all infodumps, I dropped it all on my sister. My realization that I was just like Dad. Candace's accusations. Mom's revelation. "It all hit home one night while Evie and I were at dinner. She was just sitting there, at the table, basically alone even though I was across from her. I was ignoring her because I was working, after I vowed never to be like that."

"You think you're just like Dad."

"I know I'm just like Dad."

"Then you know nothing, Alex Prescott. You stop in to see me every day, or at least you used to before you chucked your life in the garbage."

"Yeah, for genius nuggets." I did my best to smile.

"Bullshit just for genius nuggets. You make sure I have what I need, stop and talk with me, ask me if I need help with anything. You take the time to cultivate a relationship with me, your sister, because it's important to you. Dad wouldn't do that."

"Yeah, but..."

"You visit mom every day. You sit with her while she goes on about her social circles and nail polish choices even though you don't care two hoots about any of that. You aren't a surface level guy, but you are for her, because you know she needs that. Dad wouldn't do that."

I stared at me feet and searched for something to say.

"You adopted Morgan and I have never met a more spoiled dog in my life. He's sweet, but come on, this dog gets daily walks on the beach because he loves the water. And your cat? The one that's now living with Evie? I don't even know when you got him, but have you ever met a more loving feline? Let me break it to you, cats don't come like that out of the box. They have to be shown love to give love. Dad would make an asshole out of a cat. You didn't. You're nothing like our father."

"But I ignored Evie in favor of work."

"Did she care?"

The question took me off guard. "What?"

"Did she care?" Izzy carefully enunciated the question.

"Of course she cared..." The image of her sad face at Overton's popped into my head.

"She said this to you. She said, 'you're spending too much time at work and I resent it.'"

"No. But Evie wouldn't say—"

"Stop talking for a minute and listen to me. Evie's a writer. My guess is, knowing her, she completely understood you needed to disappear into your work because she has to do the same thing. The only way I see you being just like dad in this situation is because you decided you knew what was best for everyone involved and acted on it."

I looked at the dog who stared at me like the sun rose and set on my shoulders. I thought of all the time I spent making sure Mom didn't feel alone. Every time I put my notes away to spend time with Evie. The daily walks with Morgan and laser pointer marathons with Larry.

"Maybe you're right," I practically whispered. "Maybe I'm not like Dad."

"Ya think?" Izzy huffed a laugh. "You don't sound super convinced."

"I'm only overcoming years' worth of programming and negative self-talk, so pardon me if it takes some time to adjust to this wicked about-face in the way I see myself." I ran a hand through my hair. "Have you talked to Evie lately?"

"I have. She finished her book. All in all, she's doing well."

She's doing well. I smiled to hear it.

"She read your book, Alex." Warmth spread through Izzy's voice. "It left her a little gobsmacked, but she loved it."

If Evie read the book and hadn't reached out, then she must not have seen what I'd hoped she'd see. I tried to smile, but it felt like my heart was breaking in half. Like I'd failed in my mission. I checked my watch. I had to meet my agent in an hour and I was a long way from presentable.

I ran a hand over my mouth. "Hey. Listen. Thanks

for taking the time out of your day to call me an asshole."

"I didn't say you were an asshole. I said you're stupid. Vast difference."

"Not exactly." I stroked Morgan's ears. "I have a meeting. At Overton's. As much as I'd love to hang around and let you bully me some more, I'm going to have to ask you to say goodbye and hang up already."

Izzy snorted a laugh. "I love you, you big, stupid asshole."

"See! I knew it. The asshole was in the subtext."

With a quick laugh and a sharp retort, my sister said goodbye and ended the call.

It took me longer to get ready to meet Brighton than I wanted. Thoughts of Evie collided with scraps of the conversation with Izzy and kept my brain from fully processing any of it. I took longer choosing an outfit than I needed. Slicked some gel into my hair then thought better of it, only to realize what was done was done and I didn't have time to wash it out.

I parked the Range Rover in the parking lot at Overton's. A brisk wind rustled my hair as I strode up the sidewalk toward the entrance, and warmth and the scent of good food made up for it all as I pushed inside the restaurant. Brighton stood, her full, red lips stretching into a smile. Her trim figure was encased in a dress that begged for attention and giant heels put her nearly at eye level with me. I wrapped her in a hug as she purred her greeting and Bridget the hostess looked like she didn't know if she wanted to punch me or break into tears while she led us to my table at the back of the room.

CHAPTER FORTY-TWO

Evie

The drive to Wildrose happened in the blink of an eye. My manuscript sat in the passenger seat, the pages printed out and shoved into a binder. On top of that sat Alex's book, but the most important thing in the car was the sense of expectation.

I didn't know what would happen when we saw each other, only that I needed to see him. I needed to ask him why he'd pushed me away. And I hoped...

"Let's not get too far ahead of yourself," I muttered to the windshield. "Just focus on seeing him. We'll deal with any hope after that."

My phone jingled with a text, which I checked at a red light.

Izzy: Alex is at Overton's. Just thought you'd like to know. He's also missing you a lot. Thought you'd like to know that, too.

The goofiest of grins brightened my face and I adjusted my course, smiling even bigger as I pulled into the lot and parked next to his Range Rover. I'd had sex in the back of that car. We'd eaten burgers and talked about dreams and stared at stars, then steamed up the windows at Makeout Point. How could I *not* smile at the sight of his vehicle?

With both our books clutched to my chest, I pushed through the doors, smiling like an idiot. Bridget's mouth formed a surprised O, and she practically jumped out from behind her podium to block me from getting any deeper into the restaurant. "Evie! Hi!" Her overly wide eyes told me she was not glad to see me in the least.

"Hello..." The answer started on autopilot and ended in shock as I glanced over her shoulder to Alex's table.

He was there all right—with a gorgeous woman laughing at something he said. His smile was genuine and their body language said they were comfortable together and I was halfway out the door before I stopped myself.

I came here to thank him. To show him my book

and tell him I appreciated the way he ended his. I came here to see him and I would not let myself run away from the situation because it wasn't what I expected. So, he was on a date. That was okay.

I was Evie McAllister, and I was fearless.

"I'm so sorry," Bridget began. "If it's any consolation, it's the first time I've seen them here together."

"It's okay." I put a hand on her arm. "But if it's all the same, I'm still gonna go talk to him." I didn't wait for a reply. I stepped into the restaurant before I could lose my resolve. My heart thundered in my chest and that woman sitting at Alex's table got more beautiful with every step.

Turn around, said fear. *Turn around and walk away before you make a fool of yourself. He's better off with someone like her and he made it pretty dang clear he didn't want you and you're only going to regret this for the rest of your life oh and you'll probably die, too—*

"Hi." I stopped directly in front of Alex.

Shock stole his smile as his fork dropped from his hand. His eyes misted with emotion, joy and hope tugging at his lips. "Evie..."

"I won't stay long. I promise. If I'd known I was interrupting a date, I probably wouldn't have come at all, so I guess it's a good thing I didn't know because it feels really good to be here again." I turned to the woman across from Alex. "I'm Evie McAllister and, well, he's a wonderful guy and I'm sure you'll be very happy together."

Shaking his head, Alex scooted back from the table. "Evie—"

I held up a hand. "I just came to say thank you. To tell you I got your book and that it's beautiful and I'm sorry for barging into your office that day and saying all those terrible things to you about the character. I let fear speak for me and you didn't deserve that. Okay, maybe you did deserve it because you didn't tell me what you had in mind and it was kind of a shock—"

Alex started to speak but I held up a hand.

"I know I'm rambling, but if I don't get it all out now, I might never get it out at all. I loved you, Alex Prescott. I loved you in a way I didn't expect and I miss you every day, but I am so grateful to have had you in my life, even for the heartbeat of time we were together." I jostled my binder out of my arms and handed it to him. "I wrote a book and I think it might be good. Okay, I know it's good and you're in there just as much as I'm in here." I held out his book, then realized I had no idea where to go from there.

In the car, I'd stopped myself from speaking about what I wanted out of my trip to Wildrose Landing. I'd hoped to show up and say something magical that would bring Alex and me back together.

I didn't know how to handle the fact that he was on

a date and the entire restaurant watched me pour my heart out, only to walk away with my tail between my legs. Because the truth was, I didn't want to walk away. I loved it here. I loved the people, the places...

I loved Alex.

"Anyway, I guess that's all I have to say." I blinked as tears started to form. "I'm sorry to have interrupted your date, though I'm sure everyone who follows Greta's Facebook page will be thrilled for the update."

I turned to leave just in time to see Greta herself whip out her phone, her thumbs flying over the screen like a madwoman.

A chair scraped against the floor as I beelined for the exit. "Evie!"

I turned as Alex caught up to me, pulled me into his arms and kissed me until I forgot to breathe. Cheers went up throughout the restaurant. Applause broke out. Someone screamed, "Yes!" while others laughed in delight.

Chaos erupted around us, but the only thing that mattered was his lips on mine. My heart beat a triumphant rhythm, and I pressed my hands against his back, until Alex broke the kiss and leaned his forehead to mine.

"I don't think your date is going to appreciate you making out with another woman," I whispered as my breath heaved through my lungs.

A low rumble of laughter sounded in his chest. "Brighton's my agent. I'm leaving on a book tour in the morning and—"

I didn't let him finish his sentence. I kissed him so hard, so full, so deep because if he wasn't on a date than I'd been right to come see him. I'd been right when I read his book and heard, "I love you, Evie" in every single beat, chapter, and scene.

"I am so sorry for everything I said. I didn't mean it." Alex's hands stroked my face and his eyes begged me to understand. "I thought you'd be better off without me, but I'm nothing without you. I love you. I need you."

"I love you too." I placed my hand on his chest and smiled up at him. "But please, for the love of everything holy, never do anything like this again. I get to decide what's right for me."

"It's a deal, beautiful." He swept me into his arms again, his fingers threading into my hair. Another cheer went up through the restaurant, but it didn't hold a candle to what was happening in my heart.

CHAPTER FORTY-THREE

Evie

Six months later

"Izzy Prescott!" I pushed through the doors of Sweet Stuff and pulled up short to find Jude leaning on the counter and Izzy blushing from head to toe. The second she saw me, she bolted and wrapped me in a hug.

"How's my favorite writer?" she asked, her eyes wide and her heart pounding so hard I didn't know how she didn't drop dead on the spot.

"I'm fine," Alex said as he stepped into the shop behind me.

Izzy rolled her eyes and slapped him on the arm. "I wasn't talking about you. I was, in fact, talking about Evie."

"You wound me, sister." He pressed a hand to his chest. "Who'da thought I'd be so easily replaced?"

"Don't act so surprised." Jude studied the wall of gummy candy. "Evie is way nicer than you. And her book is sitting one step above yours on the New York Times bestsellers list."

Alex wrapped an arm around my shoulder and gave me a squeeze. When my debut novel launched like a rocket, he'd been so proud of me, he'd just stare at me with this goofy grin on his face. Two days after my book hit the bestsellers lists, Drew Stephens released a new book.

It flopped.

Hard.

Critics questioned if it was even written by the same person and an 'anonymous' tip leaked the truth of what he did to me. He went down, kicking and screaming while my book steadily climbed the ranks.

"Since when did you care about that kind of stuff?" Alex asked Jude.

"Since our sweet Evie started whoopin' your ass." He pounded Alex on the arm, dropped me a wink, and said a quick goodbye to Izzy before he disappeared out the door.

She sagged against the counter as soon as he was out of sight. Her attraction to him was so obvious, I had no clue how neither Alex nor Jude seemed to notice.

"What can I do for you two lovebirds on this fine summer day?" She held up a hand. "Wait, wait, wait. Lemme guess. Genius nuggets. Two bags?"

We laughed as the door pressed open again. Jack stumbled through with three shrieking children running in circles around him. He gave an apologetic glance to Izzy and broke into a wide grin when he saw Alex. "Fancy meeting you here," he said, though the rest of the sentence was devoured by an adorable little girl launching herself onto his back and begging him to be her pony.

I use the word adorable lightly, mind you.

Izzy plucked the wild child off his back and Jack raked a hand through his hair. "I told them I'd reward them for not killing today's sitter. Seeing as she only threatened to quit, and hasn't actually told me where I can shove my money, it seemed like the best course of action was to load them up on sugar before dinner."

Alex gestured. "I'd ask how things are going, but—" He trailed off as one of the little boys loudly pretended to shoot his brother with an imaginary machine gun.

"Connor Cooper! Quiet down this instant! We're in public, for goodness sake!" When the child kept belting bullet sounds, Jack excused himself to crouch in front of the child and covered his mouth. "Hush now."

Connor scowled and skulked and Jack looked devastated as he came back to stand with us. "I hate having to yell at them, man, but I get so embarrassed when they act like this. I constantly feel trapped between a rock and a hard place. I just wish Natalie was still here. She was such a good mom. They were angels with her. Not like this..." He ran a hand along the back of his neck.

Alex put a hand on his shoulder. "I wish she was still here too, buddy. But not just for them. I hate to see you like this." He gave his friend a pat, then corralled the children into a corner. "Who wants to give Uncle Alex a pony ride? Garrett? I'll just climb onto your back and..." The kids screeched and squealed as Alex chased them around the store.

"Too bad he doesn't offer a babysitting service."

"Believe me. You do not want that." I shook my head emphatically. "You'd come home to your house in shambles and your kids exhausted."

"That just sounds like a normal day in the Cooper house."

Izzy bagged up their orders and let out a long sigh as the door closed behind the crew. "I feel so bad for him. He's been struggling ever since Natalie passed. I wish I could help but I'm sure I couldn't handle those kids." She popped a double order of genius nuggets into two bags. "You guys heading home?"

"You know it." Alex grinned. "Writing calls. If my next book doesn't outsell hers, I'll never live it down."

Izzy rolled her eyes. "You guys figure out which house to live in, yet?"

It turned out that the motivated buyer who bought Sugar Maple Hill the second it hit the market was none other than Alexander Prescott. He told me he couldn't stand the thought of anyone else living there.

"Right now we're keeping them both." Alex laughed. "We can't be near each other while we're writing and not interrupt to ask questions the second they come into our head."

I laughed. "So we alternate. Some days I get the office while he sets up shop in the kitchen in my house, and other days I get the kitchen and Alex whines at the door with Morgan."

We worked all day, then spent our nights discussing our characters, our plots, our stories. When we burned out on work, we picked a book and read it side by side, then broke it apart in our own mini-book club discussion. Which, come to think of it, probably still counted as work. It just felt like play.

And then, when all was said and done, we curled

into bed and reveled in the magic our bodies made when they came together. Night after night.

After night.

EPILOGUE

ALEX

The day would forever live in my heart as the day my life officially started. *Wow, man. You sound like a greeting card.*

Light filtered through the window, illuminating the kitchen the way she lit up my life. *Better, but still a little cringey.*

Evie McAllister was the woman I wanted to spend my life with, and it was time to ask her to marry me. *Direct. To the point. No flowery language or purple prose. Go with that.*

The table was set. Burgers from Mike's. More fries than anyone could eat in one setting. Champagne.

Candles. Bouquets of flowers covered the table, the counters, the chairs we wouldn't be sitting in. Every single letter I wrote to her after she moved back to Amelia's sat in a haphazard stack. I'd never sent them, but she deserved to read them. Morgan had a bow tie attached to his collar and Larry had a matching one in tatters on the floor. Apparently, cats didn't like wearing accessories. Who knew?

Evie's footsteps sounded on the stairs and I took my place at the table.

"Alexander Prescott!" she bellowed as she rounded the corner into the kitchen. "I smell Mike's!" She pulled up short as she took in the ambiance. A curious grin twisted her lips. "Wow. Champagne *and* burgers? You really know how to spoil a woman."

Morgan wriggled his way across the kitchen, his entire body moving with the ferocity of his wagging tail. "Look at you, all dressed up," she said as she crouched to scratch behind his ears. "Did I miss an important deadline? Is it the anniversary of the first time someone mentioned Sugar Maple Hill was haunted?"

"It's an important day and I can't believe you don't know why." I shoved my hands into my pockets and slipped the diamond ring onto my pinky finger. I'd done everything in my power to make sure she didn't know why we were celebrating tonight, though I couldn't let her off easy or she'd know something was up.

A frown creased Evie's features and she cocked her head. "I feel like an asshole. What did I forget?"

I pulled her chair out for her. "Why don't you take a seat and see if it comes to you while I pour the champagne?"

With as much stealth as I could muster, I slipped the ring into the bottom of her glass, then poured the champagne over it. A ruckus sounded from the corner of the dining room and I turned to find Larry dangling from Morgan's bowtie. The cat was hissing and the dog was terrified and I ran straight into the fray to break them up. When I returned to the table, Evie placed her empty champagne flute back on the table.

"That was tasty," she said, wiping her mouth with the back of her hand.

I stared at the empty glass.

Oh, no, no, no, no, no...!

Did she just swallow her engagement ring? I blinked, then turned my attention to her, trying to decide if I needed to rush her to the hospital or...what did one do when a one-of-a-kind diamond hits the digestive track?

Evie cocked her head, blinking innocently. "What's wrong?"

"I..." I frowned. "Um...Are you...?"

She burst into laughter and lifted her hand from under the table. When she opened her fist, the diamond glittered, nestled in her palm. "I'm sorry. I was gonna try and take the joke a little further, but I don't think I've seen you look that panicked. Ever."

I dropped into my chair and put my head between my legs.

"Alex?" She laughed as she put a hand on my shoulder.

"Just give me a second. I need to recover from this heart attack." When I lifted my face, her smile matched mine. "This isn't the way I saw this going."

"What can I say?" she replied. "I like to keep you on your toes."

"That you do." I took the ring from her and stared at the stone. "You also make me happier than I ever dreamed possible and I want to keep you forever. I'll buy you flowers every day to make amends for showing up at your house with flowers for my mom and not you. I'll respect your privacy and let you decide what's best for you and I swear, we'll get so good at our cute couple thing that Morgan and Larry will learn to blush." I slipped off the chair and kneeled at her feet. "Eveline McAllister, will you marry me?"

Tears swam in her eyes as she graced me with her beautiful smile. "You better believe it, mister."

I slipped the ring on her finger, then turned on

some music, pulling Evie into my arms. I sang "All of Me" and we danced through the house as Morgan lifted his face and howled.

I hope you loved reading Evie and Alex's story as much as I enjoyed writing it! If you're looking for more time with them, sign up for my newsletter and I'll send you a Fearless BONUS SCENE right away!

Click here to sign up!

Next in the Wildrose Landing series is Jack and Amelia's story, SHAMELESS. Turn the page for a sneak peek, or click here to grab it now.

SHAMELESS SNEAK PEEK

CHAPTER ONE

JACK

Was something in the house on fire? Again?

I turned off the hairdryer aimed at my daughter Charlie's head and gave it a sniff. Nope. The appliance was ancient, but it wasn't the source of the stink. I smelled her half-dried curls and got a whiff of strawberry shampoo. Not there either, thank goodness. She'd forgiven plenty of mistakes regarding her hair, but I'd never live it down if I caught it on fire.

Her bright eyes met mine. "Whatsa matter, Daddy?"

I sniffed again. Definitely smoke coming from somewhere. "Do you smell—"

"Dad!" Connor's voice thundered down the

hallway with the shriek of the fire alarm following behind.

Charlie's mouth formed a surprised O as I handed her the hairdryer. "Stay here."

"But Daddy..."

"Just *stay*, Charlie." I launched down the hallway toward the cloud of smoke creeping from the kitchen. As I rounded the corner, Garrett tossed a cup of water into a pan on the stove.

"I got it!" he yelled, steam and smoke billowing from the mess.

Garrett snatched a stack of mail off the table while Connor hauled a chair under the screeching fire alarm. My sons scrambled up together to fan the device while I yanked open a window to let in the morning air. Birdsong replaced the fire alarm as Charlie appeared in the doorway, her hair half-dry and completely frizzed. Hopefully the babysitter would know what to do for her because there was no way I could fix that—especially considering I was already late.

"What happened?" she asked in her six-year-old voice.

I swiped a hand through my dark curls then carefully carried the still smoking pan to the sink. "I forgot about the pancakes while I dried your hair and this one burnt to a crisp."

"Oh." Charlie's face fell. "I'm sorry."

The pan hit the sink with a hiss, and I hurried across the kitchen to crouch in front of her. "No, no, no, baby. This isn't your fault."

"Yeah." Garrett bobbed his head and puffed out his bottom lip. "It's Dad's."

I scoffed, then turned to him with incredulous eyes. "Oh yeah? You think you could do better?"

"Probably." My oldest shrugged, his gaze hitting mine before rolling away. His message was clear: You're not exactly killing it, Old Man.

"Mommy always did Charlie's hair after breakfast." Connor smiled helpfully.

With a sigh, I stood, nodding. "Got it. First stuff your faces. Then fight the curl monster."

And, somewhere along the way, I needed to find time to shower, shave, and get ready for work without burning the house down. It had been infinitely easier when they were in school. Now that summer break had arrived, our mornings were unpredictable, which spelled disaster for me. I needed the structure of deadlines and schedules. This free-for-all approach to the morning was gonna kill me. Maybe I needed to tighten our routine? Set their alarms like they were getting up for school? The thought of an itemized checklist on the fridge and my kids marching through the morning in an orderly fashion was hard to resist.

Sure. Father of the year, right there.

While that would make things easier for me, it would righteously suck for the kids. I couldn't do that to them.

I ruffled Connor's blond hair, then pulled open the cupboard. "Looks like it's a cereal kind of morning."

"I can do it." Garrett yanked open the fridge and hauled out a gallon of milk, then met my uncertain gaze with a frown. "Seriously, Dad. I can do it."

As the oldest of the Cooper crew, he'd tried so hard to step up after Natalie passed, but a nine-year-old's help often led to more work on my part. Even so, the tick of the clock had me nodding my agreement as I raced back to run a comb through my hair and throw on a tie. The crash and scatter of cereal hitting the floor had my hand hitting my forehead.

"It's okay!" Charlie's voice bounced down the hall. "We'll clean it up!"

Eighteen months and I was still scrambling to fill Natalie's shoes.

The kids were falling apart.

So was the house.

And me?

I didn't have time to worry about me. I needed to hold it together and keep things normal for the kids. (As normal as possible, anyway.) They lost their mom and I'd be damned if I let them lose everything else too. They needed consistency and if that meant running around like a madman trying to fill both roles, then so be it.

My children deserved it.

The doorbell rang, announcing the arrival of the sitter, and I groaned. "Please let them be good," I whispered to my reflection before sprinting to the door and hauling it open.

The teenager I'd hired to watch the kids jumped in surprise, her eyes wide as she tore her gaze from her phone. "Oh! Mr. Cooper. Hi. You scared me." She peered over my shoulder, concern drawing her brows together as she sniffed the air. "Is something burning again?"

***

A knock on my office door had me checking the time. My appointment with the Tarringtons wasn't for another half hour, though they were often early—usually in an attempt to talk to me about their still-single daughter, Lisa. They meant well, but damn. The last thing I needed was someone else in my life to worry about. If I had my way, I'd never get serious about anyone again. Casual dating? Sure. Maybe. But not for a while. The kids didn't need me any more distracted than I already was.

I downed the last of my second cup of coffee. "Come in!"

Instead of portly Isaac Tarrington and his pencil thin wife, Gwen, Jude Malone swung open the door and leaned against the frame. He and I had been friends since middle school, along with our buddies Austin O'Connor and Alex Prescott. The four of us had gotten into our fair share of trouble over the years, usually because of one of Jude's 'great' ideas.

"Damn, Jack. You look like shit. And you smell like —" he wrinkled his nose "—burnt toast?"

"Pancakes." I sniffed my shirtsleeves and sure enough, I stank. Great. I quirked a brow at Jude. "Everything okay?"

He looked baffled by the question. "Why wouldn't they be okay?"

"Because it's nine o'clock and you're not exactly a morning person. And last I checked, you don't work here. Just doin' the math."

"I had to pop into Cheers 'n Beers and check on the ads I've got running, then look at inventory. You know, the boring owner stuff that'll steal my soul if I let it. I'll tell ya. If younger me knew what really went into running a bar, I never woulda opened the place. Thought I'd drop in on my way and be the bright spot in your otherwise boring morning. I don't know how you talk about numbers all day and don't lose your mind." He flashed me the smile he'd dubbed the 'pantydropper' and I shook my head.

"Did I miss something?" I looked over my shoulder, then down at my chest. "Did I turn into a woman over night? 'Cause I could swear you're hitting on me. Showing up at my office on your way to work. To be the bright spot in my day." I made air quotes as Jude scoffed.

"It's been a while, man. Since the only place anyone ever sees you is here..." He ran a hand through his blond hair, then jerked his thumb over his shoulder. "Tabitha said you had a few minutes, so I came on back."

I narrowed my eyes. "Are you trying to say you missed me? Is that what this is all about?"

Jude huffed as he pushed off the wall. "Fuck, man. *Life* misses you."

Ahhh, that old chestnut. Sighing, I pinched the bridge of my nose and closed my eyes. When I glanced up, my friend held up his hands, palms out.

"Look, Jack..." He stepped forward, "I know it's hard without Natalie, but you can't keep going like this. You work. You go home. You repeat. It's no way to live. You know she'd hate to see you so...I don't know. Shut down."

"I don't have much of a choice, now do I? Being a single dad is really hard. I'm exhausted all the time, just trying to keep things normal for the kids."

"Maybe, and I'm just shooting in the dark here, but maybe it's time to stop holding on to what used to be normal. Maybe it's time for a new normal." He grinned like he'd just delivered an epic piece of advice. "I know. Let that sink in a little. I'm fucking brilliant."

"Believe me, this normal is new. Nothing I've been doing for the last year and a half feels the way it should."

And I hated it.

As Jude looked shocked to learn his brilliant advice wouldn't solve my problems, Tabitha appeared behind him. "The Tarringtons are here. Early, as usual." She gave me a sympathetic smile and Jude a 'please fuck me in the conference room' onceover, then turned and walked away.

"I'll let you get back to work, but not before I tempt you with an irresistible offer." Jude's eyes lit up the way they always did when he had a great idea. "Everyone's gonna meet up at Cheers 'n Beers tonight. You should join us." He held up his hands and dipped his head. "*If* you can get free."

"If I can get free." I couldn't. We both knew it, but hey, a guy could hope.

"And if you can't, you'll be at Evie and Alex's party

on Friday, right? I've heard her friend is half crazy. Should be fun to welcome her to town."

It was right there. On the tip of his tongue. I could see it. The suggestion that Evie's friend might be the right kind of half-crazy for a lonely guy like me. I braced, but thankfully, Jude knew me well enough to keep that shit to himself. Now if only the rest of Wildrose Landing would get on board.

I sat back and threaded my hands behind my head. "Barring any fires, acts of God, or unforeseen emergencies, the Cooper family will be there."

"Great." He grinned and rapped a knuckle against the doorframe. "If I don't see you at the bar tonight, I'll see you Friday."

As he sauntered away, I dropped my hands, my eyes wandering to the last family photo we'd taken before Natalie died. Charlie had been four. She was so small, her dark hair the same shade as mine as she wriggled in my arms. Nat had one hand on each of the boys' shoulders, her face warm and genuine, her love for us shining through her eyes. Garrett and Connor had the biggest grins, their blond hair and freckles matching their mom's. It had been a while since any of us had looked so happy.

Isaac and Gwen Tarrington shuffled into my doorway and I straightened, forcing a smile.

"Jack! Long time no see." As always, his deep voice was a tad too loud for such close quarters.

I stood and shook both their hands. "Good to see ya, Isaac. Gwen. Please, have a seat."

"Straight to business, then?" Chuckling, Isaac scooted out a chair for his wife, then lowered himself into the other, arms draped over the sides like a fat, old king.

"Straight to business." I didn't have the patience for another conversation about their 'perfect for me' daughter.

"We've known each other too long to skip the small talk." Gwen folded her hands in her lap, her eyes analyzing my every movement. "How are the kids? Are they settling down, yet?"

"No, not yet," I said, forcing optimism into my tone. "I've got a girl from Wildrose High watching them today and I hope they don't traumatize her."

Gwen fluffed the ends of her bleach blonde hair. "You can't keep that up, you know. Filtering through nannies and babysitters. Eventually, the kids will—"

"The kids are fine."

They weren't.

They were loud and rude, and no one could get them to behave like they might one day grow into decent human beings, but I had even less patience for this conversation than the one about Lisa. My kids were my business. They'd been through a lot and one day, they'd settle down again.

"Lisa's coming into town next week." Gwen sat up even straighter. "You should spend some time together. See what happens."

I swallowed a groan. There was nothing wrong with Lisa. As far as I knew she was warm and kind and driven...and as her parents' accountant, I knew she came from money and stability.

But that would still be a hell-fucking-no from me.

I'd rather be lonely the rest of my life than risk falling in love with someone else and losing her the way I lost Nat. It was bad enough the kids were gonna grow up and leave me someday. That was the natural order of things, but my heart wouldn't stop dreading it. Having one person ripped from my life was enough and three more were scheduled to vacate the premises in a decade or so. Who in his right mind would sign up to let someone else in, knowing the heartbreak waiting for him when she was gone? Not this guy.

Instead of trying to explain any of that to the Tarringtons, I shrugged like it wasn't the worst idea I'd heard in a year. "Yeah, maybe."

Isaac and Gwen grinned victoriously at each other and I moved the conversation back to business, hoping nothing more would come of the Lisa situation.

CHAPTER TWO

AMELIA

The last time I came to Wildrose Landing, my best friend's life had just fallen apart. Oh, how things had changed. Evie McAllister went from living on my couch, to meeting the love of her life and living happily-ever-after in a quaint New England town.

And me?

Lately, I'd felt untethered. The optimism I'd worked so hard to cultivate floated just out of reach and the more I stretched to recapture it, the further it drifted. An old limiting belief started keeping me awake at night, one I'd conquered years before: When something good comes along, it'll just be taken from me.

The thought circled my head when I least expected it, with memories of how much fun it was to have Evie staying with me juxtaposing my now very solitary apartment. I hated it, not only because of the uncomfortable feelings, but also because it felt like going backwards.

Negative thoughts hadn't plagued me in years. I'd very purposefully become an eternal optimist, impervious to worry as long as I remembered to trust my higher self.

But still, the nagging anxiety plagued me.

Something wasn't right, and I needed a change.

After weeks of meditation, prayer, and conversations with Evie, we decided I should move to Wildrose before her wedding and open up a shop—Good Vibrations. I'd sell crystals, sage smudge kits, new age books, affirmation calendars...you name it, I'd sell it. I even wanted to start a clothing line using colors and quotes guaranteed to raise the spiritual vibration of the wearer. Amelia Brown was going into the business of selling enlightenment and I flippin' flappin' loved the idea.

Evie had invited me to live in her spare house while I got myself situated in town—that's right.

Her!

Spare!

Freaking!

House!

When I said life really turned around for her, I meant it. Her higher self had been on point to lead her to Wildrose Landing, and I needed mine to be too. Though obviously, I had no reason to doubt it was. Higher selves had this way of knowing what you needed and I wouldn't have been surprised to learn mine and Evie's were working together on this little project. The two of us settling here had been destined from the start.

I cranked up the music and grinned as I turned onto Main Street, then whispered a prayer to my spirit guides. "If it's not too much to ask, I could use a little of whatever juju you threw Evie's way. Please. I'm sure you've already got that covered, but I'm just puttin' it out there."

This was right. The quaint shops and clean sidewalks. The people waving to each other as they passed. A few even waved to me as I rolled down the road. How cute was that? Something good would happen here.

It had to.

I couldn't slip backwards into the black hole of depression that had claimed me after—

"Okay," I said to my spirit guides. "It's not that I'm doubting you because you're the ones in the know and all that, but could you please give me a sign that I'm on the right path? Just a little nudge is all I need. After that, I promise I'll relax."

I paused for a response, which was silly. The signs were never as cut and dry as "Hey Amelia! You're on the right path!" I'd just need to keep my eyes, heart, and mind open, and the sign would present itself.

On a whim, I parked in front of Sweet Stuff, a candy store owned by Evie's soon to be sister-in-law. I climbed out of my vintage convertible VW Beetle, and lifted my arms, stretching the kinks out of my body as my bracelets clinked down my wrist. A breeze rustled the boho skirt around my ankles and my blonde hair across my back and shoulders. I inhaled the fresh ocean air and tilted my face toward the sun, then straightened my tank top—one I'd designed myself—and headed inside.

Izzy Prescott looked up as the bells over the door jangled. Her brown curls were pulled back off her face and bright red lipstick highlighted her strong bone structure. She would have looked amazing in the fashion popular in the fifties. "Well hey there! Evie said you'd be coming in today, but I didn't think I'd see you until tonight's party."

"I didn't want to show up empty-handed." I surveyed the walls of candy bins, the inviting displays of chocolate and foreign sweets, the pastel neon signs and emojis on the wall. "I forgot how much I love this place."

"Once you see what I just got in, you're gonna love it even more." Izzy came around the corner like a proud momma and linked her arm with mine, walking me to a display table of exotic soda in decorative glass bottles. "Some are from Britain, others from France, Italy, Japan. They come in crazy flavors." She reached into the stack and pulled out a slim bottle with delicate designs etched in the glass. "Something tells me you'd like this one. It's elderflower and rose and I was skeptical as hell, but it's tasty."

I took the soda and studied the label. Elderflower and rose? It could be amazing...or...not so much. Either way, I had to know. I'd try anything once. Hell, maybe even twice or three times. If something kept showing up in my life, there was a reason and I'd go with the flow until I figured out why.

"Sounds intriguing."

"That's what I thought you'd say." Izzy grinned. "If you're shopping for Evie and Alex though, don't forget to grab a bag of jellybeans."

"Perfect." I pulled a giant bag out of the stack and filled it to the brim with jellybeans, then selected a wide range of soda flavors and lined them along the counter. Izzy rang everything up, then put it all in small cardboard box as the bells over the door twinkled with the arrival of another customer.

A tornado of children blasted into the store, shrieking excitement as a deep voice boomed, "Garrett! Connor! Charlie! Stop running, you knuckleheads!"

Hefting the overflowing box into my arms, I turned just in time for two little blond boys to trip each other and stumble into my path. I side-stepped, the jelly-beans and soda bottles wobbling wildly, only to stagger into a little girl spinning in circles. I lost control of the box and the entire thing crashed to the floor at the feet of their father.

The bottles shattered, spraying soda up our legs as jellybeans scattered across the floor. For a brief second, time froze. The kids stopped moving and screaming as they stared at the mess. My gaze crept up a pair of soda-covered khakis, past trim hips and a white button down, to broad shoulders, then finally to the brightest pair of blue eyes I had ever seen. Dark curls accentu-ated stubble-covered cheeks and full lips. Shock, embarrassment, and the tiniest of smiles tangoed across his face as our eyes met and all the breath left my lungs.

This was it. The sign I'd asked for. Sure, on the outside it looked like a disaster, what with both of us coated in sugar syrup and all. But the moment had this air of importance and the gravity of life-changing experience written all over it.

It was in the way his gaze skated across my face, gentle and questioning, yet oddly familiar. It was in the tired circles under his eyes and the hopeful smile quirking his lips.

This was my sign...and he was flippin' hot.

The stranger cocked his head as time thawed and the kids started screaming accusations at each other.

"Well hello there..." I lifted a hand to wiggle my fingers.

With the broken glass safely inside the box, no one was in danger of being hurt, but the mess was already big enough without three children trampling through it in an attempt to dodge blame. I reclaimed my attention from the man in front of me and turned to the kids, holding out my hands as if I was taming raptors.

"Hey now," I said in my gentlest voice. "Let's be nice to each other. You only get one family." My heart cracked at the thought, but I glued that right up with a heavy dose of staying in the moment—the sticky, sweet smelling moment.

All three children stopped moving, stopped yelling, and their father's jaw dropped.

"This is why we don't run in public." I gestured at the streaks of jellybean speckled soda decorating the store, smiling at each child in turn. "We need to fix this mess, now don't we?"

The boys nodded while the little girl bit her lip. "I'm real sorry I tripped you."

"Don't you worry your little head about it, just promise me you'll fill it with good thoughts so you'll attract good things."

Izzy arrived with a mop and a trashcan and the rest of us gathered the jellybeans off the floor. The candy coating painted our fingers in bright colors and by the smell of it, I really would like the elderflower and rose soda. Every time I looked up, I found a pair of dazzling blue eyes staring me down. I checked for a wedding ring and found nothing but beautifully masculine and definitely naked fingers, so I offered a smile, but that only made him frown and look away.

Huh.

Hello, mixed signals.

As we cleaned, the kids started to argue. "You shouldn't have been running, Connor," shouted the tallest boy.

"You ran first."

"That's because I'm older."

The little girl put her hands on her hips and blew a curl out of her eyes. "You always say that, Garrett. It doesn't mean anything. I'm older," she said in a mocking voice, then rolled her eyes.

"I say it 'cause it's true and it does mean something. Tell her, Dad."

Voices escalated. Tempers rose. The smokin' hot man with strong hands and dazzling eyes added a pulsing jaw muscle to the list of things I couldn't stop staring at. Why'd he have to give in to the angry energy? The kids were just being kids *and* were probably mirroring the way he handled situations.

Eager to diffuse the situation, I straightened, stepping over the mess to crouch in front of the trio. "Maybe we're all a little bit at fault here."

The little girl wrinkled her nose. "Why do you smell like dirt?"

"Charlotte Anne Cooper!" Her father stood, looking mortified, and started the beginnings of another apology.

I didn't need him to make amends for his daughter. Kids hadn't learned to install a filter and I loved it. The honesty was refreshing.

"It's probably my essential oil." I held out my diffuser necklace for the girl to smell. "It's vetiver and it's my favorite. Surrounding myself with things I like makes it easy to stay happy."

All three children leaned in to get a whiff.

"It does smell a little bit like dirt, but it also smells like a good memory and it always calms me down when I'm feeling stressed." I gave the necklace a sniff as the kids nodded.

"Yeah," said the tallest—Garrett, I thought. "I can see that."

"Me too." The middle child beamed at his older brother.

Charlie blew another curl out of her eyes. "It still smells like dirt to me."

Their father appeared beside me and apologized profusely, but I didn't hear a word of what he was saying over my spirit guides and higher self yammering at me. This guy, whoever he was, needed help. His beautiful eyes looked so tired. The slump of his shoulders spoke of exhaustion and fatigue, while the sadness in his voice as he asked his kids to apologize to Izzy and me made me want to hug him—and the fact that he was dead sexy didn't help.

But the cincher? The dealmaker? It was this sense of strength oozing under it all. That this man, though beaten down and struggling with something, had energy...vitality...

Whatever it was, it meant something.

"It's okay." I put a hand on his arm and tried not to react to the surge of *YES PLEASE OMG HE'S SO TASTY* zooming through my body. He offered to replace my things, but Izzy wouldn't hear of either of us spending more money. As I walked to the car, my arms once again filled with candy and soda, my head was filled with a single thought repeating over and over. "Who was that?"

Ready for more?

>>CLICK HERE<<

ACKNOWLEDGMENTS

Mr. Wonderful—you make every day the kind of day that proves I'm living my happily ever after. Thank you for your love, your guidance, and your friendship.

Thank you to my children for putting up with me wearing pjs for too many days in a row.

Thank you to Joyce, Linda, Nickiann, Stormi, Kieran, Elaine, and Suzanne. I hope you see your fingerprints in this final version!

And thank you to YOU, wonderful reader, for sticking with this story to the very end. I hope you enjoyed your stay in Wildrose Landing—because there are more books to come! If you did enjoy your time with Alex and Evie in Fearless, would you please consider leaving a review on your favorite site? It helps other readers connect with the book and you'll have my undying gratitude!

RECIPES

Drunken Sailor

This copper-cupped cocktail will bring out your inner pirate with a mix of rum, gin and ginger ale!

1 1/2 oz. rum

1/4 oz. gin

1/2 oz. fresh lime juice

Ginger ale

Glass: copper mug

Garnish: skewered slice of orange, candied ginger, lime and cherry

In a crushed ice-packed copper mug, combine all ingredients, except ginger ale. Add extra crushed ice to the top, if necessary, top with ginger ale and garnish.

Orange Chicken

This recipe is low FODMAP and is great for people with IBS.

INGREDIENTS

- 6 boneless, skinless chicken thighs or breasts (about 1.5 lbs); chopped into bite size pieces
- 1 tsp salt
- Pepper to taste
- 2 large eggs
- 1 cup cornstarch or potato starch
- Canola or other preferred oil for frying
- Chives or scallion tips, optional for garnish

For Orange Sauce: (makes about 1.5 cups sauce)

- 1 tbsp garlic-infused olive oil—Infused oils with onion and garlic are safe to eat on the low-FODMAP diet, as the FODMAPs will not absorb into the oil. This is not true for water based products and these spices!
- 1 tbsp ginger powder
- 1 tsp crushed red pepper flakes (more or less depending on desired spice level)
- ½ cup soy sauce
- ½ cup vinegar (white vinegar, apple cider or rice vinegar)
- 2 tbsp cornstarch or potato starch
- 1/4 cup water

- 6 tbsp light corn syrup
- 4 tbsp brown sugar (if you like a very sweet sauce, increase to 6 tbsp)
- 2 tbsp orange zest (about 1 medium orange)
- 1/4 cup fresh squeezed orange juice (from the same orange)
- 1/2 tsp sesame oil

Directions

For Fried Chicken Pieces:

- In a medium bowl, mix eggs, salt, and pepper
- In a second medium bowl, add 1 cup cornstarch (or potato starch)
- Heat canola or olive oil (for frying) in a wok or deep-fryer to 375 degrees F (190 degrees C).
- Working in small batches, dip chicken pieces in the egg mixture, then the cornstarch mixture and fry for 3 to 4 minutes or until golden and crisp. Transfer to a paper towel lined plate and repeat with remaining chicken. Do a few pieces at a time for maximum crispness
- Discard oil and clean wok

For the Orange Sauce

- Place your wok back over high heat and add 1 tablespoon garlic infused olive oil and ginger and stir fry until fragrant, about 10 seconds
- Add red pepper flakes then stir fry for a few seconds

- Add soy sauce and stir again
- Add vinegar and continue to stir to combine ingredients well
- Place 1/4 cup water and 2 tbsp cornstarch in a cup and stir to combine well (creates a 'slurry')
- Add the cornstarch/water slurry to the pan and stir
- Heat until the sauce has thickened on medium low heat
- Add corn syrup and brown sugar
- Add orange zest and orange juice
- Allow to thicken to desired consistency
- Stir in sesame oil

Mike's best burger and fries so good you'll sleep with them

Just kidding. I wish I had a recipe for a burger this good, but I don't! ;)

Books by

ABBY BROOKS

WILDROSE LANDING

Fearless

Shameless

THE HUTTON FAMILY

Beyond Words

Beyond Love

Beyond Now

Beyond Us

Beyond Dreams

It's Definitely Not You - Joe's story

The Hutton Family Series - Part 1

The Hutton Family Series - Part 2

A BROOKSIDE ROMANCE

Wounded

Inevitably You

This Is Why

Along Comes Trouble

Come Home To Me

A Brookside Romance - the Complete Series

WILDE BOYS WITH WILL WRIGHT

Taking What Is Mine

Claiming What Is Mine

Protecting What Is Mine

Defending What Is Mine

THE MOORE FAMILY

Finding Bliss

Faking Bliss

Instant Bliss

Enemies-to-Bliss

THE LONDON SISTERS

Love Is Crazy (Dakota & Dominic)

Love Is Beautiful (Chelsea & Max)

Love Is Everything (Maya & Hudson)

The London Sisters - the Complete Series

IMMORTAL MEMORIES

Immortal Memories Part 1

Immortal Memories Part 2

AS WREN WILLIAMS

Bad, Bad Prince

Woodsman

Connect with ABBY BROOKS

WEBSITE:

www.abbybrooksfiction.com

FACEBOOK:

http://www.facebook.com/abbybrooksauthor

FACEBOOK FAN GROUP:

https://www.facebook.com/groups/AbbyBrooksBooks/

INSTAGRAM:

http://www.instagram.com/xo_abbybrooks

Want to be one of the first to know about new releases, get exclusive content, and exciting giveaways? Sign up for my newsletter on my website:

www.abbybrooksfiction.com

And, as always, feel free to send me an email at: abby@abbybrooksfiction.com

Made in the USA
Columbia, SC
18 May 2022